To

Norma & Larry
Enjoy!

David Lyons

*ii • Mexico's Hidden Gold*

# MEXICO'S *Hidden* GOLD

# MEXICO'S *Hidden* GOLD

R. D. Lyons

DREAM PRESS
Puerto Vallarta, Mexico

# MEXICO'S HIDDEN GOLD

*She woke before the sun and gathered her infant daughters to her. Condemned to a life of servitude, she could not bear that her children share the same fate, and resolved it would not be so. Born of her union with the Invincible One, hers were the first offspring of a mongrel breed who would no longer know their own gods. The fate of her people would be to cower before a new order of the sacred and the profane, and women under this cruel regime would have but one purpose, to conceive half-caste slaves for the conquerors' rule. The young mother would not see the fruit of her womb so harshly used.*

*This was the hour of soundest sleep for those pure of heart, and the little ones murmured their dreamy babble as she lifted them from their pallets and carried them, one in each arm from the shelter to the field, and then to the river.*

*No tears were shed as tiny heads, eyes closed in complete and total trust, were held beneath the clear flowing waters, now diverted from their life-sustaining purpose. She loosed her grip and the small, sad figures drifted away. She begged their forgiveness.*

*From her own gods she begged nothing. What perverse deities they were to send such a plague as these rapacious mortals who now defiled the land with their insane greed for gold, always gold. The gods had betrayed her. And it was the gods, she was certain, who had ordained that she would be forever branded as a traitor of her own people. As the river carried away her young, she heard the cries of children yet unborn, lamenting that this paradise on earth would never be known to them.*

*She was the whore of the conquistador, her spirit doomed to wander for all eternity in atonement for those souls in wait; those souls denied their birthright. Her name...*

*La Malinche.*

# CHAPTER ONE

The air outside the adobe hut was hot enough to scorch one's throat with a deep breath, but inside neither of the two men was sweating. One stood, wearing military fatigues, displaying the calm assurance of one used to controlling everything around him—including his own perspiration. The other was tied to a chair and looked too old to sweat. The man in fatigues wore the insignia of a colonel in the Mexican Army. His black hair was neatly combed. Deep set, dark eyes were hooded by thick eyebrows denoting his Andalusian ancestry, but his skin had the pallor of one who shunned the sun. His waxy complexion gave him the appearance of a department store mannequin and he exhibited as much emotion. Though not a tall man, he towered over the pitiful creature bound before him.

"I did not order my men to tie you," he said, and with a single slash of his knife cut loose the hemp that restrained the other. The old man rubbed his chaffed wrists.

"What do you want from me?" he asked.

"I want to know where the gold is," the colonel said with a smile, knowing his words would shock, and enjoying the expression on the ancient face before him, "...our country's gold."

"I don't know what you're talking about."

"Yes, you do, Don Chuy. Yes, you do. It has been more than eight decades since Pancho Villa's death. All this time you've kept your promise to a horse thief. Your loyalty is admirable, though misguided."

"How did you—" The old man stopped. His head drooped to his chest as if he lacked the strength to finish his sentence.

The colonel pulled a weathered, leather-bound book from his back pocket and waved it before the old man. "Do you know what this is? This, my venerable friend, is the personal diary of General Alvaro Obregón, former President of the Republic of Mexico. You remember him, don't you?"

"He murdered Villa," the old man muttered.

"Possibly." The colonel shrugged. "History is vague on that point. What this little book does disclose is the theft by your Pancho Villa of the nation's treasury in gold and burying it here. Somewhere here." The colonel looked around the ruin of the hut in which they stood as if it hid the treasure trove. "The few who knew where the gold was buried died before Obregón could get the truth out of them. All but one." He thumbed the faded pages. "Right here, Obregón says that several of Villa's men spoke of a lad from Jalisco known only as 'Chuy.'" He paused and looked at the old man. "That's you, isn't it?"

The colonel reached under the chin and lifted the ancient head. It was like holding a skull in his hand. "That's you isn't it, Don Chuy?"

The eyes said it all. The old man's eyes, which could now see little more than vague shadows, displayed weariness the colonel knew how to exploit. Interrogation was his specialty. Colonel Márquez let the chin fall. He turned and paced, talking as he stared out the window of the one-room hut, slapping the side of the knife blade against his open palm.

"You were honored on your one-hundredth birthday," he said. "It made the newspapers in Mexico City. 'The last man alive to ride with Pancho Villa,' the article claimed. I might never have found you, but fate took a hand; at least," he chuckled, "took my hand."

As the colonel spoke, the old man's arm fell to the side of the wooden chair. His fingers formed around a splinter and broke it off. Hands were clasped behind his back as Colonel Márquez continued.

"I intend to see that you are appropriately honored, Don Chuy, for the faith you have kept all these years. But it is long past time the gold was returned. It belongs to the country. It belongs to us all."

When Colonel Márquez turned around, the old man sat slumped over as if he had caved in on himself. Withered arms dangled at his sides. Blood from a severed wrist dripped onto the hard dirt floor. The colonel rushed to him and felt for a pulse. There was none.

*"Damn your soul to hell!"* Colonel Márquez roared and stomped out of the hut, ripping the door off its hinges and nearly colliding with a lieutenant pacing back and forth.

"What is it?" he growled at his subordinate.

"Sir, we think they found something," Lieutenant Avila said, "in the mountains. We should hurry, sir."

The colonel looked back at the hut. "The old man's dead. Bury him, lieutenant. No, wait. Take the body back to the pueblo. Tell them that's how you found him."

"Yes sir, but we need to—"

"I want to know who his friends were; who visited him, who he talked to. He must have told someone. He must have. We'll conduct an enquiry into his death."

"Isn't that a job for the local police, sir?"

Colonel Márquez scowled. It was answer enough.

"Colonel, if we don't start now—"

"Yes, yes. Where is this place?"

The lieutenant pointed to the mountains. "There, sir. Up there."

"You are now free to move about the cabin, though we suggest that while you are seated—"

John Kylie looked out the window. There were blue skies above, gray clouds below.

"Let it be," he whispered to the window pane, "please."

Few men had John Kylie's gift for summation. His brief company policy declarations and financial analyses had not been understood by all, but over the years fewer and fewer had the courage to admit their ignorance as up the corporate ladder he flew. Had flown. Now he was engaged in prayer at 30,000 feet, a prayer for analogy; for blue skies in his future and for the clouds which had darkened so many recent months to become a distant fragment of a nebulous past. God would understand. God would forgive, he prayed. Shareholders, he knew all too well, would not.

He'd answered the subpoenas; he'd given testimony for which he was summarily fired. When rumors of indictments began to swirl he decided the best place to be was someplace else, someplace foreign.

"What would you like to drink, sir?"

He eyed the serving cart. First class offered premium brands and he pointed to the Chivas Regal. The flight attendant prepared his drink. With a smile he motioned for her to top it off, sat up straight, and sipped from the full glass before setting it into the holder on his armrest. She handed him a cup filled with mixed nuts. There was a generous quantity of macadamias and cashews, he noted. Either life was grand or life was shit. For men like him, there was no middle ground.

After a smooth landing at Puerto Vallarta's international airport, Mexican customs was a breeze, and in a show of largesse rather than laziness, he permitted the porter to carry his single bag to the taxi. He threw his sport coat over his shoulder and unbuttoned his shirt well below the neckline. In less than an hour, he had checked into his suite, unpacked, stripped to his bathing trunks, and taken his first dip in tranquil Pacific waters.

# CHAPTER TWO

High in the sierras, above the place where the old man had drawn his final breath, a truck raced over narrow mountain passes, the driver intent but distracted by the commands barked at him by the colonel at his side. 'Faster, faster' he was ordered - as if their death-defying speed could be increased. The road was still under construction and there was no traction on the loose soil. Ledges recently hacked from the mountain were steep and could accommodate only one vehicle. If there were oncoming traffic, at the speed he was traveling... The driver thought of the cross that would be placed at the side of the road as his memorial. Who would come this far to lay the flowers, he wondered.

Colonel Márquez had commandeered the lead vehicle knowing those following would eat dust. When he wasn't haranguing his driver he was yelling into the two-way radio he carried. 'How much further,' was a much repeated query. They ascended till the road was shaded by tall pines. Now they were forced to slacken their pace. Trees recently felled made it more of an obstacle course than a road. Finally they came to a halt. A civilian walked around looking dazed, screaming at unmanned construction equipment.

"Where are you hiding, you lazy bastards," he shouted.

Colonel Márquez ordered the truck to a halt and the driver made the sign of the cross as his passenger got out.

"Who are you?" the colonel asked as he approached the man.

"Engineer Diaz," the man answered. "This road is my project."

"What's the problem?"

"My men. They've disappeared."

"Probably drunk," the colonel said, turning to Lieutenant Avila who had joined him.

"Just a minute, sir." The lieutenant addressed the engineer. "You've lost your workers?"

"They're gone, vanished. Their families called our office. They haven't been seen since yesterday. There's nothing here but the equipment... and a hole in the ground."

Colonel Márquez jerked as if stuck with a pin. "Hole? Where?"

The engineer pointed with a nod of his head and the two officers ran before he could utter another word. They stopped at the edge of the pit. They could see bits of wood on the bottom. The hole was deep enough for a man to stand in unseen.

"Another one," Colonel Márquez muttered.

"Do you think it was here?" the lieutenant asked.

"Some of it. But it's not what we're seeking." The Colonel looked around him. "There's no rock. We need the rock."

Lieutenant Avila bit his lip. In this land of the most diverse geological phenomena on earth, he'd been ordered to look for a rock. He asked himself once again if lunacy was a prerequisite for command.

From the pine trees in the high sierras where Colonel Márquez had stood, to palm trees at sea level was not a great distance whatever the system of measurement, but overland treks through mountain and jungle terrain required a stamina that only indigenous peoples had once possessed, and those heartier bloodlines had been slaughtered or crossbred to extinction centuries earlier. Now, though wide-bodied jets spewed their exhaust above the cumulonimbus and traversed large territories in seconds, there remained vast areas of this challenging land on which very few feet had trodden. It was called the undiscovered Mexico.

The earliest travelers left little behind to mark their trails, but between mountain and sea, in the intended path of a road whose construction schedule would now be delayed, beyond a quiet field barely into the trees, lay a rock indistinguishable from others nearby. It was about fifteen feet tall and had a flat surface on which a dozen men could sit. Almost 2,500 years ago men did, and carved a testament to their time. Their chiseled, concentric circles may have merely been a game they played when done hunting, perhaps a symbolic offering, or a cryptic hieroglyph of a memorable event.

But to the boy, the rock's table top was a place to rest in the shade of the overhanging trees and be lulled to sleep by the gurgling waters of the meandering stream below, while his cattle grazed in the field and ambled to the brook to quench their thirst. Use of the field was granted to the small herd of his father. The land was owned by the *ejido*, the community of which they were members, in tribal fashion, and thus preserved from the incursions and conflicts of contemporary commerce. For now.

His hands folded as a pillow under his head, the boy lay resting on his rock. He opened one eye; his ears were his sentinel. He didn't move. There were hurried footsteps beneath him. Men were running past his rock with speed and purpose—no one from his village would find reason to move that fast. Orders were given with a husky whisper as if these men were... He rolled onto his side and peered over the edge of his rock. Soldiers! Federal troops! What were they doing here? This was farm country, not a hostile border. Nor could drugs be a motive for their martial maneuvers. Beer and the fermented juice of cactus were the only mind-altering substances abused by his elders.

The boy watched, barely daring to breathe. An army truck lurched over the hill, careened into the creek. Several soldiers jumped into the back, others were ordered to stay and patrol the area. Then the truck lumbered over the rise and out of sight. His refuge was again silent and still, but the boy waited till dark to return home. However many soldiers were on guard around him, he eluded them with ease. This was his territory, not theirs.

For the next several days, he led his cattle to other pastures, but would creep back to his rock just for the challenge of it. Not once was he caught. Then there was no more challenge. As they had arrived, the troops disappeared without ceremony. He was disappointed. Now he would have to return to the tedium of his rustic life. There was no evidence that "occupying forces" had ever inhabited this area. But days later he found the single trace of their brief encampment, a hole in the ground. Deep enough for a man to stand in unseen.

## CHAPTER THREE

Seeking escape, John Kylie found solace basking under the tropical Mexican sun and in the attentions of the five-star resort's solicitous staff. What he had not counted on was satellite TV. Three days lounging on the beach and at pool side restored color to his cheeks, but he blanched while surfing channels early one evening and finding C-Span among the offerings. There he was, right hand raised officiously, swearing to tell. That little ceremony should be altered to reflect its true intent, he thought with contempt. If he'd known he was going to be pilloried, he'd have extended both hands straight out as he offered his oath. He realized his cherished anonymity in this refuge might be destroyed. Hey, he chided himself, what kind of fool on vacation in paradise is going to spend time glued to the tube watching Congressional testimony as dry as Arizona tumbleweeds? But the next time he passed through the hotel's lobby, he was certain he'd been recognized. He imagined disgruntled shareholders lurking behind every column and potted palm. Trouble in paradise.

Kylie took his first meal off hotel premises, and when lubricated by several margaritas, he began to feel the magic wrought by "changes in latitudes, changes in attitudes." In a corner of the restaurant, a couple nuzzled, serenaded by a strolling trio. Above their heads, spoiling the romantic ambience, was a TV. Though mute images spared the music lovers the soundtrack of discordant news of the world, Kylie feared an errant touch of a remote control might bring a change of channels and a repeat broadcast of his own performance. He realized that to totally shun the world that had shunned him, he would have to leave his five-star existence, his aged scotch and exotic hors d'oeuvres for a place devoid of communication satellites. To live in the comfort of obscurity he'd have to adopt *la vida primitiva*—at least till newer scandals vied for their turn to strut the stage.

He paid his check and headed for the ocean shore.

Standing on the beach, Kylie's penchant for brevity would have failed him had he been able to find words to describe the sun's descent. As the last sliver of the blinding orb slipped from sight he imagined a flash of green and rubbed his eyes. From behind him, patrons at a funky beach bar saluted day's end with a round of applause.

"Did you see it?" someone said excitedly.

"See what?"

"The green flash! I've never seen it before, but there it was."

"You've been staring at the sun too long."

"I saw it. I swear I did."

"What you saw, Tommy my boy, was a glint of the sun in your beer. You were swigging it down when she disappeared. There was no green flash."

Kylie turned. At a table sat a man in his early 60's, his flowing white mane tied in a pony-tail, a Van Dyke beard extending the point of his pointed chin. As he smiled, rebuffing his younger companion in jest, he bared a set of even teeth as white as his locks, gleaming in contrast against skin tanned to burnished amber. Only the color of his hair and wrinkles at the corners of his brown eyes betrayed his years. His look, his manner, was one of eternal youth; Peter Pan with a white beard and pony-tail. He wore a sleeveless T-shirt, its sagging neckline revealing a thick growth of salt and pepper hair on his chest, in the middle of which, on a gold chain, hung a coin made of the precious metal.

The older man's companion was a man in his 30's possibly, with a face to which the aging process was as yet foreign. His chestnut hair was worn long, but more from neglect than fashion as it hung over his ears and fell onto his forehead. Though not fat, the younger man's face was as round as an apple with cheeks the color of a Mackintosh Red. A Lost Boy to the senior Peter Pan, the duo could have just dropped in from Never-Never Land. While his elder huddled over the table, seemingly protecting his bottle of beer from the elements, the younger sat up straight, as if his backbone were glued to the plastic chair. The stencil on his short sleeved T-shirt could be clearly read, if not clearly understood. "Eschew Obfuscation" it commanded. As Kylie was trying to discern the meaning of this bizarre dictate, he was caught out.

"You there," the older man called to him. "Did you see any green flash?"

Kylie approached their table, returning the elder's smile which displayed more than a hint of mischief.

"Actually, I think I did. What was it?"

"Atmospheric refractive phenomenon," the younger man said. "The sun's rays are bent, like through a prism." He fashioned pudgy fingers into a triangle, then twisted it. "Blue light is bent more strongly than red which is already under the horizon at that point."

"Ah... why then is it not called a 'blue flash'" the older man asked, stroking his beard and winking at Kylie.

"Contamination in the atmosphere. It scatters the blue and only the green gets through."

"And you saw it?" Again the older man directed his inquiry at Kylie who nodded. "I'll be damned," he said with broad grin, "Guess it's time for me to waddle on home and play 'who'd a thunk it' on the old kazoo. Care to join us for a drink before we slip away, friend?"

"I'd be delighted," Kylie said.

"I'm Raven," the gent introduced himself. "This here's our village alchemist. We call him Tommy. He doesn't use his real name."

"It's been cursed," Tommy said without further explanation. "Raven's not his real name either."

"Real name's Allen; Edgar Allen," the man said. "I got the nickname in high school; after the author. At least it's better than being called a sandwich." Kylie gave him a confused look. "Poe-boy," the man called Raven said, cackling at his own bad joke. "And how are you addressed, sir?"

"John Kylie," he said, shaking the hand offered him.

"Well sit down John Kylie. What'll it be?" Raven signaled the waiter and ordered three beers without waiting for a response.

"How do you spell your last name?" Tommy demanded.

"K-Y-L-I-E."

"John with an 'h?'

"Yes.

"Would you mind telling me your birthday?"

"Why?"

"Just humor him," Raven said, sticking his finger in the neck of his empty bottle and dangling it in front of his chest like a pendulum. "He means no harm. He pesters everybody he meets with the same nonsense."

"It's not nonsense," Tommy glowered.

"September 9," Kylie said.

"Year?" the young man persisted.

"1963."

"My god, my god, oh my god." Tommy turned to Raven. "Nine letters in his name. Born the ninth day of the ninth month in the year sixty-three. Six plus three is nine."

Raven just smiled.

"I have a middle name," Kylie offered as a spoiler. "It's Churchill." Beneath the table, he tapped fingers to his thigh as he counted letters in the name he never used. Nine.

Tommy just stared at him.

"Our young alchemist here attaches some importance to numbers, especially the number nine," Raven said. "Actually it is a rather interesting digit. Did you know every number added to nine remains the same number on reduction? Example; three plus nine is twelve, one plus two is three. Six plus nine is fifteen, one plus five is six. *Et cetera, et cetera, et cetera.*" The Latin was offered with a stage-worthy dramatic flair reminiscent of Yul Brynner's immortal portrayal of the King of Siam.

As he listened Kylie did the math. Including his middle name there were eighteen letters in all. One plus eight. Nine. He felt a chill as the evening breeze pushed waves gently onto the shore.

"Nine is the force of the outgoing; the beginning and end of each experience;" Tommy said, "the compassionate and benevolent energy of resolution."

The waiter set their beer bottles on the table.

"Best you focus your energy on the resolution of *this.*" Raven handed Tommy his beer. "With compassion and benevolence, of course."

"You laugh. Things *happen* around him," Tommy said, nodding to the new arrival.

"That true? Things *happen* around you?" Raven mimicked.

"Look guys, I'm just here for a little R&R."

"Down here that means rum, and well, more rum," Raven chortled.

"That sounds fine too," Kylie smiled. He was enjoying the banter of these eccentrics who he figured would be the last on earth to take interest in the mandates of Congressional committees. "...as long as I have a place to sleep it off."

"You don't have a room?"

"I'm stuck in one of the resorts. I was thinking of looking for something a little more ethnic."

"Just how "ethnic"?" Raven leaned forward conspiratorially.

"No, Raven. Don't." Tommy was ignored.

"I have a dream," Kylie mugged. "Thatched huts. No phone. No TV. Especially no TV."

"We got no TV, 'cause we got no electricity!" Raven slapped the table and laughed. "There's a pay phone in the village, but it hardly ever works."

"Where's this haven?"

Raven extended his arm and pointed a long finger out toward the huge bay's far southern shore. "Yelapa. Last piece of yesterday on the whole coast. Won't be much longer though. Goddamn road's coming. When it does it'll be paradise lost. You want to check it out before it's ruined for good, be back here at noon tomorrow. We're here to do some shopping in the morning, then we're taking a panga back. Right now at least, only way to get there's by water. Might not be enough action for you, though we do have an interesting little band of players in our small community, don't we Tommy?"

Tommy just frowned.

"Sounds great," Kylie said. "Do I need to bring anything?"

"Two things. Your sense of adventure and your sense of humor," Raven said. "We'll supply the dancing girls."

A most amusing fellow, Kylie thought. One was never sure when he was kidding.

## CHAPTER FOUR

Kylie made a long distance call from his hotel room.

"Mexico? What the hell are you doing in Mexico?" his lawyer barked at him.

"I need a break."

"You're set for depositions this Friday. I can't postpone them again."

"What happens if I'm not there?"

"Don't even think about it. They'll move for contempt and the judge will issue a bench warrant for your arrest. John, don't screw with contempt. They can keep you locked up till doomsday. If you're not here Friday, you'd better learn to speak Spanish. What's the phone number there?"

He gave the number, but not his plan to seek new quarters.

As he checked out, Kylie tried to give assurances that his early departure was not a reflection on the resort or its staff. The young executive at the front desk was offended when offered a tip as proof there was no complaint, but the porter who carried his single bag and an extra on the scene with no function but to open the taxi door had no such reservations when a fistful of pesos was offered.

Raven and Tommy were waiting outside the bar where they had met the evening before.

"Ready to rock 'n' roll?" Raven grabbed the knapsack at his feet in one hand and a bag of groceries with the other. "Give Tommy a hand with the other bags, will you?" The remaining sacks were parceled as Raven strode away; the elder, the leader. He turned away from the beach and pier where fishing boats lacking a day charter bobbed as useless as driftwood.

"I thought we were going by boat," Kylie said.

"Not from this place." Raven didn't look back, already a dozen feet ahead. "Only tourists head out from here. We take a bus to a village called Boca de Tomatlan eight miles down the coast. Fare's cheaper there."

It was a hike to the bus stop through searing heat and wilting humidity. Kylie did not possess a T-shirt with the name "Puerto Vallarta" stenciled across the front, as did the two men he followed. On his own shirt Ralph Lauren had affixed his logo to a fabric which now clung with sweat to his chest and back like Saran Wrap. The cotton chinos he wore were the most casual pair of slacks that had hung in his home's ample closet, but he wished for a pair of draw-string shorts like those Raven and Tommy wore. His Italian loafers had cost him Eight Hundred bucks at Neiman Marcus and at that moment he would have traded them for a pair of Two Dollar rubber-soled sandals. What he did have was enough money in his pocket to make up any difference between the fares charged to tourists and locals, but as he hastened to match Raven's brisk stride and inform him of this fact, his grocery bag broke and contents clattered and scattered on the sidewalk.

Raven turned and stared. "Glad I got the liquor," he said and continued on his way. Kylie scrambled after the scattered groceries.

They waited 20 minutes for the bus as Kylie, his café-crème colored Polo shirt transformed to a dripping chocolate brown, ruefully eyed taxi after taxi passing them by, fingering the now soggy peso notes in his sweat-dampened pocket, imagining how far the bills could have taken them in comfort. The bus rattled to a stop and all clambered aboard. There were women with children, women with groceries; men with the tools of their trade and the fruits of their labors. A diver carried a small inner-tube, mask and flippers—and a lethal spear-gun which he endeavored with varying degrees of success to point at the vehicle's ceiling. Several men had strands of freshly caught fish, and one dangled a small gelatinous octopus from his line. There were tourists, young tourists, boys without shirts and girls whose bathing suit tops left little unexposed, both sexes with tattoos on various parts of their bodies, several sporting metal loops and rivets in ear lobes, rings in eyebrows and lips. The capacity of the vehicle seemed to be at the discrimination of the driver, and this driver was indiscriminate. The bus was packed till any change of position was impossible. Kylie was forced to stand immobilized with his suitcase between his feet, a damaged bag of groceries in one arm and the other raised, hanging onto the handrail for life itself as the bus lurched its stops and starts and sped around bends in the road with the driver apparently bent on mass murder. He blessed his height, which gave him access to hot but fresher air blowing in from open windows, muting the pungent mix of perspiration, sea creatures and suntan oil the seated passengers were forced to inhale. He pitied the shorter Mexican gentleman pressed against him who tried with desperation to keep his nose out of Kylie's aromatic armpit.

He was able to catch occasional glimpses of the coastline as they sped on a parallel course. Deep green, jungle-covered mountains fell to the sea, gentle white lines of surf demarcating the azure waters, the far horizon crisp and even against a sky of blue. It was not only the suffocating condition of his transport which took his breath away.

At last, the bus came to its terminus and disgorged its contents. Raven was waiting to lend a hand as Kylie stepped off the bus.

"Amusement parks would charge you five bucks for a ride like that," Raven said grinning. "You got it for 45 cents. Stay here. Tommy and I will get us a panga."

Kylie stepped away from the bus, looking for the nearest shade. He spied a small store and entered. Here he found everything he needed and his new wardrobe totaled less than 25 dollars. For one to whom frugality had never been a priority, especially where personal appearance was concerned, he was pleased with his bargains. When Tommy came looking for him, he stepped out in a white sleeveless T-shirt with an anchor on its chest, baggy draw-string shorts and flip-flop sandals. He smiled as if ready to parade down a cat-walk, but the young man took no notice of his new attire.

"We forgot the mosquito repellent. Better get all they got to sell us."

This was not exactly music to his ears.

They were waiting for their panga, one of the open boats which carried passengers along the coastal villages, to collect a full complement of passengers. The passage of time was accompanied by a round of beers on the beach.

"I'd put some repellant on," Raven said, "no-see-em's are pretty thick around here. It's all these mangy stray dogs, I guess."

Kylie sprayed his bare ankles and legs.

"They're not as bad where we're going," Tommy said, reading his mind.

"But they ain't exactly extinct there either," Raven said, quick to dispel glad tidings.

"Why do you live there?" Kylie asked. "I mean, what's the attraction about a place with no electricity and mosquitoes?"

"I can only speak for myself," Raven said. "One word. Overdose." He paused. Kylie prepared himself for an addict's—or reformed addict's—confession.

"I got an overdose of man's inhumanity." Raven said, sitting on the edge of his plastic beach chair, his legs spread wide. He bent over, elbows on knees and studied the sand at his feet. He had nothing more to offer.

"How about you, Tommy?" Kylie asked.

"I guess I've got one word too. Mushrooms."

At this Raven sat up and burst out laughing. "I told you Tommy's our alchemist. He searches the jungle night and day for mushrooms but he hasn't brought back a single one yet. What do you do, eat them raw? That would explain a lot, you know." Raven turned to Kylie. "Actually, he was a doctor in real life, isn't that right?"

"I was a doctor, so what?" Tommy said, then pointed at Raven, "And he was a Colonel. Colonel E. Allen, US Army. I saw it on that duffel bag he keeps hidden under his bed."

"It's not hidden." Raven stood up grabbing his knapsack and groceries. "It's just none of your goddamned business." He walked to the water line, climbed into the panga and growled at the boat's owner, who was suddenly compelled to wave for all to board.

"Touchy, touchy," Tommy sing-songed.

There was little conversation during the half-hour ride over water, not only due to the chill in comradeship, but the roar of the twin outboards and the splash of waves over the bow. Raven broke his silence twice, first to point out to Kylie a giant manta ray, not at all unusual in these waters, and a gray whale, unheard of at this time of year.

"He's sick," Raven said. "He's stayed behind to die." Then he added, "Like me, I guess."

They were discharged in the middle of a crescent beach, clean sand the color and texture of brown sugar, nestled into a cove with rugged hills on both sides, perhaps two miles across its mouth. Kylie missed his timing getting off the boat and landed in water waist deep, losing his balance and taking a dunking. A pretty Mexican girl retrieved his flip-flop before it floated out on the tide. Raven stood on the shore and guffawed at the awkward landfall. The boat's mate handed Kylie his suitcase when he retrieved his balance and he sloshed up onto the beach.

"Welcome to Yelapa," Raven boomed, notifying all in earshot of the new arrival, assuming the role of a one-man chamber of commerce. "You have these restaurants here on the beach, don't be seen in any of them before four in the afternoon or they'll think you're a tourist. Cruise boats drop the water rats off here in the morning and pick them up, thank God, in the afternoon. After four, the beach is ours. There's a hotel down there at the end, and rooms for rent behind these restaurants here if you don't mind sleeping in a hammock."

"Where do you stay?" Kylie asked.

"Tommy and me share a house other side of town, over there. Oh, there are a couple bed and breakfasts in the hills, but you might want to get the lay of the land before you choose one of them. They're not cheap, though I suppose it's all relative. Anyway..."

"I think I'll try a hammock," Kylie said.

Raven smiled. "Good choice. Next day or two we'll find you something else; that is, if you decide to stay."

Kylie turned his head from side to side taking in the vista and said, "Who knows? I just might like it here."

## CHAPTER FIVE

His accommodations were unlike any place he had ever laid his head; thatched roof, dirt floor, and except for one wobbly wooden chest which leaned forward tipping its drawers open, everything hung from the ceiling. A hammock, a queen-sized bed shrouded in mosquito netting, and a swinging chair woven from the same hemp as the hammock, all were fastened to the rafters with thick ropes. The young boy showing him his quarters mechanically withdrew each loose drawer from the chest and turned it over, thumping the wooden base of each though all were empty. The purpose of this unique housekeeping ritual he explained with a single word. "Scorpions." That also explained the elevated furniture.

Cocktails are at five, Raven had said, which gave Kylie several hours before his first social engagement. He placed his suitcase on top of the battered chest and opted for the hammock rather than the bed with once white sheets, washed probably bi-annually in muddy river water and no doubt crawling with microbes possibly unknown to science. No, the hammock was highly preferable and, the siesta being one cultural adaptation he'd already made without difficulty, he was soon asleep.

Kylie woke with a start and sniffed the air. What the hell was that? He sat up, swaying in the hammock, looked down before placing his feet, slipped on his sandals and stepped outside. Horses. Fifty of them at least, in close proximity, and with the afternoon tropical heat, their collective stink was overpowering. He hadn't noticed the fenced-in patch of dirt earlier. Obviously it was a corral and the animals had been put up for the night. Here was one more reason to "get the lay of the land" and find a place soon. But he'd stay here tonight, just to prove to Raven he could endure, though why he had to prove anything to the quirky old coot, he couldn't figure.

The beach was almost deserted. Lounge chairs in which day tourists had earlier sat broiling were now folded and stacked against each other like muskets at bivouac. Two vendors with sample cases of silver jewelry sat in the sand, eyed him as he took a seat at the table nearest the water line, decided he wasn't worth the effort and continued their conversation. It was nearly five. The sun hung high over the hills on the southern half of the cove, still hot enough to make one appreciate the shade of an umbrella, which he adjusted against the glare. Kylie sat facing the sea. Though not yet sure why he had come to this single spot out of all the other destinations on earth he could have chosen, he knew why he would stay, at least for a while. Here was serenity unmatched. Here one might perhaps slow the spin of the Great Mandala long enough to get one's ship off the shoals and chart a new course. Perhaps.

"Mind if I join you?" Raven's voice was almost a whisper. "I hope I'm not interrupting meditation."

"You're not," Kylie motioned to a chair, "though this would be the perfect time and place for it."

"Yes, we know. How are your sleeping quarters?"

Kylie turned and faced him. "Where the hell did those horses come from?"

Raven chuckled. "The tourists that don't plop on the beach trek on horseback up to the waterfall. I forgot to tell you about your evening neighbors."

"Well between scorpions, horseshit, and that god-awful community toilet, I can tell you I'll be seeking a change of accommodations first thing tomorrow."

"Of course you will. But just think how much you'll appreciate whatever you move to. Hell, you'll praise the Lord if you've got a cement slab for a floor."

Kylie smiled. The logic was irrefutable.

"Just one thing," Raven said, "when you get up to pee tonight, look to the heavens. You'll forget about the discomforts, believe me."

"Where's Tommy?" Kylie asked.

"Roaming the hills, I guess. He doesn't feel much inclination to tell me what he does."

"You're a strange pair."

Raven reached out and clenched Kylie's arm, fingers digging into flesh and muscle. "We are not a pair," he growled. "Get any thoughts like that out of your head right this minute. Understand?"

"Hey!" Kylie swatted at the hand and the grip was loosened immediately. "I didn't mean anything. I don't give a rat's ass what you are...or aren't."

Raven sat back. He slumped and looked sheepish. "I'm sorry," he said. "I get a bit touchy on the subject. Old man, younger man living together. Easy to think we might be a couple of gays. Everybody here knows we're not of course."

"Like I said, I don't give a rat's ass." Kylie said, rubbing his arm.

After several minutes of silence, Raven whispered, his voice barely audible over the gentle surf advancing with stealth towards their toes. "I really am sorry," he said.

Kylie stared out to sea, his thoughts his own.

"Hey Raven, sun's over the yardarm, boozer's lamp is lit."

Further back from the waterline, a group was gathering around three tables set end-to-end. One hooted his invitation. Having anticipated and prepared for their evening arrival, a waiter had set out glasses and now carried pre-mixed pitchers to his regulars.

"Come John," Raven said softly, his embarrassment still written in the sand and not yet washed away with the tide, "come meet some friends of mine."

They were eight (Kylie was relieved the number was one less than the mystical digit) and he had never seen much less joined a more motley looking crew, save two, one with skin white as pearl, the other of honey. To the ladies he was introduced first.

"This is my friend John Kylie," Raven did the honors. "He might be staying a while. John, this is Priscilla" (she of pearly luster), "don't ever call her 'Prissy' on pain of death. This is Malin," The honey-hued Mexican lovely had a name that sang like an arrow from a bow, Ma-*leen*. "The rest of these sorry bastards will answer to anything if someone else is buying. They can introduce themselves."

Raven sat at the head of the table, obviously his custom. Kylie was offered a chair at the opposite end. The women, as if their presence was being shared equally by all, sat across from each other dead center.

"Where are you staying?" Priscilla asked.

"Right behind the restaurant here."

Priscilla turned to the head of the table. "Raven, you didn't stick him with the horses."

"Just for tonight. He'll go looking for something else tomorrow. Pass him that pitcher Toad, you've got the manners of a goat."

"It's Tod," the man said to Kylie, offering the pitcher of margaritas. "Welcome."

Kylie nodded his thanks and filled his glass.

"Alice would like to have a lodger up at her place," another said as pitchers were passed and poured.

"Alice would like something more than a lodger. Hi, I'm Fred. Hell, she'd invite him to her parlor to watch TV and he'd never come out alive." This drew a chorus of knowing chuckles.

"I thought you didn't have TV, or electricity," Kylie said, almost with alarm.

"Alice has a bed and breakfast up in the hills," Priscilla said. "She has her own generator. We don't get reception out here; she just shows videos on her TV. She's really a nice person, though she does get a bit lonely."

"Well, she's not lonely now and she's not looking for a lodger," a man who introduced himself as Jerry offered. "She's got one. Ain't that right, Malin?"

Malin nodded her head. "*Mexicano*," she said.

"Mexican?" several hooted in unison. "She get herself a beach-boy?"

"No," Malin said. "An army officer on vacation. A colonel, I think." Raven raised his eyebrows.

Kylie stared at the woman. "Malin, you look familiar to me. Have we met?" This of course elicited derisive laughter and comments about tired pick-up lines.

"We didn't meet," she said. "I was on the beach this afternoon. You fell and lost your sandal in the water. Remember?"

"Oh yes. I wanted to thank you."

It was a prime moment for a zinger, and in this gathering such moments did not pass without comment. "My God, she saved his sole," Toad quipped and Kylie blushed.

"Well," Raven said after a healthy chuckle, "any other ideas for a roof over our visitor's head be sure and let him know. Now it's time for our evening toast and getting this rot-gut roto-rootering down our gullets." Glasses were raised as he stood. "Thanks for the grace we've been granted, bumping gently into kindred spirits here in the land of lost and found, old sorrows lost, new treasures found with each day's rising and setting of the sun."

After solemn clinking, Fred said, "And here's to shorter toasts."

"I'm working on it," Raven groused.

The toastmaster seated himself and banter buzzed genially round the table. Raven ignored those seated with him, frowning as he watched a man walking the north end of the beach alone. Even the casual stroll betrayed a characteristic that men cut from the same cloth notice instantly. One old soldier can always spot another. The man did not venture closer, in fact walked away, though turning to watch the revelers. Raven maintained his focus until interrupted by a scream from a Mexican woman running towards them. One of their favorite locals, she was the lady who sold slices of homemade pie on the beach every day. Her shrill cry was one word repeated over and over as she ran towards them. *"Muerto, muerto."* Confused by the meaning though the message was clear, all remained seated until the heavy-set woman reached their table, gasping for breath.

*"El es muerto,"* she managed to expel between gasps.

"Calm down, Teresa," Raven said. "Who's dead?"

*"El señor Jeb,"* she said, then with one breath delivered a torrent of details. Malin listened intently then translated for the rest.

"Jeb's body was found in a cleared field in the jungle between here and El Tuito. He burned to death in a fire."

"My God," Priscilla said.

"Burned?" Toad asked. "How can one burn to death in the jungle?"

Teresa, obviously understanding the question in English, offered another rapid fire narration in Spanish for Malin to translate.

"They think he was sleeping. The farmer didn't know he was there. He set a fire to clear his field for planting. Jeb never woke up. They found a bottle of tequila by his side."

A discordant chorus of "how the hell could..." began, but Raven raised a hand for silence. "Come on, we all know Jeb was a drunk. It's possible."

"Who found him?" one asked.

"They are not sure," Malin said. "Teresa said someone came across Tommy walking in the jungle. She says Jeb's body is with the doctor in El Tuito."

"Guess someone will have to collect Jeb's stuff, notify his kin," Raven said.

Not knowing the man, not emotionally invested in his demise, Kylie watched the expressions of those at the table. Priscilla wiped away a tear.

"He drank too much but he was nice," she whispered. The other faces were expressionless. Kylie guessed that every one among them was thinking "there but for the grace of God go I" as they stared at their glasses.

Malin got up without a word, left the table without looking back, and an odd comment was offered by a man at the end of the table whose name Kylie hadn't caught.

"Guess your house hunting just got easier, Mr. Kylie," he said.

Priscilla addressed his puzzled look and explained. "Jeb rented his place from Malin. She'll be looking for a new tenant."

Teresa withdrew, saying in broken English that she was sorry but that she had pies to bake. The silence in her wake didn't last long.

"What the hell," Toad said. "Pass the pitcher. Last thing Jeb would want would be to come between us and our evening salute. Bet he's standing over our shoulders right now." He filled then raised his glass. "Here's to Jeb. May he rest in peace."

The toast induced reminiscences of the departed, and indeed, Jeb did not come between his comrades and their evening ceremony.

Kylie rose from slumber twice that night, the second time drawn to examine the stars beyond number. With no man-made light for scores of miles, he was treated to a view of the astral plain not visible through civilization's corruptive filter. Immersed in total blackness, one could erase eons and experience a vista unchanged since before primordial life began, unvarying throughout man's insignificant calculations of time. Nothing on earth could compare. During the first of his nocturnal sojourns, he listened as horses rooted feed from their trough and heard the soft voice of Priscilla somewhere in the dark. He wondered who she was with, and yes, what they might be doing. He'd already observed that mourning was the briefest of rituals among this expatriate group. Returning to his hammock he almost ran into someone creeping silently in the dark. Startled, he jumped. A horse whinnied.

"Sorry,' the shadow whispered before dissolving into the night.

From the single spoken word he knew it was her.

Malin.

## CHAPTER SIX

Despite death's appearance at the previous night's gathering, it was an ode to the joy of living John Kylie whistled as he walked the beach early the next morning wading up to his calves in the light surf. He counted three mosquito bites; right thigh, left cheek, and elbow. It could have been worse—he had forgotten to spray himself before sleep. There was no one stirring at that hour, though a small fishing boat was leaving the village pier across the cove to join two others already in his line of sight off-shore. Fishing might be an activity to pass the time, he thought, but not in the uncovered pangas that the fishermen used. He would ask for one better equipped, certain that his request would be passed along the local grapevine like wildfire, much like the messages of the dogs he had heard in the night. A single bark would set off a chain reaction and have curs howling to each other over a radius that must have covered 30 miles along the coast and into the jungle. And when the dogs stopped, the roosters would start. But oh, those moments when all was still, when the rustle of palm fronds alternated with lapping waters on the beach. His last night at the resort, though no further from the ocean, he'd fallen asleep to the hum of an air conditioner.

He was hungry but there was nothing open yet and Kylie set out to do some preliminary exploring. The north end of the beach offered the hotel Raven had mentioned, a quaint collection of bamboo huts, a last option if he found nothing else today. Past the restaurants heading south, the beach was undeveloped, ending abruptly at a cliff face, and in this direction he headed. A hundred yards before the cliff the shore yielded to a river, which merely trickled to the sea this morning, but which no doubt would expand to a torrent when rains fell in the mountains. As he looked to the hills and tried to gauge their distance from where he stood, he saw something coming out of the jungle onto the path leading to the village. He rubbed the sleep from his eyes, looked again and saw Tommy with a limp bag over his shoulder walking to town.

He forded the trickling stream and came upon a set of hand-hewn steps. These led up to a trail which became the dirt path which became the cobble-stone walkway through town. He huffed his way up the last of the steep steps and nearly bumped into Tommy, who jumped like a frightened cat to the opposite side of the path.

"Good morning, Tommy."

"You startled me."

"Sorry. Headed home?"

"Yes."

"Mind if I walk with you?"

"I don't care one way or the other."

"We heard about Jeb's death."

Tommy turned his head, glanced at him without comment.

"They said you went with the body to...I forget the name of the place."

"El Tuito," Tommy said. "No, I didn't go there. It's too far at night for me. The farmer went for the local doctor. There was nothing I could do, so I left."

"Any idea how he died?"

Tommy shook his head, but not in negation. "Something funny about it."

"Like what?"

"I'm not sure he died in a fire. The body wasn't completely burned and there were lacerations of the scalp. Anyway, that's for the doctor in El Tuito to decide. I'm no pathologist." Tommy stepped up his pace, as if walking away from the subject.

"How was the mushroom hunting?" Kylie asked, matching the reticent Tommy stride for stride.

"Terrible. Something's out there digging up the land like I've never seen."

"Pigs hunting truffles, perhaps?"

Tommy tutted with disdain. "I don't know why you're here or why you've decided to stay, John Kylie. You just go your way and let me go mine. OK?"

"Of course. I didn't mean to be rude. It just seems everyone here likes to joke about things. They even take death casually."

"That's why I don't spend much time with them," Tommy said.

The buildings on both sides of the cobble-stone walkway grew from one to two stories, several with shop fronts at ground level. The center of commerce was only 40 feet on one side of the path. The few stores were not yet open. The only hints of trade were suppliers' advertisements stuck to crude wooden doors. Further along the path whitewashed buildings shrunk back to single-story dimensions. As they passed through the village outskirts small plots and low fences divided the residences from habitations that catered to the tourist trade, offering the ubiquitous "bed and breakfast" with hand-painted signs. The path narrowed and again became a twisting trail along the bluff leading back out to sea, the southern arm of the cove. Various elevations offered views and relative privacy to those who had chosen to place homes here and there on the slope. Still Tommy walked.

"There's not much to see from this point," Tommy said. "Our place is over there, the last one on the bluff. Maybe you'd better go back now. I'm sure Raven's still sleeping."

"Tommy," Kylie said, "Raven mentioned a road being built. Maybe you saw the work of road crews, you know, clearing the land."

"Nope. Too scattered." Now it was necessary to step carefully over stones and exposed roots of trees. "The rock tells of alien visitation. Maybe they've come back."

"The rock?"

"A petroglyph on the other side of the mountain. Maybe 2,500 years old. I'm sure the carvings on it are space craft."

"Really? I'd love to see it."

Tommy stopped and turned to face him. "Not many know about it. To those that do, it's a place of spiritual, even cosmic significance," he said. "That must be respected. Now, if you'll excuse me."

Kylie watched Tommy wind his way through the brush, then turned back toward the village. The only thing of cosmic significance to John Kylie at that moment was breakfast.

❖

Kylie selected one of the beach restaurants for breakfast. A young man leapt to his first customer of the day.

"Good morning, sir."

"Can I have some breakfast?"

"Anything you like. As long as it's ham and eggs and beans and tortillas. Oh, and coffee of course."

Kylie smiled, going along. "And can I have my eggs any way I like?"

"*Absolutamente*, as long as you like them fried or scrambled," the waiter joshed.

"I don't suppose," he reached into his pocket, pulled out a fifty peso note and wafted it over the table, "that the cook could be induced to sauté some of your fine local mushrooms with my eggs, could he?"

"Local mushrooms?" The boy's look of befuddlement was as sincere as his longing for the fifty peso note waving in the breeze. "We got no mushrooms around here. The closest you gonna find local mushrooms is Morelia and that's at least a day's drive. This is jungle, man. Mushrooms don't grow in this heat. But..." he extemporized an alternative, "we could throw in some *jalapeños*."

"No. Thanks anyway." Kylie put the bill on the table not back in his pocket, thus extending the possibility for prompt and courteous service—and retaining the young man's good humor. He fully intended to reward him for the ounce of knowledge dispensed, knowledge which deepened the mini-mystery—what did Tommy do in the jungle and why did he lie about it? He pondered this question while eating his breakfast. With little to do to occupy daylight hours in these parts, finding the answer might be a source of some amusement—after he addressed his first priority, securing a place to stay. That prospect brightened as he saw her coming his way. Malin.

In some people the defining genes lie recessively in wait for generations, then burst forth like desert flowers after centennial rains. Malin's elemental beauty was pure, the product of a conception so unadulterated that, though without doubt of this land, she was less seemingly of this time. It was not merely the hue of her skin, that meld of maize and cocoa no artist's palette could produce, or her high cheekbones, or the regal slope of her forehead. It was not her deft, elongated fingers which one could imagine her using in preparation of her table, plucking a flower or strangling a chicken with equal grace. Nor was it her shapely legs narrowing to thin ankles, sculpted feet with arched insteps which could dance on a beach at twilight or stand spread in fearless defiance of both man and beast. To be sure, Malin inspired physical longing, but there was an almost subconscious recognition that this female was reserved for the leader of the pride, whoever, wherever he might be, and to approach her was to invite that spirit to spring from the shadows in a dual to the death for primacy. For between the loins of such unique women as Malin lay the seeds which could ensure the survival of man in the form first intended. This quality was her curse. Malin was a prize to the victor in a world of the vanquished.

Kylie watched as she walked along the beach, the undulating waves a perfect backdrop to her ambling ballet. She approached his table without hesitation or reserve.

"Good morning," she said.

"*Buenos días*, Malin. Would you care to join me?" He stood and pulled a chair away from the table.

"I don't want to disturb your breakfast."

"I've finished, but would you like something?"

"I'll join you in a coffee."

He waved to the waiter, holding up his cup and pointing, indicating the need for a second. The boy was quick to their table with cup and coffee pot, and though he must have known Malin, he said nothing, backing away after he'd poured the coffee, bowing as if in the tent of a potentate. Kylie raised his cup to her in salute.

"I managed to sleep last night," he said, "but I'd like to find another place today—as far from the stables as possible."

"I can help you," she said. "Raven expects people to look out for themselves, and Tommy, well...," she rolled her eyes. "There's a small house up there," she pointed behind his back. "You can't see it from here, but it has a view to the ocean. The path is a bit steep, maybe a hundred and fifty steps. I hope that's not too much of a climb."

"I could get used to it."

"Jeb lived there. I got his things together last night. Does that bother you?"

"Not particularly. I mean, I didn't know him but I'm surprised the news of his death was taken so casually."

"He was a foolish man," Malin said, "always drinking and going out on his own. The country is still wild around here. Snakes, animals; there are many dangers. It's dry now, even in the jungle. The farmers are burning their fields before the rains come and accidents happen. Anyway, the house is secure, has a good foundation, and the roof doesn't leak; two rooms, and the toilet is inside. There is a porch to watch the sunset, and flowers I planted myself. And the rent is cheap."

"Where do you live?" Kylie asked.

"Further back in the jungle. I enjoy my privacy more than most people here."

"Let's finish our coffee and have a look." He turned his gaze to where she had pointed, a steep hill covered with lush vegetation.

❖

"I warned you."

Half-way up the hill he had started breathing heavily, now huffing as he followed closely behind her, the attraction of this elevated vantage point clouded by respiratory challenge. But he could see the house. "I can make it," Kylie wheezed, forced to divert his gaze from Malin's pleasing rump to the uneven steps leading upward. "This must be a bitch in the dark," he mumbled.

"There's a flashlight in the house," she yelled back. "Don't leave home without it."

The steep grade at last turned to gentle slope and he stopped for breath and a look at the house, little more than a hut, but a Fifth Avenue penthouse compared to last night's lodging. Raven had been right on that account.

"You are welcome, come in," Malin invited, already through the front door.

Kylie stepped up one high but manageable step onto the veranda and turned seaward. The view was stunning. Then he entered. Light from three windows illuminated the first room. The furniture was *equipale*, the barrel shaped Mexican design of cheap but serviceable local materials, two chairs and a small sofa arranged around a low table of unfinished wood. Fresh wild flowers in a clay vase adorned the simple table. He was charmed by this gesture. A slightly larger table for dining, with two straight-back chairs, was placed against a wall. There was a sink, and behind a plastic curtain in the corner a drain in the floor gave clue to the purpose of a rubber hose hanging from the ceiling—a shower stall.

"Jeb built that," Malin said. "There's a gas heater outside and a water tank. Hot water is very much appreciated. He used to let me bathe here sometimes."

"I just bet he did," Kylie smirked to himself, thinking that extending shower privileges would be the perfect way to repay her efforts this morning.

In the second room was the bed, and stuck in a corner, that essential eyesore, the modern toilet. A covered barrel contained non-potable water for flushing. He'd have preferred this fixture to be outside, but maybe there was more out there in the dark than he'd imagined.

"You need to bring up your own bottled water," Malin said, "and I don't know what happened to the grill. That's OK, we can make another. They're simple. Most everybody eats their main meals at the restaurants on the beach, but there's a gas hot plate somewhere in here, enough to boil water, cook eggs."

"It's perfect," Kylie said. "I'll take it." He felt the urge to at least share an embrace in this suddenly intimate moment, the first shared under the roof that he would now call his own, but with his decision to rent the place, Malin became no longer friendly guide, but landlady.

"We'd better go then," she said, "there are things you will need to buy and the stores close for lunch."

And so they went down the hill, along the beach, then trod up the cliff-side steps into town, purchased the few necessary household goods, non-perishables and the 20 liter bottle of purified water which Kylie hoisted on his shoulder, wobbled back down the steps with, lugged across the length of the beach, and, with it feeling like it weighed a ton, nearly dropped on his return climb to his new abode. The few items were put away and, bidding adieu, Malin gave him a kiss on the cheek for welcome and good luck, which he accepted with a wan smile. As soon as she was out the door he collapsed, exhausted.

It was late afternoon. Lying in bed, his first conscious act was a deep intake of breath. The air was fresh and clean with no equine odors. He listened; there was barely a sound outside. At this time of day even ocean breezes were stilled. Kylie got up and walked to his veranda to revel in his vista. Though he had a blissful view of the far horizon, trees obscured the beach below as well as the few dwellings on the hillside beneath his. He could stand stark naked on his porch and not give offense—or invitation. Here was solitude encased in natural grandeur and glory. He pulled a chair to the point where he could best see the cove, sat and stared, allowing the retreating sun's harvest of diamonds on the liquid emerald plane to wipe his mind's slate clean. The poet Frost might have reproached him for his shallow watch, neither out far nor in deep, but he was ready with his retort. After schlepping a 20 liter bottle of water across a beach, up a mountain and into the jungle, he was entitled. It had been quite some time since he could boast of so tangible an achievement, and this recognition drew him towards a swirling eddy of remembrances—but a life preserver was thrown just as he began to sink into his own nostalgia.

"Haloo. Is the laird in his castle?" Someone was scraping up the path.

"Raven, is that you?"

"It is I, huff-puffing up the hill." His white crown first appeared, then the man came fully into view. Raven was walking with a staff, and Kylie noticed a game leg.

"Are you alright?" He stood and started towards him.

"Stay where you are. I'm fine. Twisted my knee is all."

Raven hobbled to the veranda, accepted a hand up, and didn't wait for an invitation to sit. "Malin told me she showed you Jeb's place. I guess it is about the best available at the moment." Raven leaned on his walking stick as he sat. He took several deep breaths, then spoke. "Seems his death might be more than a case of passing out at the wrong time and place. Tommy told me he met you this morning on his way home."

"He made a few observations, but I don't know if I can believe our misguided mycologist's opinion on much of anything; a mushroom hunter who doesn't know they don't grow here. Why does he lie about whatever he does at night?"

Raven sighed. "Look John, Tommy's still a bit disturbed, OK? What he came here to forget has still got him a little unglued. He doesn't do any harm walking where he will, when he wants. Here he can roam jungles and look for mushrooms or whatever, instead of staring at the inside of a rubber room like he'd be doing if he was back up there. I look out for him. I know how to handle boys like him. I've seen enough of them; bodies unscarred but minds blown away. Survival can be a high price to pay when you slog through hell every waking hour of the rest of your life. But Tommy, he's got a chance to get himself back. This is a good place for him, a forgiving place. We do a lot of that for each other here; forgiving." Raven looked at him, waiting for a response.

"Like I said when I met you," Kylie smiled, "I'm just here for a little R&R."

"Reminds me," Raven said, "I brought a housewarming present." From his pocket he pulled a pint-sized bottle. "Bacardi *añejo*; don't need a mixer, or ice—neither of which I expect you got—and if you don't have glasses yet, take the first slug, just save me a drop." He handed his gift.

"Thanks Raven, and thanks for telling me about Tommy. I'll humor him." He took a hearty swig, then passed the pint back.

Raven opened his throat and poured, the bottle never touching his lips. He swallowed loudly. "If you want to help him, don't just humor him. Show him a little respect. Act like you believe what he says."

"Like his crap about flying saucers? Supporting delusions is not the road back to mental health. The shrink I went to for marriage counseling told me never to do that, and my ex wasn't nearly as delusional as Tommy. She didn't see flying saucers anyway; she just thought I was the Bank of America."

Raven chuckled. "That's a delusion many of us deal with one time or another. But Tommy doesn't say he's seen flying saucers, he says he's seen *evidence* of them."

"There's a difference?" Kylie chugged down the last gulp, to Raven's chagrin.

"If you ain't seen the evidence son, you can't dismiss the possibility."

"If you're talking about the mystic rock, I told Tommy I'd love to see it. He refused to show it to me."

"I can show it to you," Raven said.

"When?"

"Tomorrow soon enough?"

"What about your leg?"

"It'll be fine in the morning."

"Maybe we'd better do it tomorrow then," Kylie said "before my dance card gets too full."

Raven chuckled again. "Your "dance card" might get a little fuller than you expect, if you can keep your timing right. Malin had the first samba, Priscilla's waiting for a slow dance. She's good in the clenches. Watch out John, they're both circling your tent."

Kylie started to respond to this veiled, what, threat? promise? but Raven stood. "C'mon, let's get down this hill while the light's still good. Oh, guess I should warn you; there's a game the boys play with the new kid on the block. They try to get you to tell all about yourself."

"That won't be easy," Kylie said. The last thing he wanted to do was talk about himself.

"You think not?" Raven dug his staff into the dirt then stepped tentatively off the veranda. He turned. "I know your name, middle name included, that you're divorced, and that you've got—or at least had—money. I also think there's some reason you don't want a TV in the neighborhood. And I don't even play the game. I'm just warning you, it's trickier than you think."

"I'm forewarned. I guess I can play the game with them, too?"

"That'd be interesting." Raven's voice trailed off as he led the way down the hill. "And don't forget your flashlight," he yelled back.

"Never leave home without it," Kylie quipped.

# CHAPTER SEVEN

Unvarying from the evening before, Raven's reverential toast was followed by a plea for a shorter one, this too apparently a part of the group's nightly rituals.

"How 'bout this? Thank God we're in the pink. Thank God we got a drink," was offered by Fred in replacement. This was followed by howls of scorn, honored tradition again prevailing. "At least it's shorter," the poet mumbled in defeat.

Their numbers were diminished by one. Malin was absent. Kylie sat mid-table, next to Priscilla. He recognized the perfume she wore, Nina Ricci's *L'Air du Temps*. He'd bought more than a few of the Lalique birds-of-a-feather-topped bottles over the years as gifts. He even knew that the inspiration for the bottle's design had come from the writings of Omar Khayyam. He was tempted to compliment her and impress with his knowledge, but the opening gambit announced that tonight's game was afoot. The first shot was fired before the initial round of margaritas was poured.

"Heard you rented Jeb's place. Bet it's a come-down from what you're used to," Jerry said.

Kylie had expected something more subtle. Maneuvering the questions and answers he turned the game around without much effort. He learned that Jerry, sporting the most tattoos in the group, had been in the building trade when he offered an opinion on the structural integrity of Malin's rental property—which, with some pride, he admitted building. From the corner of his eye, Kylie could see Raven cock his head, the classic "not bad, sport" expression on his face. One down, five to go.

Tod, or Toad to all but himself, revealed an English teacher's background when Kylie asked to borrow some paperbacks. Fred, who had introduced himself the night before, was induced to admit that he had sold real estate in northern California. The lug known as Barf was mentally excluded from the game for fear any probing might expose the source of his revolting nickname. The final member of the group was Owen Ford, DDS, and thus introducing himself, he too was excluded. Maybe he forgot about the game or just didn't care. The dentist, in addition to his profession, revealed something else about himself—a drinking problem. At this early evening hour he was already sloshed, but nobody seemed to mind. In fact it seemed as if several were playing catch-up. And so they drank, laughed and dined till the hour was late and it was time to return to their respective homes.

"You did pretty damn good," Raven congratulated him. "It took months to get that much out of them when they first got here. Now, get on home and rest. We've got us a hike tomorrow. Meet me here for breakfast. Can you wear a size ten shoe?" Kylie nodded. "Good. Wear your jeans or whatever long pants you've got. Don't forget your socks."

Priscilla went round the group, kissing cheeks, bidding goodnight. When she got to Kylie, she planted one alongside his left eye and whispered a husky, "If you need anything..." Then she turned and skipped down the beach with Barf on one arm and Toad on the other.

❖

It had been a fun evening, and with the tequila and Controy, Kylie was in high spirits. Tiki torches lit his way along the beach past the bamboo hut hotel. Behind it he reached his path and switched on his flashlight. There was no light.

"Damn it."

The tenderfoot had forgotten to check the batteries. But the moon was full, he'd made this trip several times already, and with Dutch courage supplied by pitchers of booze he proceeded with caution. The moonlight affording limited field of vision, he slid one foot forward in minesweeper fashion till it bumped, indicating a step up. This was painstaking but there was a deliberate sort of progress. Actually, it was rather pleasant. Over his shoulder he could see the moon's reflection on the water and the flickering torches on the beach. He stopped. This spot could be a scenic rest on one's way up or down he decided; if not to lessen fatigue, then to simply enjoy a different perspective of the magical cove. As he enjoyed the view, he heard steps below, coming towards him. At first he was relieved, thinking someone with a flashlight could help him at least part way to his new home. But as the hurried steps came closer, he saw no light, heard only urgency. Someone rushing in the night. Kylie stepped off the path and crouched in the brush. Seconds later, the man raced past him. Alarmed by his urgency, he gave plenty him of head-start before stepping back on the trail, feeling with his toes the rest of the way through the darkness. There was something about the man in the moonlight, Kylie thought. He did not look like a villager.

He was pleased to see Malin next morning and again invited her to share breakfast with him on the beach.

"How did you sleep?" she asked.

"Great. We missed you last night," he said, the third person plural masking his personal disappointment.

"That is not a nightly ritual for me," she said, implying that it should not be for him either.

"I can't see much else to do around here."

"With eyes blinded by alcohol there is much that isn't seen."

It was a bit early for a temperance lecture, Kylie thought, and besides, he had adhered to his practice of moderation, and no one had really gotten out of hand, much less "blinded"—though the dentist was probably headed that way.

"I'm sorry," Malin said as if she'd telepathically received every unspoken word. "I like those people better during the day. I don't understand most of their jokes anyway. Perhaps you would let me show you other ways to spend an evening sometime." Eyes lowered, she smiled at the eggs on her plate.

"I'd like that," he said, immoderately emptying the salt-shaker on his own sunny-sides as he stared at her.

"Good morning folks." Raven seemed to materialize at their table. Neither had seen him coming. He dropped the bag he was carrying to the sand with a soft thud and sat down.

"Hope you don't mind us ordering," Kylie said to him, then to Malin, "Raven and I are going—"

"Fishing," Raven interrupted. "We're going fishing." A not-too-hard kick to the shins was administered under the table as Kylie gagged and choked.

"*Aaaak.*" Kylie grabbed his throat. "Salt," he croaked, reaching desperately for his coffee, the only liquid in reach. "Too much damned salt on my eggs."

"Whose fault is that I wonder," Raven asked, picking up and examining the empty shaker.

Malin smiled coyly. She had finished her breakfast and had no interest remaining in the company of men setting out to do manly things. She excused herself from the table. "I wish you good fishing," she said and strolled off down the beach.

"Sorry about that," Raven said, "but the natives don't like us making a fuss over their rock. Some of them think it's sacred. It's better if we don't advertise where we're goin'. Hope I didn't kick you too hard."

"So I should keep it a secret from Malin?"

"I think a lot of things should be kept secret from that woman. But I'm no Ann Landers. You decide for yourself what to tell, what not to tell. I need some salt." He called the waiter.

They set out after Raven had shoveled his eggs down, Kylie wearing a rather worn but comfortably fitting pair of size ten walking shoes provided by his guide.

"How's your knee?" he asked Raven, who again walked with a staff.

"It's fine. This is for hiking up the mountain. We'll cut you a walking stick when we get up the hill a ways. We've got a tricky path ahead of us."

"Where are we going?"

"See the tallest peak dead ahead? Up and over. Not too late to turn back, city boy."

"Just lead the way, Kimosabe."

Mosquitoes dogged them the first half hour as they trudged through salt grass alongside an algae-covered lagoon formed when the dwindling river flow could no longer batter down the natural wall of beach sand and reach the cove. A flock of egrets stood as still as statues on spindly legs in the mirror-smooth brackish water, eyeing their passage, no doubt communicating the approach of strangers. There was no shelter from the sun, and though it was early morning, its rays beat fiercely on the back of Kylie's neck and uncovered head.

"I'm going to have to get me a hat," he said.

"Yup," Raven acknowledged without sympathy.

But as soon as they reached the jungle Kylie noted immediately how much cooler it was. In the shade, slight breezes wafted damp air in nature's climate-controlled environment.

"I didn't expect it to be this cool in the jungle," he said.

"Unggh," Raven grunted as if the further from civilization, the more he regressed. When they began to climb, he cut a branch off the first hardwood tree they passed, whittled it into a staff and handed it to Kylie.

"Watch me," he said. "Use it like I do. Don't look down."

Kylie kept up with Raven's pace, and they were going up at a pretty fair clip. Raven remarked on this when they finally stopped for their first break.

"Toting a 20 liter bottle of water uphill conditions you pretty fast," Kylie said. "Plus, all those years of Wyoming corporate retreats."

"Watch out," Raven said, "you're giving it away."

"What? That I'm from the business world? I'm sure you figured that out. That's a pretty big world, Raven. I'm not giving away much. Besides, you said you don't play the game. I trust that about you."

"Well just so you know," Raven picked up his staff to continue their trek, "I always believed a man with a briefcase could steal more than a man with a gun any day. I'm careful who I trust." And he continued the ascent.

Reaching the summit, they stopped and gazed at the ocean's vast reach. "Closest thing to heaven on earth," Raven said. "Sailing the Pacific, if you're lucky you can go weeks without seeing another ship. No sign of man anywhere. Almost like looking at the stars. Did you do like I told you and check out the sky that first night?"

"Yes. I thought the same thing; a view that hasn't changed since time began."

"Let's get on down. You're gonna see something else that'll have you thinking about time and its mysteries."

How different the back of the mountain was from its coastal face. There was no jungle on the inland side; they could have been in the foothills of Colorado as down they went. The slope seemed gentler, softening into undulating hills and dales reminiscent of Virginia. The path led them to a forest.

"It's through this stand of trees," Raven said, stepping across a narrow brook, whispering as if entering a church. Under the shade of tall trees was a shadowed sylvan scene of primeval tranquility; a Disney setting which prompted visions of fawns and squirrels coming forward to eat out of one's hand. No wild woods these; there was a sense of acceptance and shelter for all living things and as he felt his pulse slow with each step, John Kylie felt a need recognized a number of times since his arrival, a need to stop and give thanks just for being, and for being here.

"There it is," Raven said, stopping in the shade of a stone monolith. "Come on."

They walked to the rear of the rock where a small tree had affixed itself like a vine, now one with the stone, a servant shielding its master's upper surface—and providing supplicants a natural ladder. The two climbed and crawled onto a flat surface perhaps 25 feet across. The first design to catch Kylie's eyes was nothing more than the shadow cast by leaves rustling in the wind. Then he saw them. There were circles carved into the rock, six or more, some nearly faded away. The largest were almost two feet in diameter, with a bull's eye center, and pie-shaped sections fanning outward, resembling a wagon wheel. There were smaller circles of one continuous line swirling in on itself. They could have been anything, and yes, they could have been UFO's reduced to pictographs by primitive hands with primitive tools.

"You remember Mexican jumping beans? " Raven asked. "One theory is that they played a game with 'em right here. Put beans in the center and bet on which one jumped out first. Sounds dumb to me, but who knows. Here, look at this."

The largest carving was impossible to decipher. From one angle it looked like the side view of a carriage, a phallus-like object between the two 'wheels.' From another angle it looked like a dancing figure, from yet another, an ornate helmet. Its artistry bore a singular similarity to Aztec ceremonial depictions, but Raven dispelled any direct connection. "These carvings pre-date the Aztecs by almost 2,000 years. Over here. What do you think this is?"

Away from the drawings was a square with barely visible markings, by far the most angular of the carvings. It might have once been detailed, but had weathered away and was barely visible.

"Tell you what I think," Raven said. "I think it's a calendar, telling when those circle things whatever they are, appeared. "This crazy thing over here, I have no idea. But if somebody says it looks like a primitive effort to depict an alien being, who am I to argue."

And whether he shared Tommy's belief or not, Kylie was not going to argue either.

Raven whispered. "All the history, all we've built up and all we've destroyed in 2,500 years. And these carvings are still here, still trying to tell us something. Will we ever figure it out? Come on," Raven snapped back to the present. "We've got to eat. It's a long walk home."

"Eat?"

"The village of El Tuito is just a couple clicks from here. They make a good cheese. We'll get some tortillas, couple of beers and eat as we walk back."

The first hole was encountered as they walked to the village. "Damn, that's a blight on the land," Raven said, eyeing the gaping gash. "Don't know what they were looking for, but they left in too big a hurry to clean up their mess. Folks around here aren't usually like that."

The pueblo of El Tuito had the archetypical plaza and church around which the homes and shops of the residents clustered. At one of these homes Raven, standing on the street under a window, yelled in Spanish to the lady of the house, who came to the door with the requested item for her customer, the local *panela* cheese. Passing a dark closet of a store under the covered walkway on one side of the plaza, Kylie noticed tack and farm tools and poked his head inside. He purchased a broad-brimmed cowboy-style straw hat.

They bought tortillas and beer on the plaza, greeting women and men in groups as they passed them. Both the men and the women stared at Kylie. In a doorway a group of men huddled. An ornate black bow hung above the transom. Raven whispered to the group and was answered. After a sharp intake of breath, he bowed his head in silent prayer and nudged Kylie to do the same. They began to walk away. A man in the group ran after them. The Mexican spoke in low tones but his facial expression and hand movements were animated. Raven frowned, nodding and shaking his head gravely.

"What was all that about?" Kylie asked when the man had left.

"Don Chuy died; the most revered man around here. More than the priests, more than the landowners. He fought in the Revolution. Over 100 years old. He was the last to fight with Pancho Villa. I used to walk over here just to talk to him. Think about it. He was actually in cavalry charges with Villa. Cavalry charges on horseback, among the last in modern warfare. There were some firsts back then, too," Raven continued, enjoying this subject. "In the Punitive Expedition, Pershing's hunt for Villa after he raided a couple U.S. border towns, we had our first motorized assault in military history. A couple of 1916 Dodge touring cars were used in an attack by a young lieutenant named George S. Patton. Pershing used tanks for the first time, but not as armor. They were used to pull supply wagons. It was also the first time U.S. military aircraft received enemy fire, also from Pancho Villa's men. Man, I enjoyed talking to that old dude. Now he's gone. Fellow who just spoke to me said there were "suspicious circumstances." Said he saw soldiers taking the old man away."

After a moment of silence, Kylie said, "Raven, was it just my imagination, or were those people back there staring at me?"

"It's your watch," Raven said. "The gold on your wrist could feed a couple families in this village for a year or more. There was a lot of gold dug out of these mountains. People here can't look at a wedding ring without wondering whether it was part of the treasure stolen from them centuries ago. You know, before the Spaniards, a man caught stealing gold was flayed alive and sacrificed to the patron god of goldsmiths, Quetzalcóatl. That's who they thought Cortez was when they let him in, and he turned out to be the biggest gold thief of all time. Who knows, what you're wearing might once have hung around one of their ancestor's necks. Gold is indestructible. It doesn't rust or deteriorate. If it doesn't end up at the bottom of the sea, it's just melted, used over and over and..." Raven's voice trailed off as he walked ahead.

A more direct route to the mountain path took them across a large field charred by fire.

"Farmers burn their fields this time of year to clear them for planting," Raven said, stabbing his staff onto the hard earth as punctuation. "Gets out of hand sometimes when it's this dry. Certainly possible that old drunk Jeb could have died in a fire, but who knows." Raven stopped suddenly. "Damn. Here's another one."

The two stood on the side of another large hole, recently dug—though timing was a guess since the dry clay was only proof that no rains had fallen since the excavation.

"What on earth are they looking for? And who the hell are they?" Raven pondered out loud.

"Just don't tell me this is another UFO," Kylie said.

"No, no. Plain old shovels dug this. Pretty big hole to dig by hand. Specially in this hard ground."

"KRAACK. Pfft." The first sound came from a distance, but the second, like a distorted echo, spit into the ground only feet from where they stood, kicking up a tiny dust cloud ankle high. Raven threw himself against Kylie and both tumbled into the hole.

"What the—" Kylie gasped.

"Somebody's shooting at us."

"How'd you know?"

"I've been shot at before. Seems like someone's pretty partial to this damn hole. You alright?" Kylie nodded.

They sat up. Shards of rotten wood littered the bottom of the pit. Raven reached under him and scraped the dirt from a broken plank. "…plosivo" was stenciled in faded black ink. Another splinter showed only the bottom half of the letters and could barely be made out to read "…public de…"

"What's it say?" Kylie asked.

"My best guess, this one, 'explosives,' and this one, 'Republic de Mexico. Another guess, this wood is old. Real old."

"Maybe a farmer set off some old explosives."

"Not from this hole. Nothing exploded here," Raven whispered as he crawled up the side. "Give me your hat," he ordered. Kylie handed him his new straw sombrero. Raven lifted it above the surface with his walking staff. Nothing.

"We have three choices," Raven said, lowering the hat. "We can wait and see if somebody comes and shoots us in this ditch, we can wait till dark and scoot, or we can get the hell out of here right now. I think they were trying to scare us. I say let's get out of here."

"You've got more experience than me. You lead the way."

"OK. When you're up, start running in a crouch behind me. I'll head for the first cover. Let's go."

They clawed their way out of the pit, then began running, hunched over as low to the ground as possible. There were no more shots. They reached the cover of trees at the foot of the mountain.

As they climbed, both were silent. Finally, Raven speculated, "Maybe they dug up a box that said 'explosives' but didn't contain explosives."

"Like what?"

"Like something worth killing for."

## CHAPTER EIGHT

Kylie hoisted himself up the mountain with the aid of his staff. As they reached the summit Raven stumbled on a loose rock and fell down hard.

"Can't do it," he gasped. "Knee. I twisted it again back in that damn ditch. Been trying to ignore it, but... Aaagh!" He gasped with pain as he tried to stand.

"Why didn't you say something?"

"Thought I could make it home."

Both looked down the mountain. The village was directly below, but the path down, steep and rocky, had been a challenge for the able.

"Maybe if you put your arm around my shoulder—," Kylie began.

"Don't even think about it. Trail's too narrow for two abreast, especially with me having to hop. We'd both lose our balance and end up on the rocks."

"Well what do you propose?"

"Leave me here."

"Forget it. We don't leave men behind. Not in this man's army."

"No, really. You go down alone and bring back some help, make a stretcher."

"Yeah," Kylie yawned, "In the morning. I think I'll just stay here for now and make sure you get a good night's sleep. I'm too tired to crawl down there and back up again today. Besides, there wouldn't be enough daylight for the return trip. I'll head down at sunup and be back with help at mid-day. They won't even miss us. Not for one night."

"Tommy will fret himself to death," Raven said.

"You're lucky to have someone who cares."

The gentle breezes of late afternoon died away to nothing. The sun fell to the horizon as both men rested. There was nothing left of the day but scarlet banners draped across the background of deepening blue when Kylie opened his eyes.

"Raven. You OK?" he whispered.

"Fine."

"How's the leg?"

"Why are you whispering?"

"I don't want anyone to start shooting at us again, I guess."

"I told you they were just trying to scare us away."

"Raven?"

"Yes John."

"I think that whatever they're looking for, they haven't found it yet."

"That's possible."

"I think if someone stumbles across it before they do, that someone is going to get himself shot."

"That's also possible."

"Raven?"

"What is it now John?"

"I sure wish we were talking about flying saucers."

Raven chuckled. "Man is about the scariest thing in the universe, isn't he?"

"Tell you what; I'm not leaving the beach again unless it's to go fishing. No one shoots at you for trying to land a marlin."

"Wouldn't mind a bit of that myself. Yeah, let's get us a boat, catch a couple big ones and smoke 'em on the beach. It'll be a good excuse to have a party."

"Like we need an excuse," Kylie said.

Through the early evening there was no sound other than their own breathing, but darkness settled and air currents rose, caressing the mountain top, causing boughs to creak and branches to shimmy. Leaves whispered their secrets to the wind, causing a lone owl to answer, "I hear you, I hear *youuu...*"

"John," now it was Raven breaking the silence, speaking barely above a whisper, "you don't have to answer, but I've got a question."

"Yes?" Kylie whispered back.

"You made it to the top in the business world, didn't you?"

"Yes, I did."

"Did you kill anyone to get there?"

"No."

"I did. In my profession that's what you did."

"*I hear you. I hear youuuu.*" The owl hooted his acknowledgment of the old soldier's confession.

"I suppose though," Raven said, "you must have made enemies too."

"Sometimes an executive has to be prepared to end a competitor's life for the corporate good, his business life anyway. I did do that. Plenty of times. But that's commerce."

"Do you know where they are, those men you laid to rest—commercially speaking?"

"I didn't always know who they were, much less where they ended up."

"Well I've got that over you," Raven said, twisting his torso to relieve the pain in his shoulders and back. "I knew where mine ended up. Right where they fell." There was silence in the darkness, then Raven added, "But sometimes I feel they're standing alongside me. Every one of them. Like now."

Kylie shivered in the cool mountain air. "I'm the only one here, Raven."

In fits and starts they slept; one waking, whispering low to the other, trying to fall back asleep when no answer came.

Raven whispered in the darkest hour before dawn, "John, you awake?"

"Yes."

"I was thinking of Malin. Maybe you should tell her what happened."

"Why?"

"She might know what the hell's going on back there."

"I can ask. What do you know about her Raven—or do I have to play that game with her too?"

"She's from here. Full-blooded member of the tribe that owns all this land. Lost both her parents when she was a kid, I don't know how. Anyway, she was selling flowers and trinkets on the beach and an American couple took a fancy to her. They arranged with the village to pay for her schooling—she's very well-educated you know, I think she might have even gone to Vassar, or one of the Seven Sisters. Anyway, she came back here, to her home, and couldn't get along with her own people. She was shunned, can't get a one of them to tell me why. Full grown woman, and they gave her a new name – La Malinche. It was the name of the indigenous mistress of Cortez.

That's what they call her in town. We shortened it. She seems to enjoy our company, when she wants any company at all, and she knows she's welcome."

"Why does she stay here?"

"Can't figure it," Raven said. "She's not one of us, not with them, and she stays. Living alone in the jungle, a beautiful woman like that. I don't know, she doesn't claim to practice witchcraft—there are a couple women in town who do—but she just seems to have that kind of aura about her. You know what I mean?"

"Does she sleep with anybody?"

"Well I ain't been there, but a couple guys have. They didn't talk about it. And they didn't stick around afterwards."

"Maybe they weren't asked," Kylie said.

It's not only always darkest just before the dawn but coldest as well, and both men woke shivering in the gray prelude to day. Kylie jumped up and stomped the blood down to his feet and toes while slapping feeling back into his upper extremities.

Raven got his juices flowing by laughing heartily at his comrade. "Might be good enough for the locals," he teased, "but not for Riverdance. I'd have to give you a four out of ten."

He could stand. With the help of his staff he could take small steps and though he winced in pain with each footfall, Raven swore he could make it, so down they went, Kylie leading the way. Raven was never more than an arm's length behind, a hand on the younger man's shoulder when traversing particularly treacherous stretches—and there were many. Kylie enforced stops and breaks every half hour, enquiring with each stop of Raven's fitness to carry on. Finally, the village of Yelapa was near, the *palapa* rooftops of the beach restaurants in plain view.

"I think we're going to make it," Raven said. "Let's stop and rest one more time." They took a longer break, though hunger and thirst were now restive spirits in both. "Now we go." Raven stood and took the lead, walking with hardly a hitch in his step. One who had not been with him through the night might have thought his earlier wincing was an act, but Kylie knew better. This was not a man to parade his weakness through town.

"You sure you're alright now?" Kylie asked. They had come to the path leading into the village.

"I'm fine," Raven said. "I'll see you for dinner tonight."

"Unless I get a better offer," Kylie said with a smile.

"Well, man's gotta do," Raven said. "I'm going to see about a fishing boat."

"Raven, you're going to give that knee a rest. I just dragged you down a mountainside. I don't have the strength to pull you from the ocean."

"To get a good boat takes a couple days notice anyway. You rest up matey; it won't be sardines we'll be going after."

"Aye aye, Cap'n." Kylie saluted, clicked heels and walked towards the beach. He turned once to watch Raven head towards home. The man was practically skipping.

The day-trippers were on the beach in force and, though breaking the locals' taboo by patronizing one of the restaurants during tourist hours, Kylie was suffering too much from hunger and thirst to wait any longer. He found a table in the shade away from the sun-worshipers and ordered a hearty meal and two beers at one go, both of which he guzzled. Upending the second, he noticed a man standing at the corner of the building, near the toilets— "for costumers only," the hand-painted sign read. The man stared at him, just stared. Kylie knew he had seen him somewhere before and lowered his chin to scratch his forehead, masking his own stare. He lifted his eyes and squinted at the sun on the sea as he reflected. Head down but looking up at the man he tried to focus till his head began to ache with the effort. Could he have been one of those people staring at him in the village? Not likely, unless he'd made the all night trek over the mountain too. And if he had... Kylie covered his watch with his right hand. "Enough gold to feed a couple families," Raven had said. He watched out of the corner of his eye as he ravaged his lunch. Two more beers and the man was still there, still watching. After four beers, Kylie had good enough reason to approach him, and headed to the toilet. But he bumped into a tourist rising from his chair and after glancing away a split second, the man was gone.

Could he be mugged for his watch on his way up the path to his house? He thought about carrying something for protection, recalling that, 24 hours ago, someone had shot at him. They were only trying to scare, Raven insisted. But could it have been for the gold that he wore on his wrist?

## CHAPTER NINE

Lieutenant Avila stood stiffly before Colonel Márquez.

"You shot at them?" Colonel Márquez asked.

"Yes," the lieutenant answered. "They found one of our excavations. I wanted to uh, discourage them from taking any further interest. I did manage to scare them away."

"What were they doing in El Tuito?"

"They bought cheese, beer, and a hat, and visited with those mourning the old man. I spotted them as they came into the village. They had walked. Over the sierra."

"They walked all the way from Yelapa?"

"Yes sir."

"For cheese??"

"It is very good cheese, sir."

"Ridiculous. What did they say to the mourners?"

"Nothing. They offered a prayer and went on their way. Oh, one man ran after them and said something to the older gringo, the white-haired one. I have learned that he and the old man were friends; that the gringo is a former soldier himself who often called on him. I followed them. When they stopped at the excavation, I—"

"You shot at them. May I ask you Lieutenant, what did you fear they would find? We took everything that was there, what little there was."

"I don't know sir. I just thought—"

The colonel waved him silent, stood from the canvas and wood folding chair. "In future, no guns. We don't need to shoot gringos. It might attract attention, and it's unnecessary."

"Sir?"

"They are careless people. Accidents just seem to happen to them."

The younger man returned his commander's crooked smile. "I ordered one of our men to follow them. He will report any "accidents." He started to leave, then stopped.

"Sir, how can you be sure there is more gold to be found?"

Colonel Márquez gazed past the younger man. He pulled the worn diary from his pocket and held it up. "Because of this, I am sure." He handed the book to his subordinate who held it in his open palm. Aware of its obvious antiquity, he was too timid to turn a page.

"What you hold, Lieutenant, is the personal diary of General Alvaro Obregón, President of the Republic of Mexico when he wrote much of it. The last entry was made the day he was assassinated, July 17, 1928."

The young man lowered his hand as if with these words the book took on weight. He turned to the last page. "It says, 'banquet at La Bombilla Restaurant.'"

"Where he was shot," Márquez said.

The lieutenant placed the book on the desk in front of him.

Márquez paced, his hands folded behind him, the back of one hand slap, slapping against the open palm of the other, "I will tell you something very few men have known;" He inhaled deeply as if needing lungs full for his narration. "… a tale that I alone am left to tell. Don't ever think of betraying my confidence, Lieutenant. Don't ever think of it."

"I swear, sir."

The gaze of Colonel Márquez was piercing as he took the last full measure of the man before confiding. "You remember Venustiano Carranza," he said, "our first post-revolutionary president and how he was forced to flee the capital by train, the 'Olive Train'." Avila nodded. "You remember when he fled he took the nation's entire treasury in gold with him."

"I remember it was returned after he committed suicide," Lieutenant Avila said.

"Did you never think of that as curious? In a time of upheaval and lawlessness, an unarmed escort returns the nation's treasury in gold through still hostile territory. And we were made to believe that fairy tale. Did you know the leader of that selfless band of heroes was not even a soldier? He was an accountant and as unlikely a politician as ever there was, yet he himself became President of the Republic three decades later? Can't you see the irony? Can't you smell the deception? I'll tell you what really happened. Pancho Villa stole the country's gold and got away with it. This was kept secret. The truth would have undermined the government so soon after the Revolution. Obregón tried to induce the old bandit to give up its location, tried for years. But the fool was obstinate. Patience finally ran out and Villa was eliminated."

The gore of Villa's slaughter had been caught in sepia images and was part of the nation's collective consciousness, the photographs indelible in the mind of every Mexican. Still Márquez paced.

"With Villa gone, Obregón began the search. He found men who had served under Villa; men who were with him when the gold was plundered, when it was hidden. He bribed some, he tortured others. Certain hiding places were revealed, like the ones we have discovered these past few weeks. But the bulk of it," Now he stood before his subordinate, his hands in front of him, his right hand forming a fist which he pounded into the palm of his left, "we have not found. Yet. Villa's men spoke of a rock—"

"Sir, there are rocks everywhere in this country. I've tried—"

Colonel Márquez raised his hand for silence. "The men Obregón questioned spoke of a man who knew where this rock is found. It holds the key."

"But surely sir, any such man would be dead after so many years."

"He is now," Márquez said. He paused and sighed before continuing. "General Obregón's diary tells of a 'lad from Jalisco, called Chuy.' That's all he had to go on. Do you know how many Chuy's there are in Jalisco? Obregón never found him. But then his time was cut short. *Hecho*. With his death the gold was forgotten; the few men who even knew of the theft of our nation's treasury, all dead. All but one."

Márquez took a cigar from his pocket, lit it and watched the smoke curl to the ceiling. "I grew up with the story. It was my fantasy to find the gold, for the real truth to be known."

"But sir, if no one knew of its existence, how did you know?"

Márquez smiled. "Remember I told you of the man who took credit for returning the gold, who was ordered to perpetuate the deception and was later rewarded with the Presidency for his role? He did not marry my mother, but—"

Lieutenant Avila stared wide-eyed at the biological son of the former President.

The Colonel continued. "I happened to meet one of Obregón's descendants in Mexico City. He was a contemporary of mine. He told me about the diary, and lent it to me. I never got to return it. Poor man fell to his death from his balcony; 20 stories high."

Colonel Márquez picked up the diary and waved it in the air. "Who could find a man known only by one of the most common of nicknames? I too thought he had to be dead after so many years. Then," Márquez smiled, "the old buzzard had a birthday."

"I'm sorry sir, I don't understand."

"A local newspaper," Márquez said, "reported the birthday celebration given for one Don Chuy of El Tuito and claimed him to be the last man alive to have ridden with Villa. The article made the papers in Mexico City where I saw it. I knew immediately the old man was the one in the diary." Márquez's voice lowered to a whisper. "He's the one who knows where it is. The rock. The gold."

"But he's dead, sir."

"Ah yes, and that's a pity." Márquez seemed to slump but then stiffened. "But he told someone, I'm sure of it."

"Who sir?"

Márquez frowned, his thick eyebrows forming a 'v' over the bridge of his nose. "Maybe that gringo with the white hair. The one you shot at. Nobody walks that far for cheese."

As he finished his lunch on the beach, Kylie imagined that others too were staring at his gold watch. After he returned home he even looked for a place to hide it. What was time here anyway? He had no particular sentimental attachment to the piece. He could afford another with ease if it came to that. But damned if he would remove it. No, the overriding factor, the single rationale which had in the past led him to advance rather than retreat, to fight rather than surrender, was the simple belief that life's predominant purpose was two-fold, acquisition and then retention. The first phase was a battle; the second, war without end. Whatever you acquired, there was always someone trying to take it from you. He'd not always won the struggles to keep what he had gained, but he'd never given anything up without a fight. And so, though he might easily give the watch away tomorrow as fancy, even conscience might dictate, no shadow-man was going to scare it off him today. He adjusted it on his wrist for good measure.

But as sleep came that evening—an evening which had brought no "better offers," just a crushing fatigue that kept him from joining the beach crowd—he asked himself whether a fight for something so irrelevant, so immaterial was not itself doomed to defeat whatever the outcome. That seemed a question worthy of further consideration and he had time to ponder it. He had an abundance of time.

Next morning, there was not a muscle in his body which didn't throb with pain. Kylie knew the only cure was to get up and move. The shower contraption and the hot water it dispensed was not only cleansing but soothing to his aches, and after debating whether to shave or give in to a decades-old temptation not to, he scraped his face clean of stubble, and dressed.

The beach was again deserted but, as before at this hour, fishing boats were heading out from the town pier across the cove. He spied Raven talking to a fisherman preparing his panga. "I don't want one of those old things," he muttered and picked up his step toward the town. He met Raven on the path, headed his way.

"I got us a boat," Raven said.

"Not the one I saw, I hope."

"That?? Naw. Neither you nor I have the stuff these fishermen have. How they can sit out there, exposed to the sun hours on end, is beyond me. He's got a friend with a good boat. It'll be a regular charter, full complement of equipment, protective cover, twin outboards. I like to fish, not suffer."

"Good. When do we go?"

"Thursday."

"What day's today?"

Raven chuckled. "When you have to ask that, you can consider yourself a local. This is Tuesday." They walked.

"How's your knee?" Kylie asked.

"Still hurts."

"Then why aren't you home resting? Raven, I—"

"Because I'm steering clear of my damned roommate. That's why."

Kylie smiled, tempted to speak, but knowing what a flashpoint this subject was.

"It's not just that," Raven said. "He has patients today."

"Patients? I didn't know he had a practice."

Raven's gait was slow and uneven. "Tommy's been making a study of herbal medicines," he said. "He just wants to help people. I think it's as much therapy for him as for them. He's especially good with the kids. The Mexicans love him."

"Did he look at your knee?"

"Not yet. I'm waiting till he cools off. I know what you're thinking." Raven raised his hand, waving off the inevitable observation, spoken or not. "We are an odd couple—like in the movie," he added as a pointed clarification.

As they were already in the village, they chose a gringo-owned and operated bed-and- breakfast for their morning meal. They were served by a gentleman so thin a customer might have had reason to fear there was no food at the inn. This was far from the case, the establishment claiming justifiable pride in their eggs benedict.

"Tommy was upset?" Kylie asked as their breakfast was served.

"When I told him I took you to the rock, he exploded. Said it wasn't for any goddamned tourist."

"It seems to me that Dr. Tommy is just as judgmental as he accuses me of being."

"He does tend to become attached to his opinions. Usually he can defend them."

"I think I'll have a talk with him," Kylie said.

Raven smiled. "Sooner than you think."

Kylie turned to see Tommy on the cobblestone path at the entrance to the restaurant. He knelt before a little Mexican girl, talking to her, pointing at a bandage covering her shin. He smiled as he pushed a wisp of hair from her face. He stood and waved as she skipped away. His smile vanished when he saw Kylie. He quick-stepped across the small patio directly to their table. Kylie invited him to join them. "We were just talking about you."

"I sensed that," Tommy said, drawing a chair from under the table and sitting down.

"Thought you had patients this morning," Raven said.

"Just that little girl." Tommy studied the menu.

"Interesting case?" Kylie asked.

"Skin infection," he said. "I try to help the local kids when I can. They don't get to a doctor all that often."

Like a crouched runner waiting for the starting pistol, Kylie suspended comment while Tommy ordered. As soon as the proprietor who doubled as waiter had left them, he spoke. "I saw the rock," he said.

"I know," Tommy answered.

"I'm glad I did." Tommy looked warily at him. "I didn't know what to make of the carvings, still don't, but I felt something as I was sitting up there." The expression on his listener's face relaxed as Kylie continued. "I felt insignificant."

"Good. It should make one humble," Tommy said. "You respect it, then."

"I do." Kylie extended his hand and Tommy took it.

"Gentlemen," Raven said, "I think civilization is a crock, but I do believe in civility even among outcasts like us. You two agree?" They nodded. "Good." He paused then added, "You remember my friend the old revolutionary soldier?" Tommy nodded. "He's dead. Some folks suspect he was murdered. "I think you should be careful on your jungle walks. There's something funny going on around here."

Tommy was served his breakfast and, in the manner of rural villages, the morning news was offered with their meal. As he set down the plate, the proprietor asked, "You guys hear about the disappearances?" When all three shook their heads, he sat down. "Fourteen men disappeared off a road construction project last week, up near San Sebastian. Now, the wives and kids of ten of the men who disappeared, they're gone too. Vanished. Our maid's cousin was one of them. Just about every Mexican in town has a relative or knows somebody who's just... 'poof.'"

"Epidemic of some sort?" Kylie offered.

"Alien abduction," Tommy whispered. The other men turned briefly to him, then away, rejecting his suggestion.

"You said the wives and kids of only ten of the men?" Raven asked.

"Yeah. A few of the wives are still there. Don't know why."

"Not the best specimens," Tommy said without looking up from his plate.

The commentator ignored him. "Anyway, it's big news. Fourteen men disappearing down a hole, then entire families vanishing. Not your everyday story. You'd think the government might look into it but our maid says no one's doing a thing. Authorities are pretending it didn't happen."

"Government denial in such cases is standard," Tommy said. "Roswell, Site 54..."

"UFO's?" Kylie said with a smile.

"Absolutely," Tommy said. "What other explanation could there be?"

"Thanks for telling us," Raven said to the newscaster. The proprietor departed. Raven frowned.

"I'm almost afraid to ask," Kylie said.

"Yeah, well I'm going to tell you," Raven said, looking at Kylie. "Isn't it funny we've got holes being punched all over the countryside all of a sudden?"

"When they land they make holes," Tommy offered.

"Tommy, shut up for a minute, OK? We're not talking about UFO's. What I saw yesterday was a plain old ditch dug out of the plain old ground with plain old shovels. Nothing more. If those men who disappeared found something—"

"They might have been shot," Kylie said.

"Yeah," Raven said, "but wives and kids too?"

"Anybody who'd kill 14 wouldn't stop at more."

"But what about the women left in the village? Women running around screaming for their husbands. Don't you get it? Their husbands abandoned them. Others took their families with them. I think those workers found something. Something that paid for their ticket out."

"Raven," Kylie said softly, "look slowly around to your right. Inside the door of that little store across the street. You see that man in there? He's been following me."

"The rock," Tommy interrupted. "It's all tied to the rock."

"Tommy, will you shut the fuck up?" Raven cursed.

"Uh-oh. What happened to civility?" Tommy said.

"Sorry. Would you *kindly* shut the fuck up?"

"He was on the beach when I was eating," Kylie said. "Just standing and staring at me. I think I saw him when we were in El Tuito, then again the next morning. If I'm right, then he followed us."

"I don't see anybody," Raven said.

When Kylie looked again, the man was gone.

For several minutes Raven was lost in musing and chin-scratching. Then he leaned forward and whispered,

"Let's go to San Sebastian."

## CHAPTER TEN

"What is San Sebastian?" Kylie asked.

Raven leaned back and tilted his chair even further, balancing on two legs, letting Tommy answer.

"It's an old mining town in the high Sierras. Tommy said. "Had a population of 5,000 at one time and was one of the first cities in Mexico to have electricity. Only a few hundred people live there now; a sleepy colonial village that's being rediscovered as a tourist destination."

"How do you get there? I'm not climbing any more mountains."

"There's a small plane service that takes the tourists—" Tommy began.

"And there's a bus," Raven said, bringing the two front legs of his chair thumping to the ground. He left no doubt which mode of transportation they would take.

As Raven's proposal hung in the morning air, Kylie inhaled deeply. He exhaled his response.

"I came here for relaxation. I came here—"

"to get away," Raven said. "I'm not sure from what, but I bet the law has something to do with it." He slapped his palm on the table, startling both men. "Not that I give a damn. Most people here are running from something. I give 'em credit. Anybody who's got the courage to try on a new life deserves the chance as far as I'm concerned."

"Damn it," Kylie said, "I'm not trying on a new life. I just came here to get—"

He stopped in mid sentence. Raven smiled.

"Like I was saying, I give credit to anyone who's trying on a new life. But what I can't stand, you know, is indolence."

Both Kylie's and Tommy's eyebrows rose.

"Yeah," Raven said. "Indolence."

Tommy leaned back. "You've got about the most indolent group of characters you could ever hope to meet sucking down margaritas with you every night of the week. Why are you picking on poor John Kylie? He just got here and you haven't even given him time to relax, much less become indolent."

"Shoot. I took him on one little hike and he's whining," Raven said. "He's getting paranoid too; seeing people staring at him wherever he goes."

"Now just a minute buddy," Kylie said. "That wasn't paranoia back in that field. Those were real bullets."

"Somebody shot at you?" Tommy said. "Raven, you didn't tell me."

"Thanks," Raven muttered. "Something else for him to go on about. OK; maybe indolent is a bit strong. But that's where you're headed Kylie, if you're ready to just turn your back on something like this. And what if you're right? What if someone is following you—or us? You're not gonna do anything about it? You think you're gonna sleep at night up there all alone in your little shack?"

Kylie sighed. "So where do we catch the bus to San Sebastian?"

It was an involved process, retracing the route that had first brought him to Yelapa; the water taxi, then the crowded city bus. When they were back across the bay in Puerto Vallarta, a shopping trip was necessary before heading into the mountains. Kylie bought his own pair of hiking boots. A sweater was advisable for the elevation where they were going and Raven threw a waterproof poncho into the shopping cart, reminding that the seasonal rains would begin any day.

"That's why we've got to get up there now," he said. "One good rain and there'll be nothing left of that ditch." Raven was certain the mountain ditch would bear similarities to the ones they had seen, and Tommy was just as certain it would prove his own theories. Kylie was along for the ride.

"Why are we doing this, Raven?" Kylie asked. "Tell me again."

"You have to have a reason for everything?"

"Yes."

"A little while longer with us and you'll realize that's no way to live. It's the hunt, the chase, the risk, not the reward. Hell, do something for its own sake. Life's in the doing. That's living."

"You really like to get him wound up, don't you?" Tommy said.

The ride into the mountains promised to be more comfortable than Kylie's previous experience with public transport. Yes, the bus was old. Its metal sides were dented, and rust had eaten through its frame, fenders, even the passenger steps. Inside, a covering of fine dust discolored the olive seat-covers to a mustard yellow, except where the fabric had been worn or torn away, exposing rotting sponge padding and corroded spring coils. But one could avoid these unsightly inconveniences because this bus was practically empty. Kylie breathed a sigh of relief as the driver pulled away from town. Less than a quarter of the intended capacity was on board. One could sit where one wanted, having a full bench to spread out. It was mid-afternoon by the time the bus left from the coast, heading toward the mist-shrouded mountains.

"Tonight," Raven said, "we will rest in the style of 19th century gentry. We will lodge in a hacienda built in 1840, enjoy a gourmet meal, and I for one intend to get good and liquored up. You're going to discover, John Kylie, how deeply one sleeps in the upper elevations."

"I had that dubious pleasure two nights ago."

"It's better with a bed," Raven said with a grin.

Not quite an hour from town, the bus turned off paved surface onto dirt. The driver didn't feel that the change called for diminished speed, and they raced through back country dirt roads just as they had over asphalt. The vegetation at roadside was the same color as the interior of their conveyance, every leaf covered with mustard colored dust chewed up by vehicles transporting persons, livestock, lumber, and produce between country and town. Further from the road, beyond the settling dust, the country was verdant, faded somewhat from months with no rain, but thriving, hardy. Life here didn't offer the lush existence of the tropics. This land yielded its comforts only with time, effort, and patience. If the jungle was a plush armchair, this land was a cane and wicker rocker. But its yield was plentiful, as evidenced by fields of avocados, mangos, and corn, and small ranches where cattle grazed, where sows wandered filthy, fat and sassy. Kylie rattled contentedly along with the other passengers; shaken by the rough bumpy road, but not stirred to complaint.

But they hadn't reached the mountains yet. First the trail took dips as small streams were forded, splashing hundreds of butterflies from waterside sanctuaries in bursts of fleeting color. Then came sharp turns, some to avoid deep ruts, some to cling to the sides of the peaks they were beginning to climb. Now Kylie could look out as they careened around the mountains and gain a broader perspective of the landscape, and the horizontal vista was recommended. The vertical, a shear drop. He had to squeeze his eyes shut, and when the bus had to slam to a stop because something of equal size and weight was coming head-on around the bend at the same speed, all the passengers gave a collective gasp. He'd steal a glimpse at his traveling companions. Tommy's eyes seemed glued shut throughout and his lips trembled, not mumbled, in prayer. Raven looked ahead wide-eyed like a demented kamikazi pilot. On the downward slope of a long incline, he said, "This is the best part. The river crosses at the bottom here. We've got to get up enough speed going down to make it up the other side. Sometimes the passengers have to get out and walk up. Don't think so today though. We don't have a full load."

True enough, the bus hurtled down the mountain and hit the river, skimming across its surface like a smooth stone. Then it slowed. Gears ground as the driver manhandled the tortured transmission as if he were beating a team of stagecoach horses already giving maximum effort. Black smoke coughed from the exhaust.

"It's like its having a heart attack," Kylie said, looking back.

As the angle became steeper, velocity lessened. They were coming to a stop, the old horse now broken and winded, unable to climb any further—and it was a long way back down. At last the road began to level out. Slowly the vehicle crawled around a bend and the driver proclaimed victory with yet another punishing shift of gears.

"Made it," Raven said. "Cheated death once again. Not much further now."

Kylie withdrew into silence. Every journey has one, he thought, maybe not so dramatic, maybe not even perceptible; that moment when there's no turning back, when the risk has been assessed and taken, and bets placed. Maybe the bet is no more than the price of a ticket, a tank of gas; maybe the bet is a sliver of time from one's life— or one's life itself. But the moment comes when the player can only hope he holds the best cards and says to his god—or his devil—"it's your ante" hoping to win one more hand, one more day, one more year, one more chance. In the high Sierras of Mexico, Kylie realized that, if he played his cards right, there was hope for one more chance for him too. And in that moment he loved with all his heart this country that had helped him recognize that saving grace.

"We're getting off here," Raven said, hoisting his backpack and walking to the front of the bus.

"Here" was nowhere as far as Kylie could see, just thick growth and mountains. But as Tommy made no protest, he had little choice but to join them. The bus stopped and the three passengers disembarked onto a hard clay road.

"San Sebastian's up ahead a couple kilometers. The hacienda's over there." Raven pointed to nothing more than a corn field. "Come on."

Across the road, a rusty gate led to a path, ruts sculpted in damp weather now hard as rock. The gate was hinged by a length of chain draped over a nail in the post, as impotent a security measure as ever devised. Raven opened the gate and when all were through, closed it, replacing the chain as he had found it. If they were now trespassers, they were at least respectful ones, Kylie thought. The path wound through the cornfield a kilometer or more, then descended down a gentle hill. It transformed itself into a cobblestone drive that narrowed over a gently arching bridge, flanked by hip-high flagstone walls covered with downy moss. A stream purled below the bridge and willow trees on the bank draped their weepy strands over a tableau that Monet could have landscaped.

At the end of the drive, weathered wooden gates hanging open between columns chipped and cracked by time and the elements bid a muted, weary welcome. Flower-bearing branches peeked from behind the gate like shy young mistresses of the house, curious but timid. As one entered, passing between a smaller and a larger building into an open courtyard, bougainvillea, jacaranda and mimosa exploded into view, shouting their greeting in brazen scarlet, purple and pink. In front of a small building to the left, which had once served as either a carriage house or servants' quarters, a small citrus orchard offered oranges and limes, and the air was perfumed with their scent.

A pair of black labs padded to them, sniffed, wagged tails and followed Raven as he stepped onto the veranda and yelled, "Chester, you old bandit. You got clean sheets on those moth-eaten mattresses of yours?"

One black lab did a dance at Raven's feet, a raised voice being a signal either to play or eat, as a grizzled old man shuffled out through an open doorway, his unhurried movements emphasizing that *he* set the pace here and if so inclined, answered to no one. He was much in need of a haircut and shave and wore baggy white muslin matching shirt and pants, which he hoisted up above his paunch while looking downward at the feet of this intruder, as if footwear established the criteria for entrance to his domain. A cigarette hung from his lips, and without touching it he inhaled, then exhaled, leaving a cloud of smoke behind as he approached.

"Got reservations?" He looked past Raven to the other members of the trio, frowning as if he'd caught them stealing fruit from his orchard.

"Hell, Chester. This time of year? I didn't think we'd need—"

"No reservations, no room." The keeper of the inn turned away.

"Brought you a bottle of Jack Daniel's," Raven said.

Chester stopped, turned to face him, and growled, "Which I guess you expect me to share with you."

Raven nodded, and the two stood silently before one another; a face-off.

"Shit, Raven," Chester whined, breaking the impasse, "why the hell don't you ever call first? I don't have food for you and the cook's in town probably getting drunk. We like to offer dinner to our guests, dammit."

"How 'bout if you make it up to us with breakfast in the morning?" Raven asked, turning to give his *compadres* a quick wink. "Our friend John is new here. I told him all about your hospitality."

Chester appraised Kylie. "Alright," he said. "You know where the rooms are," and walked back into his residence.

"Which ones are vacant?" Raven asked.

"Hell, they all are," came from inside. "You know what time of year this is."

❖

Kylie was given the nickel tour of the old building. A front veranda was large enough for the *patron* to sit with friends and family, and looked out onto the courtyard, a faded remnant of what it must have been when *caballeros* on prancing stallions once called on the master of the house. The ground floor contained a dining room, drawing room, and master's study. Wooden tables were decorated with relics dug up presumably on the property; rusty keys, old irons, even corroded metal skeletons of antique firearms. On the walls hung photos of Chester with Hollywood legends of another age, and faded letters expressing gratitude for his hospitality and friendship. All rooms led out to the back patio, where a massive oak sheltered a tranquil sitting area. A wing at the far side contained the kitchen and rooms for the help and at the sound of their voices a sleepy young Mexican walked out from one, yawned a greeting and offered to show them to their quarters. Back stairs ascended to the lodgers' rooms on the second floor. There were three; large and with fireplaces in each. Hurricane lamps provided the only light—there was no electricity—and in the semi-darkness Kylie studied the remains of wall decor a century and a half old; painted wainscot, crown molding, and earth-toned accent walls. He chose the center room, tested the four-poster piled high with blankets and down comforter, sighing as he luxuriated in the lumbar support of modern bedding. With hot water from a gas heater and adequate water pressure, he couldn't ask for anything more. After a shower, and siesta, he joined his friends on the patio.

Laughter rolled like rocks down a landslide when Chester delivered the punch line to an anecdote as Kylie seated himself. Proper introductions were made, Chester disclosing that he was from a long line of Boston Brahmins, had escaped his legacy and its mandates, and had bought the hacienda 40 years ago after his first trip up the mountain from the coast on horseback. More biography was not needed; the walls of his labor of love were testament to a life lived full, and far from the madding crowd. Raven then offered a tale of his own, and for the next two hours it was good-natured combat between dueling raconteurs as the quartet made quick history of the bottle of Tennessee's pride. Kylie's sides were aching from laughter when Raven finally said it was time to head into town for supper. Chester offered the use of his old jeep—as long as Tommy did the driving—and retired with courtly grace, reminding them that breakfast would be waiting for them in the morning.

The boy sent into town for provisions had also informed the owners of the town's restaurant of the new arrivals' dinner plans, and their tables were waiting.

"Wait till you see what's for dinner," Raven said as he hobbled in. It was anyone's guess whether his unsteady gait was due to bad knees or good sour mash. "This gal's a master chef."

To Kylie's surprise, Tommy carried on an animated conversation with their chef and hostess in Spanish, then translated their conversation for his benefit. She and her husband had left behind stressful professions and Guadalajara's urban chaos for the ambience and mores of the 19th century mountain village. There were enough tourists to justify her culinary efforts and her husband—though she didn't know how he spent much of his time—acted as tour guide for small groups, and was the happiest she had ever known him to be. She offered her mate's guide services, assuring that there was much to see while they were here; an old church where a miracle had occurred, the view of the coast from the bluff where natives had watched the fleet of Sir Francis Drake sail into the bay, and of course the local moonshine still. Raven politely declined.

"Ask her if her husband can tell us where the road's being built," Raven whispered.

She answered in English and quickly outlined a simple route. "The people think it's a bad place. No one will go near it and they are having difficulty replacing the workers who disappeared. Three whole families from the village have vanished, and two local women have been widowed."

"God, I'd love to talk to them," Raven muttered.

"The widows? They don't speak English but they might talk to you, sir," she nodded to Tommy. "They feel they are being ignored by the authorities. They'll talk to anyone who will listen to them."

"Perhaps we could go to their homes in the morning after—"

"No," she said. "I will ask them to come here. Will you excuse me now? Your dinners are almost ready."

# CHAPTER ELEVEN

It was a cool, damp morning and dew on the leaves of plants and ferns gave a waxed, polished look to the foliage as the sun's rays pierced through tree cover. Breakfast was *du luxe*; the finest Paris hotel could not have done better than the rustic old hacienda. Second cups of coffee were half finished when Raven hustled them away, Tommy again the designated driver.

Finding the road under construction was a simple matter of a few kilometers, two turns and they were on its graded surface. "Now we just drive until we see something," Raven said, and not another word was spoken. It was hard not to feel that all this was a shame, this construction, however beneficial the long term results might be. The mountain was wounded; deep gashes cut into its flesh left uncovered and bleeding, mounds of rocks and dirt pushed to the sides like piles of refuse. Trees that had been felled were likewise simply pulled out of the way and, for now at least, left to rot. Branches withering but still breathing life seemed to cry out in their extended agony, pleading for a swifter death.

They came to the unattended road building equipment, helpless prey to vandals and thieves. Size, complexity, and this remote location was the only protection these behemoths were offered. Tommy stopped the jeep and the three got out.

"They didn't get any further than this," Raven said. "Fan out; keep your eyes open."

This they did and it wasn't minutes before Kylie on the right flank called out, "Here's the ditch." The others ran to his side. This one did not resemble the others they had found. It was deeper, and one side of it seemed to have caved in near the bottom. "It looks different," Kylie said. Raven stared at the pit, frowning.

"There were 14 men down there. That's a bunch of men in a ditch." He took a flying leap as Kylie and Tommy gasped. Such a fall could cripple. But the ground at the bottom was soft, and Raven sunk in dirt up to his knees. He looked up. "There's another difference. They found something here. They dug it out of the side. That's why we've got all this loose dirt at the bottom. There's a shovel in the jeep. Get it for me." Tommy was away and back in a flash and handed it down. Raven dug several spades full. He sifted through a shovel of dirt, held something in his hands, the size of his palm. He put it in his pocket. "Help me up." Kylie held the handle of the shovel; Raven grabbed the heel of the blade and walked up the side.

"What did you find?"

He pulled a sliver of wood from his pocket. It was a mere splinter, but something had been stenciled into it. The fragment read only '1917.' "This looks like that wood I found in the other ditch," Raven said. "I swear it's just as old. What was going on in these mountains in 1917?"

The three stood in silence. A crow flew over, mocking with its '*caw, caw.*'

"1917 was the year the Mexican Revolution ended, at least officially," Tommy said.

Revolution; that anarchic period of a nation's history when destruction, slaughter, and deprivation are utilized as weapons for social change. As the three men stood looking down at the hole in the mountain, images of Pancho Villa and Emiliano Zapata, of *federales* and peasant armies, leapt to mind. But the minutes of morning ticked away and they were no closer to an explanation for the disappearance of so many men, women, and children. And it was time for their meeting with the widows.

◈

The restaurant was open, but the tables were empty.

"They're in back," the owner whispered. "Señoras de la Cruz and Villareal." The trio walked to the back. They were stopped. "Only him," she said. Tommy went in alone. He came out almost an hour later, shaking cobwebs from his head. Raven and Kylie sat nursing a beer.

"I need one of those," he said, and grabbed Raven's bottle and upended it. The two eyed him curiously. "Jeee-zus," he said. "Those two would drive the dead wild." He sat down heavily, ordered a round of beers, and left his comrades on tenterhooks till the proprietress had served them and was out of earshot. Tommy leaned forward and whispered.

"They don't give a damn about their husbands, whether they're dead or alive, on this planet or any other. They want their paychecks, their pensions; they want money and they want it now. I tell you one thing, those two haven't been widowed. They've been *dumped.* I've never heard two members of the species maligned as much as their poor husbands, and if those men had a chance to get away, they grabbed it and I can't blame them one bit." Kylie had never heard Tommy string so many words together since he'd met him.

"So they weren't much help then," Raven said.

"Maybe. They told me where two of the families that disappeared live. They said the houses are open. Want to go?"

Raven was out the door.

The homes were both on the same street, only doors away from each other down one of the narrow cobblestone paths that emanated from the central plaza. They entered the modest dwellings with their adobe walls and dirt floors. The homes were practically identical in every way, even to the niches in the walls for votive candles and shrines.

In the second of the two houses, Raven noted, "Ever been in a Mexican home where there are no pictures of the parents, the wedding or the kids? They took the Virgin with them too. Oh, they left things they didn't need, or could buy new. Look at this." He dangled a cheap necklace from his index finger. "I can almost hear the husband saying to his wife, "Leave it, I'll get you something prettier." Well, I didn't have much doubt before but I'm now sure. These families pulled up stakes. And nobody's doing anything about their disappearance because they know it."

"Guys," Tommy whispered, "Let's get out of here."

It seemed like a very good idea.

⊰◈⊱

The bus ride down from the mountains was long but uneventful. When they reached the coast the regular water taxis had stopped running to Yelapa, but the men were so anxious to return home they paid a fisherman's exorbitant fare to take them back across the bay. The sun had set below the horizon but was taking encores in reflections of mauve and violet in the clouds above, when the craft pulled to the beach and the three jumped into the whispering surf. The usual retinue was in place for end-of-day observances. All turned to watch their arrival.

"Hey Raven," Jerry called out, "did you buy any whiskey?"

"Bought it and drank it," he answered, then lowered his voice and said, "We went to the mountains for a change of pace. Period. Whatever went on up there is none of their business. Right?" There were nods of agreement.

As Kylie walked from the surf he could see Malin's warm smile. She looked pleased to see him. Sitting across the table from her, turning to face him, it seemed the same could be said for Priscilla.

"What's it to be, John Kylie," Raven asked as they approached the table, "the lady or the tiger?"

"I don't suppose you're going to give me a clue which is which."

"Sorry. That would be against the rules of engagement."

The minute he sat down, Kylie wanted to leave. He'd tired of the game, the collateral snooping that the men at this table played with strangers, in fact, he'd had his fill of male companionship for a while. Rather than ribald laughter, he longed for promises implied through half-smiling lips, subtle offerings with eyes lowered coyly, suggestions hinted with a movement or a touch, while scents alien to all manly things teased his nostrils and spun in his brain. He returned Malin's smile, and Priscilla's, but could do no more. Not here. Not now. He gazed out to sea almost wistfully—and was briefly blinded by a vein of white light searing the heavens. Seconds later came thunder so loud its vibrations were felt.

"Wow," Toad said. "We're going to have some weather tonight."

It was enough to bring the evening's social activities to a sudden close. The season's first storm was best viewed from one's home for several reasons, one of which was to observe where the leaks came in, where repairs would have to be made when the rain stopped. High temperatures and the long dry spell from autumn to summer brought cracks in roofs and walls, and after the first storm, a flurry or repair work would be undertaken to shore up for the inevitable rains to follow. Goodbyes were said hurriedly. All but two lived in town or on the southern arm of the cove and headed homeward in a group.

Kylie and Malin began walking in the opposite direction. He turned and called out, "Raven, are we still going fishing tomorrow?"

"Not if it's raining," Raven yelled back.

Malin stood at his side. "You two seem to do a lot of fishing," she said.

"No, tomorrow will be the first time—" he said catching himself, remembering their deceit two mornings ago, cursing Raven for his silly little lie.

# CHAPTER TWELVE

The storm approached. Five seconds separated lightening from thunder. A thousand feet per second, one mile away. The wind picked up, whipping the surf from its languid whispers to rhythmic whooshing rasps as waves grew in stature and threw themselves on the sands like breathless messengers laying down their lives with their warnings. The first drops of rain felt like pellets pummeling the backs of their necks as they walked the beach.

"Let's run," Kylie said and held out his hand for hers. Malin ignored it, running on ahead. Now lightening and thunder were simultaneous, right above them. Blinding light, deafening cannon-like roars, as if heaven was determined to show its might and cause all living things to cower before it. They reached the dense jungle brush and turned back to look as a bolt of lightening struck one of the smaller beach *palapas* built as permanent shade for sun-worshiping beach-goers. The woven palm fronds burst into flames as the wooden post cracked and tumbled to the sand like a fallen soldier.

The two stood in awed silence. Rain fell in torrents and even from where they stood, in the flashes of lightning they could see water rising over the banks of the lagoon at the far end of the beach, carving its sluice through the sand and now, at last a river, rushing into the cove. Branches and brush were swept up by raging waters and carried out to sea. Safely removed from this terrestrial carnage, they stood beneath the trees, rain falling from leaves and branches above them in a steady but gentle warm shower. Without a word Malin turned to climb the path in the dark. Kylie had no flashlight. He could not see the trail. But nature, as if sensing his limited acuity, illuminated all around with blinding flashes of lightening, allowing him to scamper up several yards at a time as thunder seemed to nip at his heels. Malin, darting ahead, did not look back.

Breathless from running in those instants when lightning afforded him a brief field of vision, Kylie reached his house. Malin was walking fast, passing the veranda, her shadow visible in the glow of a soundless flash preceding the thunder's roar.

"Malin," he called to her, "why don't you stay here for a while. Let the storm pass."

She stopped and waited for him to reach her.

"Please," he said between gasps, "stay for a while."

"Why did you lie to me," she asked, "about going fishing?"

"First," he panted, "let's get out of the rain."

The tempest passed as quickly as it had come. The night was still but not silent as creatures, the insect world well represented, collectively celebrated the return of water to their parched domain. Crickets chirping, frogs croaking, and geckos with their shrill smacking lip sounds provided the back-up chorus as free-range hounds howled their solos throughout the jungle one after another.

"Umm, I like this," Malin said.

Leaning against an arm of the couch, she rested her legs on the small settee. Kylie sat across the coffee table from her. The glimmer of a single candle added texture and tone to the intimate vignette in the calm aftermath of the tropical storm. Her praise could have been a comment on the mood or the moment, even the cup of tea he'd managed to fix for her, but she was fingering the lapel of the terrycloth bath robe he had lent her after her shower. Kylie explained its origins.

"That's from the Peninsula Hotel in Hong Kong, one of my favorite hotels in the world. I remember standing at the window of my suite, looking over the harbor and watching a storm just like we had tonight."

"What were you doing in Hong Kong?"

"I spent a lot of time working in the Middle East and Asia. Hong Kong was just a stop along the way to break the monotony."

"I can't imagine what could be monotonous about traveling. You must be going mad with boredom here."

"But I'm not." Kylie leaned forward. "I'm fascinated. Really."

"And what has fascinated you? Other than fishing, of course."

He sat back. "I'm sorry about that. Raven took me to see a rock. A petroglyph. He thought you might be offended by a couple of gringos crawling all over something that might have spiritual significance to uh, your people."

"What did you think of it?"

"I was fascinated. An antiquity so untouched by time."

"It is so untouched because it hasn't been trampled on by tourists through the ages."

"We did nothing to damage it in any way," Kylie said.

After a sigh and a moment of silence Malin said, "I fear what may happen to it when the road comes. I used to go and sit there at night. Sometimes all night. You wouldn't believe what a night in the woods will do for your imagination."

"Oh I believe it," Kylie said. "We spent the night out coming back because Raven twisted his knee. I was certain somebody was watching us."

"Or watching over you."

"Not exactly. After getting shot at, you don't imagine benevolent spirits."

"Shot at? Who shot at you?"

"We don't know who and we don't know why. We were looking down at this ditch in a field, then bullets were kicking up at our feet."

"Ditch?"

"A hole somebody dug in the ground. We jumped in to dodge the bullets. Nothing in there but a few splinters of old wood. Raven thought they meant something. That's why we went to San Sebastian."

"Wait, wait." Malin lowered her feet to the floor and sat up. "What does all this have to do with San Sebastian?"

"Ditches. There was a big ditch near San Sebastian where the road is being built, where men disappeared. Raven wanted to compare ditches."

"This is crazy."

"No argument about that. But we found the same kind of wood up there as in the first ditch. Just a small piece. It had numbers printed on it. We think they found something in the San Sebastian ditch and ran away to enjoy it. Maybe buried treasure or something. What are you doing?"

Malin was standing. "I have to go home. It's late." She slipped into the bedroom then out again in less than a minute.

"Your clothes aren't dry yet," Kylie said.

"I'm fine. Dampness is something you'll have to get use to if you decide to stay here longer."

"I'm not planning on going anywhere," he said. He walked her to the veranda. She stepped so close he could feel her warm breath on his face. The glow from a candle made her eyes spit fire.

"There is much treasure buried throughout this country," she whispered. "Aztec gold stolen by Spaniards; Aztec gold hidden from the Spaniards. Much was hoarded by those who dug it out of our mountains centuries ago, rather than sending it over the ocean to their king. During our revolutions people hid their wealth, and many died leaving it buried. I believe treasures returned to the earth are meant to stay where they lie. There's a story of an order of Franciscan monks who came upon gold buried under their mission. They decided to keep what they found for themselves and abandoned their order. A few years later, one came back. The last one still alive, he was a babbling mad man. After confessing, he knelt before the altar of the church he had abandoned and prayed for forgiveness. He died on that altar. Those people in San Sebastian, perhaps they thought their discovery would bring them salvation. What they found is a grain of sand for which they will pay with their souls. Don't get involved with this, John Kylie."

Malin turned from him and was gone in one fluid motion, swallowed by the shadows.

The morning dawned with a coolness to be savored. Kylie groped without opening his eyes, feeling for the single cotton sheet he had kicked off in the night. Finding its hem, he pulled it up to his chin with a smile. The intermittent morning song of a bird outside the window reminded him more of a soothing snooze alarm than a jarring wake-up call.

"John Kylie, are you awake?"

It was a female voice, but not the voice that had stayed with him through the night in sleepless visions; a silhouette behind the shower curtain, sculpted legs stretched the length of the settee, black hair gleaming, glistening in the candle light.

"Hey. John Kylie. Time to get up."

He propped himself up on his elbows. "Who is it?"

"Priscilla. Are you decent? Hope not. I'm coming in anyway."

He leapt from the bed and scrambled for his shorts, hopping on one foot then the other, barely slipping them over his buttocks as she entered his bedroom.

She stood in the doorway, surveying the small room with obvious familiarity. "You know why Jeb put the toilet there?" she asked, nodding towards the porcelain bowl.

"Uh, no." His shorts pulled up and his hands free for other tasks, he rubbed his eyes, partly in wonder at this bold intrusion.

"For us, of course. Les gals. It serves as a bidet after sex, not that many *mujeres* around here know what that is. Bidet I mean," she giggled, "not sex." She walked to the window. "I thought it was quite considerate of him. Saving us a walk out there, barefoot in the park so to speak. I wouldn't have it moved if I were you."

He just stared at her.

"Anyway, I was on my way to Alice's, and—"

"Is there something I can do for you Priscilla?"

"I ran into Raven in town. Since I was coming this way he asked me to give you a message. 'Fishing trip's on. Get your ass out of bed.' That's it. Message delivered." She turned to go.

"Uh, Priscilla, wait." He followed her to the door. "I'm sorry, I was asleep. Would you like—"

"No thanks," she smiled, looking into his eyes but taking in his body. "I'll take a rain-check." She stepped from the house with the walk of a woman accustomed to the gaze of men. Kylie did gaze, but it was with the glassy stare of a sudden awakening.

Yawning, he turned and stared at the interior of his shelter, trying to determine if he owned anything that might be serviceable on a fishing trip. As the fog cleared, the answer was easy. No.

The boat had left the town pier and was approaching the beach. The captain had backed his boat into the shallower water, cut the engines then lifted them to protect the propellers. He rode the crest of a gentle wave to the shore and his mate gave Kylie a hand into the boat.

"Good morning, John," Raven said. "Traveling light I see."

"Yeah. I thought there might be a sporting goods store somewhere in the neighborhood but I must have missed it." He surveyed the craft; twin outboards, two rotating chairs facing aft with metal cups for holding reels and eyes for latching harnesses when the big ones struck. A cover over the cockpit allowed for some shade, and a dash over the wheel displayed a suitable complement of navigation equipment. No cabin cruiser, it was certainly adequate for the day's activities. Raven looked no better outfitted than he was, wearing faded blue swimming trunks and a sleeveless T-shirt. He did sport a cap and boat shoes.

"Bought you a hat," he said, motioning to a plastic grocery bag, "and suntan lotion. Put it on and lather up. Mind the sun. Even with the cloud cover we have, it'll get brutal out there."

"Thanks," Kylie said, grateful for the consideration, amused at the inconsistencies in this gruff old lizard's nature.

The mate jumped into the water and pushed the boat off the beach, hoisted himself up and lowered the propellers back into the water. Engines were fired and Kylie watched the shore recede, their wake expanding outward to infinity. They picked up speed as they passed the cove. The swells were larger than when he was last out in the bay, but with more powerful engines than the ferryboat pangas they cut through them with ease. Waves crashing against the shore's cliffs and jagged rocks confirmed the high seas. The water around them tended to gray-green rather than blue, reflecting the clouds above. They sat in the fishing chairs, Raven with his feet on the stern, scouting the horizon.

"Not the best weather," Kylie said.

"Maybe not for sunbathing. It'll be fine for fishing. Won't get as hot either."

"What's there to catch?"

"Bonito, dorado, red snapper, maybe tuna. We'll go out near the mouth of the bay, another 15 miles or so, no further. This is a good little boat, but I like a little more wood under me in the open ocean."

"You do much fishing?"

"Some."

The single syllable response was a wet blanket to further conversation, and the two sat in silence as they motored west. The mate busied himself baiting the hooks of four reels. Suddenly the boat veered to starboard. They both turned to the captain who pointed to the horizon. Kylie saw nothing. "School of something," Raven said squinting, but when they got there the water was calm and after several minutes with no action on the lines, the captain turned and headed once more to the mouth of the bay.

"I told Malin we went to the rock," Kylie said. The captain had slowed down as they trolled lazily.

Raven fixed his eyes on the sea.

"I told her about the ditches too."

"What'd she say?"

"She said what they found up by San Sebastian was 'a grain of sand' and that the rest needs to stay where it is. She said they would pay with their souls."

Raven turned to face him. "She said that?"

Kylie nodded. Raven said nothing more.

They motored for hours, drifted, cruised, and even sat bobbing like corks on the water, but nothing, not a nibble from the meandering residents of the briny deep. Hunger was assuaged by sandwiches Tommy had made for them, and thirst quenched by cans of beer that even on ice seemed not to get cold enough till Kylie clicked to the trick Raven had kept to himself: Drink 'em faster. Hot sun, cold beer, and languid seas loosened tongues as mid-day deepened into afternoon.

"So," Raven said, apropos of nothing, "did you abscond with the church funds, run off with the Senator's wife? I'd like to think that you killed someone. It's the romantic in me."

Kylie eyed him.

"Casa Blanca," Raven grinned. "Claude Rains as Inspector Renault. People always want to know where the stranger came from and what made him leave there."

"Oh," Kylie said, suddenly dizzy from sun and suds. "Casa Blanca."

"OK, OK." Raven said. "I'll go first. West Point grad. Made bird colonel. Then War College at Fort McNair in D.C. I was on the fast track to a general's star. Tour in Kosovo. Lost ten of my men in a skirmish one morning, and discovered a mass grave that afternoon. Ethnic cleansing. Women and children mostly. The women had been tortured and raped. Little girls, too. Next day we ambushed the bastards that did it. I killed a number in hand-to-hand."

"That's what a soldier does in war," Kylie said.

"I had this feeling that the whole world was watching and applauding me," Raven said. In one hand he held a beer, in the other, half a sandwich. He crammed the bread in his mouth. "They said I cut out their commander's heart after I killed him. I don't remember that, I kinda flipped out. After that I was on the fast track to an early retirement."

Kylie felt a wave of nausea.

"OK, *compadre*," Raven said. "That's my story. What's yours?"

Kylie lifted the beer can to his lips and sipped.

"I uh... I uh."

"Jesus, it must be bad," Raven said.

"I certified false accounting statements," Kylie said, clenching his jaws.

"You what?"

"...and falsified annual reports."

"Felipe!" Raven called to the captain. "Throw this man overboard! He's one *baad hombre!*"

"A lot of people lost their life savings. Retired folks lost their pensions."

"You steal it from them?"

"In a manner of speaking, yes."

Raven began chuckling. "So one might say there are a lot of folks back there who'd like to cut your heart out?"

"That's a fair assumption." Kylie said.

"Hey, don't look at me like that. I'm retired from active duty," Raven chuckled.

"*Amigos.*" The captain pointed, and turned the boat about. Raven pulled a rod from its holder and Kylie did the same. This time they could see the waters churning as birds circled and dove.

Minutes later Kylie heard the *ziingg* of the reel as a fish took the bait and the line went taut. He gave a yank, setting the hook, then let the line play out; then reeled in, played out, reeled in. It was a fighter. Then another *ziingg* from an untended rod. The mate quickly grabbed it handing it to Raven in exchange for the one he held in his hands and Raven began his own duel, bending forward, pulling back, rod bowed and line taut. The two men now bobbed in unison with arms cranking furiously at the spinning reels. Both fish were soon brought flapping to the surface, still full of fight.

"Tuna," Raven said. They were in a school of them.

The next half hour was one of frantic activity as they remained centered over the agitated waters. As soon as a fish was brought aboard, the rod was handed to the mate, who ripped the hook from its mouth, threw the flapping fish on deck, handed over a fresh rod, then baited the one in hand ready for the next catch. It was like reloading single-shot muskets in defense against an advancing army. The action was too fast to even catch a complete breath. Finally Kylie wheezed.

"Stop. I can't do anymore." Kylie said. Both were gasping for air, barely enough strength in their arms to hand the mate their rods. "I think we've bagged our limit." The back deck of the boat was covered with squirming, shimmering silver fins and scales, wide mouths agape, gills opening and closing like accordions.

"Gonna have us a fish-fry tonight," Raven said, but as soon as the words left his mouth he hit the deck, cowering, crouching as low as he could get; an instinctive reaction to a sound which would haunt him for as long as he lived. Kylie looked up to see a helicopter fly over their heads.

"*Chingon*," the captain cursed, raising his fist to the sky.

"What is it?" Kylie asked.

Raven rose from his crouch and stood to his full height. He shielded his eyes with his hand as he gazed out to the open sea, and then quickly rummaged his bag for a pair of binoculars. "I see it," he said, handing the binoculars to Kylie, uttering one word. "Pirates."

Kylie brought the image into focus. There it was, several miles out to sea. It had to be a large ship to be visible so high on the horizon from that distance. The helicopter, now a dot in the sky, was returning to it. The pilot had grabbed a cell phone from the dash and was shouting. He set the phone down, still cursing.

"Modern-day pirates," Raven said, answering Kylie's unasked question. "Japanese, probably. They use copters to hunt tuna and spread out nets ten miles wide or more. It's illegal and they're in Mexican coastal waters. He just called the Navy. Doesn't do much good though. It'll take the fastest boat they've got three hours to get from port to where that boat is now and it'll be gone in minutes. Boat, shit, it's a floating factory. Local fishermen can't compete. That thing can suck out all the tuna in the bay in a single afternoon."

"Pirates" was an antiquated term, Kylie thought, but no less valid today than 200 years ago. He'd been called one himself.

## CHAPTER THIRTEEN

It was a grand party, fish for everyone, and even those Mexican locals who rarely socialized with gringos showed up in force. They made it a party with their guitars, songs and dancing. The only ones who didn't enjoy themselves to the fullest were Kylie and Raven. They were too exhausted.

"How do the fishermen, the charter boat crews, how do they do it day after day?" Kylie asked. "I tell you Raven, I'm too tired to climb the hill to my place. I think I'll just grab a hammock back by the stables."

"You wuss," Raven mocked, but when he tried to stand, his knee buckled and he fell to the sand in a heap. Several men came running, Tommy in the lead and yelling.

"What'd I tell you? What'd I tell you? I told you to rest, but oh no, not you. You've been over-doing it ever since this guy joined us and you just had to go off fishing. Serves you right. Serves you right if you never walk again."

"Doctor Foster Quentin Briery," Raven growled, "alias 'Tommy,' will you shut your fucking mouth and help me up, or get out of the way so someone else can?"

Tommy's round face flushed with anger. "You have no right to talk to me like that. I'm the only one who looks after you old—you old—" He muttered under his breath as he turned and walked away. Raven was helped to his feet.

"Did you ever know anybody scared of the sound of his own name? Looks after me? The little shit. I don't need some looney like him looking after me."

"You're tired Raven. And you've had a lot to drink," Kylie said.

Raven glared at Kylie, then realized that two men were supporting him. He could not stand on his own.

"Maybe we'd better get you home Raven," one said.

His shoulders slumped. "Yeah, I am kinda tired." He looked down the beach. Tommy walked towards the jungle, refusing to turn around as his name was called. "Guess he's gone looking for mushrooms. I'll apologize to him in the morning. You guys want to help me home?"

His arms draped across their shoulders, Raven hobbled but was mostly carried to his house. Kylie stumbled his way to the hammock in which he'd spent his first night and was asleep long before the revelers ceased their music and laughter. Hours later he awoke with a start, not sure where he was in that first moment of consciousness. He opened his eyes but there was nothing to see in the total darkness. Immersed in total silence as well, it was his aching muscles that assured him he was not suffering a loss of all senses. Then he heard a horse snort. And another. There was the thump, thump of hooves stomping on the firm ground, then one whinnied. The animals were scared of something out there. Then it sliced the night, a scream which stilled his heart and stopped the flow of blood through his body. Staring wide-eyed into the black nothing, his fingers clenched, nails dug into the soft flesh of his palm. Kylie had never felt such stark terror. There was the sound of running feet and shouting. Beams from flashlights piercing, pulsing. Yelling in Spanish. Someone stuck his head in the doorway of Kylie's hut.

"*Señor*, you OK?"

"I'm fine. What was that?"

"*Pantera*. She gone now."

"A panther?"

"Yes. But don't worry."

Don't worry. Killer cats on the loose and he'd been sleeping out under trees; now in a shanty with a door that barely even closed. What was he doing in this place? Kylie asked over and over again till blessed sleep returned.

For once, the roosters got it right. Since his arrival he'd heard them crow at all hours of the clock except early morn. Last night he'd not heard a one but this morning they trumpeted the dawn right on cue. Rarely had their pronouncement of the coming of day been more welcome. Kylie rose from his hammock and stretched in the doorway of his hut. A sleepy-eyed Mexican leaned against the corral gate after having stood guard over the horses during the night. He yawned and waved a good morning.

Kylie relieved himself, then walked to the beach. The pain this morning was in his shoulders, and he swung his arms around in the widest circles possible. He pulled off his shirt, kicked off his sandals, walked to the water, waded, then dove, swimming to work the stiffness out of his muscles. The cold salt water revived him, but not as much as the chill morning air when he emerged remembering he had no towel. He jogged up and down the beach to dry off and spied Priscilla coming his way. He thought this an unusually early hour for someone like her. She was running toward him.

"Did you hear it?" she said when barely in speaking distance.

"You mean the cat?"

"You bet I mean the cat."

"I sure did. Sounded like it was right on top of me. Do they get that close very often?"

"Right in the village? Not since I've been here. But you don't have to go too far into the jungle to find them. Hey, you're shivering. Get some clothes on."

He recovered his T-shirt and sandals. "I need to get back to my place. I hadn't planned to sleep on the beach."

'I'll walk with you," Priscilla said. "I'm going up to Alice's hotel. Care to join us for breakfast?"

"Sure, after I shower."

They walked a short ways in silence but Kylie could feel the woman at his side was bursting with commentary. She blurted out, "Raven and Tommy, they were sure acting like a couple of queens last night. What kicked that off?"

"Raven was tired. He had too much to drink. Everybody gets cranky once in a while. And I wouldn't call them queens if I were you," he said.

"I didn't call them anything; I just said they were acting strange. And whatever they are, I couldn't care less. Other people's private lives don't offend me. I believe in sexual expression, in case you haven't noticed."

He couldn't help but smile. "I did catch a subtle hint."

"Oh damn, was I being subtle again?"

Kylie said, "I don't know either one well enough, but maybe Raven gets a little tired of looking after Tommy all the time."

"Raven gets *what?* Boy, you sure don't know them well enough. I'd say that shoe was on the other foot. Raven was a basket case till Tommy moved in with him. That kid, he's a natural care-giver. I live near them. I see him looking after the old guy. I see him with sick kids from the village. I got typhoid last year and was pretty bad off for a couple weeks. You'd have thought Tommy had moved in with me, he spent so much time at my place. He seems embarrassed to let people know he has medical training, but I've never met anyone with such a natural inclination."

"That's funny," Kylie said, "Raven gives the impression that Tommy is so dependant on him."

"Well don't tell him you heard different from me."

They reached the path and started to climb. Kylie had a vision of Malin bolting ahead of him in the storm. He recalled her saying that she lived alone in the jungle—where the big cats roamed. He mentioned his concern.

"Sometimes I think Malin's part panther herself," Priscilla said.

"Let me clean up. I'd like to go check on her."

Priscilla was waiting for him on the veranda. "Mister, you do clean up good. My, my but you cut a dashing figure for this backwater. This poor little gal's heart is just a thumpin'. Here. Feel."

She stepped towards him, reaching out for his hand and bringing it to her bosom. She pulled him to her. Her sudden and unexpected kiss was ardent.

"Next time," he gasped as she released her embrace, "give me a little warning." He inhaled deeply. "So I can take a breath first."

There was a certain swagger to his step as they left his shack to check on Malin's well-being. John Kylie, man among men, protector of the fairer sex. Full of himself as they ventured into the brush, he tried to ignore the fact that it was Priscilla who led the way. Fifteen minutes into the jungle seemed like a very long time and a great distance. Humility returned as Kylie followed, admitting to himself that this was not a journey he would have undertaken alone.

"I'm not worried about her," Priscilla said. "Malin told me that she sleeps with a flashlight in one hand and a knife in the other."

"Then she's seen cats out here?"

"She wasn't talking about cats at the time."

They came to a small clearing and a bamboo hut similar to those of the hotel on the shore, but larger. The thatch covering had more of a roof line and windows were cut into the bamboo walls. Flowers framed the winding stone path to the front door, and wild orchids hung from the posts which extended from the roof to form a covered porch.

They walked to the entrance of the house. "Malin, it's Priscilla and John Kylie." There was no answer. "Maybe I'd better go in first in case she's uh, got company." The front door was nothing but woven wicker that flapped back and forth like a leaf in a breeze. Priscilla pushed it open and went in. Kylie peered into the dark after her. "Malin?" Kylie paced back and forth in front of the door. Priscilla came out. "She's not here."

"Any signs of anything?"

"No. She's just not home."

Kylie wasn't entirely relieved. This was inconclusive, like when a threatening hurricane shifts its course, but the warning remains in effect.

"Let's go," Priscilla said. "Breakfast is waiting and I'm hungry."

Though breakfast was delicious and Alice a charming and gracious hostess, Kylie had come to this rustic end of the earth to do as Romans when in Rome, not to dress up a movie set. The oak table and chairs, hunt-scene place mats, Wedgewood flatware, and polished silverware were a bit much, and when he'd eaten, and engaged in polite conversation sufficient to show he was neither ill-mannered nor ungrateful, he was ready to be on his way. He knew after bidding *adios* that he would be the subject of their prattle. That was fine. Alice made no bones about being a widow living on memories. Priscilla with her exaggerated hussy act didn't fool him either. She could play the licentious strumpet but, like the older woman whose company she obviously enjoyed, she was lonely. Just lonely. Even in paradise, there was a lot of that going around.

# CHAPTER FOURTEEN

That afternoon as he walked down the hill, Kylie was not looking forward to spending another evening with the eccentrics who gathered on the beach to bid the sun *adios*. They were already ensconced in their customary places. Seeing him approach, Priscilla got up from the table and walked to greet him.

"We have some MIA's this evening," she said. "Malin's not here, nothing too unusual about that. But Raven's not here either. He's home worrying."

"About what?"

"Tommy. Nobody's seen him since he stomped off last night."

"Shouldn't we be looking for him?"

"Ask them," Priscilla said, nodding to the group. They stood together at the end of the table. As he looked at the men with the question in his eyes, Tod spoke.

"I was with Raven less than an hour ago. He said Tommy's just doing this to get back at him. I think he's probably right."

"Tommy's always staying out all night," another said. "He knows his way around the jungle better than any of us. Besides, what could we do now? It'll be dark soon and look at that sky. We're in for another storm tonight. A big one."

A look to the heavens confirmed this forecast.

"He could be out there injured," Kylie said.

"Yeah, and he could be sitting in a hotel somewhere laughing at us. I say we give him tonight to come home. Then we tell the police."

Suddenly Kylie had no wish for the company of these men. "I'm going to go see Raven."

"Can I come?" Priscilla asked, but knew it was not a good idea. Raven, as they all were well aware, preferred solitude for his suffering.

Kylie left them to their ritual, which, like most rituals, served through its observance to deaden senses to life's realities. As he walked away he belittled their evening entertainment. Just how much of a leap backward was it from toasting with alcohol the sun's nightly departure to deifying the fiery ball of gas? How much different were their raucous jokes and drunken laughter from trances and chants induced by mind-altering herbs and plants used in the search for that which can never be found in the here and now? Raven was right. Civilization was a crock.

He walked through the village and found the path he and Tommy had trod that first morning and followed it to its end. The home the two men shared occupied the most strategic location on the cove, if not the entire coast. The spit of land extended further into the ocean than any other outcropping, and their residence was at its tip, built almost to the edge of a rocky cliff. Approaching, the home looked like a concrete bunker, a dwelling so inhospitable at first glance that it not so much welcomed as dared man, beast, even the elements to cross its threshold. Kylie took the dare and knocked at the most solid wooden door he had seen in these parts.

"Raven, it's John Kylie."

"It's open."

Kylie stepped inside and gasped with wonder. The house was a pentagon with the seaward exterior like the bow of a ship, two angled perimeters built out to a point, made entirely of thick floor-to-ceiling glass. The sea and sky made the entire exposure a moving tapestry. Large windows in the northern and southern walls provided cross ventilation and gave one the feeling of outdoors, but this was a clever fiction. One wasn't just sheltered, one was encased in this structure. In one corner was a metal spiral staircase descending down to a lower level where, Kylie guessed, the sleeping quarters were found. Raven sat in a huge over-stuffed *equipale* arm chair near the glass wall with his legs stretched out on a matching ottoman, staring directly into the setting sun. He did not get up, did not even turn to face his guest.

"C'mere. Quick," Raven said. Kylie crossed the room.

Even overcast skies at this hour became tableaus of striking color. The sun had broken through a mass of purple clouds and was sinking into the horizon where a clear band allowed an unobstructed view of its final moments. They watched as the sphere of flaming crimson sunk slowly out of sight.

"Hah," Raven said. "No flash, green or blue or candy-fucking-apple-red. I don't believe there is such a thing."

"Well if you haven't seen one from here, I doubt you ever will. Raven, this is fantastic. Why the hell do you ever leave this place to watch sunsets from the beach?"

"I don't like to be alone," he said.

If sorrow had a sound, Kylie had just heard it. "We're all getting a little worried about Tommy," he said. "Has he stayed out this long before?"

"Never."

"Shouldn't we do something?"

"I can't," Raven turned to him, his eyes glistening. "I can't walk much just now." An elastic support was wound tight around his bad knee.

And there was the truth of it. The man was helpless and Kylie surmised there had been no immediate offers on the part of the others. Well, in fairness they would have allowed till mid-day or even later before giving cause to worry, and for obvious reasons, Raven had not gone looking for help.

"Perhaps I should go look for him," Kylie began.

"Don't be stupid. You don't know your way in the jungle and there's a storm coming. You, I'd worry about. Tommy's just got me pissed off."

"So we wait?"

"That's all we can do." Raven continued to stare at the horizon. "Wait till he comes back. If he comes back."

"What do you mean, if? He's going to—"

"There's nothing in this house he can't live without," Raven said. "Nothing he couldn't turn his back on forever."

"Can I get you anything?" Kylie asked softly.

"Cabinet under the sink. Bottle of Smirnoff."

With misgivings, Kylie brought him the vodka.

"For relief of pain, this sure as hell beats aspirin," Raven said with a wink and sly smile as he upended the bottle to his lips.

Kylie left Raven to whatever peace he could find this coming night. On his return, he made a wide circle to avoid the group still gathered on the beach for whatever solace they sought in each others' company. It was a long walk home.

The jungle was full of sound most nights, except in the calm before the storm. This had passed and Kylie lay in bed listening as breezes blew;

first whispering then howling up the mountain, shaking the roof over his head. Imagination runs wild when solitude's uncertainty is enhanced by darkness, and he couldn't sleep as he tried to identify the noises in the night, trying to differentiate the shrill whistling of wind through the trees from screaming gusts which his frightened fancy tried to convince him were four-legged predators circling, circling. The screen door rattled against its ill-fitting frame. The latch was broken—not that it did much to secure the door in place anyway. Occasionally a gust would whisk it open and slam it shut. He made a mental note to attend to it in the morning. An annoying *slam* caused him to open his eyes and he knew his imagination had taken hold. In the total darkness he thought he saw shadows. Shadows in the dark. Something was coming toward him, approaching the foot of his bed, now circling it. Kylie swore that this would be the last night he slept without a flashlight in one hand and a knife in the other—but perhaps this was to be his last night. The shadow circled the bed. He could smell its presence. This was no fantasy. A pale arm, luminous in the pitch black, reached down to where he lay, grabbed the sheet under which he cowered. Someone sat down on the mattress.

"Scoot over, cupcake. You've got company." It was Priscilla.

He heard the rustle of her clothes as she slipped out of them. She leaned into him, the curves of her body melding into his. A hand reached across his chest, fingers dancing down to his stomach. Kylie grabbed her wrist.

"Priscilla," he whispered. "It's not going to happen."

"I've lost out to her already?"

"What are you talking about?"

"Never mind. Can I just stay here tonight?"

"If you're good."

"I'm better when I'm bad."

"Do you want me to walk you home?" He propped himself up on his elbows.

"Alright, alright. Go back to sleep. I'll be good."

With first light Priscilla jumped from the bed and made her way to the shower. She needed no instructions in the use of the artful plumbing. Kylie remained in bed, still not trusting his uninvited overnight guest.

Wrapped in a towel, she walked to the veranda. Anticipating, she caught the screen door as it closed behind her to keep it from slamming. Kylie was unnerved at her familiarity with his home. He rose from his bed, pulled on his shorts and joined her.

"Priscilla, about last night. I didn't mean to be rude."

"You were the perfect gentleman," she said flatly, not looking at him.

"Would you like some coffee?" he asked. "I've got some instant." "No," she turned to him. "I've already abused your hospitality. Let's go see if anyone's heard from Tommy." She brushed past him, her fresh-washed scent teasing his nostrils. "I'll get dressed now. No peeking." Her hint of a smile was not one of defeat.

They walked to the beach and saw several of their colleagues seated with Raven at the restaurant. Even from a distance, their postures said it all.

"Nothing," Raven said as they came to his side. "Nobody's seen him." Propped next to his chair was a single crutch, a real one.

"Then we have to go looking for him," Kylie said.

There was no argument. Two men ran off to get the others, giving Kylie time to wolf down breakfast. They returned with the remaining members of their little band, save one. Malin had also gone missing, and for the same length of time. Kylie asked if anyone had seen her. They hadn't but there was no concern over her absence, she was frequently gone this long or longer.

They left the beach as a group. Reaching the river, they decided to split up and follow it into the jungle. Leaning on his crutch, Raven took command.

"Two groups. One on each bank. Stay close enough to hear each other. Sound off every 15 minutes at my call. Got that?" Raven set a pace which even the unimpaired struggled to keep up with.

Swollen with rains from the recent storms, the river raged, carving, defining new banks as it tore at the silt loam and ripped shallow-rooted plants, shrubs, and trees from their tenuous moorings. The river ran brown with occasional dark patches of foliage clumped together, branches, even trunks of trees. And there was the detritus of the humanity upstream; plastic bottles, aluminum cans, and polyurethane wrappers of various foodstuffs. What was not trapped in logjams, remaining and despoiling the land, would be carried out to man's largest dumpster, the open ocean. Walking the river, watching the free-flowing garbage was like walking through a battlefield after a calamitous engagement. Waste. So much waste.

They had set a goal of 20 kilometers. Raven halted for a rest at one of the many bends in the river, a point where it narrowed enough for them to communicate without having to cross. The water was murky and fast flowing. The risk of wading in was not warranted. Several drank from makeshift canteens fashioned from bottles of purified water; others had simply purchased containers of Gatorade and strung them around their shoulders. They refreshed themselves in silence. No one had seen anything worthy of conversation. A waterlogged tree trunk meandered around the bend coming their way. The currents caused it to turn in the water and still more waste could be seen wedged in its branches as it continued its march to the sea. All eyes watched as it slowly passed. It came to a halt, momentarily trapped between two rocks. Rushing water gave it a full turn as if an invisible lumberjack was doing his acrobatic log rolling. Submerged branches turned up and reached out of the water as if begging. Twisted in one, hanging limp in the open air, was a hand.

Raven yelled, pointing with his crutch. Kylie jumped in the water and was followed by three of the men. Their feet sunk in the riverbed beneath them but they were able to wade in waist-high waters to where the log had jammed between the rocks. Kylie broke off the branches freeing the hand and arm as the others leaned into the tree trunk, turning it over, bringing the body fastened to its side to the surface. It was Tod who looked to Raven on the shore and simply nodded his head. They had found Tommy.

"Don't touch it! Don't touch the body," Raven yelled, then jumped into the water. He dragged himself through the current to where the log was pinioned. "Give me your shirts!" he demanded of those holding the log in place. With curious looks they pulled off upper garments and in consternation watched as Raven seemed to engage in mummification, wrapping cloth around all exposed areas of the body. Only when this was done did he ask for help in moving the remains to the shore. The shrouded body was laid out on the bank. "We must make a stretcher," Raven said, "and take him to El Tuito. Don't touch the body." This seemed a macabre excess of protectionism, then he explained.

"HIV."

# CHAPTER FIFTEEN

It was a strange funeral cortege that trudged along the swollen river, men stripped to the waist, the deceased swathed in faded T-shirts, the lone woman following behind the crude stretcher made of driftwood. The dirge to their mournful march was provided by Raven, hobbling alongside the body, giving the eulogy. He spoke in meter, in time with the slow placement of halting steps in the damp, muddy earth.

"His specialty was pediatrics," he said with measured cadence. "In the last month of his residency a woman was brought to emergency, near death and pregnant; gunshot. She died on the operating table, but he was called in to save the baby. All in a night's work. Anyway, Dr. Briery got married just after he finished his residency and began to build a practice, and a life. A year later his wife's pregnant and they discover she's HIV positive. He's the carrier. They abort the child. Word gets out and worried parents find new doctors. Seems the mother of the child he saved that night in emergency had AIDS and in the chaos of trauma, who knows, a pin prick through a surgical glove, the splatter of a single droplet on a superficial cut. Anyway, his wife contracted AIDS and died. He lost his practice. He could no longer bear the sound of his own name. Every time it was uttered it was with a curse."

"Why'd he spend so many nights alone in the jungle?" Tod asked.

Raven sighed. "Maybe he was looking for a cure. Maybe there he could forget." They walked in silence for several minutes, each left to his own thoughts. A question seemed to hang in the air above their heads. Raven mumbled.

"What'd you say Raven?"

"We were not lovers," he said.

"Raven, none of us ever really thought—" Priscilla began.

"But I loved him. I did love him so."

They halted on the outskirts of El Tuito for many reasons; to avoid scaring children, to retain a modicum of dignity, and because they could see a procession and an event of some importance had already drawn the local populace to the church and plaza.

"That's either a wedding or a funeral," Raven observed from the field where they had stopped. "Look," he said, "Kylie and I will find the doctor, and there has to be a truck somewhere. Wait here. We'll be back."

"See if you can find us some shirts too," was yelled after them.

The entire town had gathered on the plaza. The mood of the crowd was not festive. Raven spotted familiar faces and walked to the gazebo in the center of the square where the pueblo's notables had gathered. Kylie stood back and watched as he drew one aside. The man nodded and ran off. Raven walked from the plaza and waved him over. Kylie met him at the door of the store where he had bought his hat on the previous visit. The door was open but there was no one to wait on them, commerce having taken a back seat to whatever the village occasion was.

"That was the village doctor," Raven said. "He went to get a truck. He'll meet us and bring the body in."

"What's going on over there?" Kylie asked.

"Memorial service for Don Chuy."

"Well he had a long life."

"Some are still saying he was killed," Raven said.

"I can't imagine anyone harming a hundred year old man."

Raven shrugged. After several minutes waiting for the shopkeeper's return, they simply selected several cotton shirts and left an ample payment under the cash register.

They returned to the others moments before the doctor arrived with his pick-up. The body was placed in the truck bed and everyone jumped in the back. It was a short drive to the physician's modest residence. Doctor Garcia motioned for them to go around to the back, where a rear bedroom with its own entrance had been converted to an office. Raven informed the doctor of the virus Tommy carried and he nodded gravely. He bid all to wait outside while he examined the body, then came out and addressed them in English.

"You will have to remain with us while we wait for the police. Your statements will be necessary. There may be arrests."

"Arrests?" Raven said, "For an accidental drowning?"

"He does appear to have drowned, but how accidental is going to be disputed."

"What do you mean?"

"It seems there was a struggle. There is human flesh under his fingernails. Also, someone tried to cut off his tongue," Dr. Garcia said.

Despite their screaming at the lack of logic in their being treated as suspects—they had brought in the body—they were placed together in a single cell that could have been a set from a 30's B western and served as little more than a place for the town drunks to sleep it off. The gang of gringos were gawked at like celebrities—especially Priscilla. One by one they were taken from the cell and ordered to strip in front of the doctor, searched for scratch marks on their bodies. Their incarceration by the local sheriff lasted the entire night, with the exhausted doctor forced into duty as translator. When morning came, interrogations were completed. They were free to go.

The shortest distance home was between two points, but there was mountain and jungle between those points. Raven was in pain—in more ways than one—and all were dead tired. A 40 kilometer bus trip to the resort town preceded a half hour trip by water taxi across the bay as they made the triangular return. Along the journey, nothing was said. Finally they reached their familiar shore. Several workers from the restaurants came running to the boat to receive the news and hung their heads when told of the young American's death. A small Mexican woman offered summation in her simple English. "He seemed sad, but he was a kind man." Like any who had become a part of this disparate community tucked snugly into its remote corner of the world, he would be missed, silent nods assented.

Raven announced that he would be going back across the bay in two days to recover the ashes, and asked all to attend a memorial service, the exact time and place to be announced.

"Now if you all don't mind, I'm going home. I'd like to be alone." He refused offers of help and made his solitary way along the beach and into town.

As the others began to disperse, Kylie asked, "Has anyone seen Malin?"

No one had.

Priscilla and Kylie shared a quiet dinner before retiring to their separate residences. They finished their meal, too tired to speak but when Kylie called for the check, Priscilla said, "Two dead, one missing. Do you have any idea what's going on around here, John Kylie?"

Kylie took a deep breath and looked out to sea. Beyond the cove far across the bay was the silhouette of a single sail, the craft barely moving in the gentle breezes of sunset. "I had thought this place was a paradise where the world could be forgotten," he said. "I thought there might be purity, a cleansing, living without modern conveniences. Pretty naive, huh?" Priscilla nodded. He continued. "You know, some people think that the road and electricity will destroy this pristine beauty. It's more basic than that. It's greed. Before the road is built, before the first power lines are laid, greed will have changed this place beyond recognition."

"John, what are you talking about?"

He told her of their discovery in San Sebastian.

"Maybe I'm just tired," Priscilla said, "but it doesn't add up. Are you saying Malin dug up something and that's why she's missing too?"

"I don't know how Malin fits in. I think Tommy found something, maybe Jeb also, and they were killed. The people in the mountains were luckier. Malin said what they found was 'a grain of sand.' Anyway they got away with it. Malin seemed to know what they discovered. A little knowledge can be a dangerous thing."

Priscilla toyed with the uneaten food on her plate. She stared down, moving cold French fries around as if pieces of a puzzle. "Jeb died during one of his jungle jaunts. Tommy's dead, another death in the jungle." Kylie nodded. Priscilla lifted a French fry saying, "This one's Jeb," putting it in place, "and this one's Tommy. Now of all of us in our little sunset group, the only other one who also likes roaming the jungle, lives in it all alone in fact is—" She put a final French fry in place, forming a triangle. "Connect the dots, it seems to spell Malin," she said.

Kylie was given no chance to counter, as the waiter appeared and whisked their plates away. "Your French fries don't add up," he said. "First, we're not even sure if she's missing. She could be on a trip, or she could be lost, dead, or dying herself. All we do know is there's something out there somebody will kill for."

"Maybe more than one 'somebody.' Did you ever stop to think that what someone wants to find, someone else might want to keep hidden?"

Kylie sighed. "I haven't because I'm just too damn tired. Priscilla," he stood, pulling money from his pocket to pay for dinner, "do you mind if I—"

"I don't mind. I think we all want to be alone tonight. For the first time since I've lived here, I'm going to lock my door."

On opening his eyes next morning, Kylie recognized that life continued, but there was less comfort in its continuity. He thought of moving on, of leaving this place. But where would he go? Back home awaited subpoenas, indictments, and the deposition his lawyer had warned him not to miss had come and gone. He was not ready for what awaited him back there. Anyway, would the most remote Pacific isle be any different than this? Not unless it was uninhabited. He got out of bed hesitant and lethargic, able though unwilling to face a day, an existence, so complicated by the misfortunes of others—and those who fed on them. He had tried to escape all that. He fixed coffee and took it out to the veranda to admire his view with meditative tranquility. No, this would have to do for now. He would just withdraw from the society of men. Completely. But perhaps it was the devil himself laughing at such a plan, at man's folly believing he could take his destiny into his own hands. Devil or no, there was laughter, crazed laughter coming up the hill as Kylie sat and sipped his coffee.

"John Kylie, get your ass up."

He sat calmly. Raven came over the hill and approached. Quickly. He had no crutch, carried his walking stick but seemed to use it hardly at all. His limp was barely noticeable, and 12 hours earlier he could barely hobble. There was a ruddy glow to his complexion, even a glint to his eyes. The worry and misery that had lined his face was gone. This man could have just returned from a week at a spa and Kylie was perplexed at this overnight transition. He'd expected him to be prostrate with grief. Raven carried a notebook in his hand and waved it over his head.

"Look what I found," he said, almost skipping to the house. "Tommy's notebook." He jumped—yes, jumped—onto the veranda and pulled up a chair. "I was going through his things last night. Poor boy didn't own more than three sets of clothes." He waved a notebook in Kylie's face. "It's kind of a log. Where he went in the jungle, what kind of plants he found; you know he did experiments, mixed up stuff for the potions he gave to people for skin problems, rashes, ringworm—"

"Raven will you slow down? How about some coffee?"

"OK," Raven said and caught his breath. He was ready to proceed when Kylie returned with his coffee, had even turned to a page and was drumming it with his index finger. "Here. Here he talks about a place and he says, 'Men digging at night. Heavy equipment in the jungle.' This was written a couple nights before he died! He even gives directions to the place." The cup of coffee which he really didn't want was placed on the ground. It interfered with his histrionics. "Don't you see? I was such an ass that night after all that beer and tequila, I didn't give him a chance to tell me what he'd found. They killed him. John, the bastards killed him."

Kylie just sat and continued to sip, staring at the man across from him. What a wonder of recuperation Raven was, vanquishing severe depression, even debilitating physical affliction, in the course of a single night. But then, the elixir he had administered to himself was one of the strongest known to man, so potent that armies filled with it overcame insurmountable odds, leaving death and destruction behind their frenzied advances. Its powers could grant man the closest thing to immortality; feeding on it could keep one alive. Raven had drunk deeply from the chalice of hate and now found his sustenance. Pure unadulterated hatred had restored him, given him new reason to live.

"I'm gonna get them," he growled.

Kylie's immediate responsibility was to talk him out of such madness. His first tack was the wrong one. Raven would not be convinced of his limitations. Age, physical condition, the fact that he would be one against an unknown number didn't matter.

"You cannot imagine the things I've been trained to do," he said, "the things I'm capable of doing." Kylie could imagine. The picture of the bloody Kosovo battlefield came to mind.

"But Raven, there might be many people involved in this." He shared Priscilla's observation about someone wanting whatever it was to remain undiscovered. Raven stroked his beard thoughtfully.

"There was someone who didn't want it found," he said, "but he's dead now."

Kylie just stared at him.

"I'm gonna tell you something, John Kylie. First, I gotta ask you a question. How much do you know about the history of Mexico?"

# CHAPTER SIXTEEN

"The history of Mexico?" Kylie said. "I know Cortez and Montezuma. Remember the Alamo. That's about it."

"It's a pity," Raven said, "that we're so ignorant about our southern neighbor. You want to get yourself another cup of coffee? The lecture's about to begin. I don't want to be interrupted."

"I'm good," Kyle said. "Begin, professor."

Raven leaned back in his chair. "Military history has always been a hobby of mine. I told you I used to enjoy visiting Don Chuy, our deceased revolutionary hero on the other side of the hill. I wanted to learn all I could from him about the cavalry charges he was in; Pancho Villa's tactics. Actually, there wasn't too much to learn about those, Villa's only strategy was to mass his troops and charge. In the end, that wasn't enough. He would—"

"Raven, is this going somewhere?"

Raven sighed. "Show a little respect. Don Chuy was living history. I respected and admired him. He came to trust me with the secret he carried to his grave. I'm sure it was why he was killed. They found out he knew."

Now Kylie sighed. He looked at his watch.

"You got an appointment?" Raven asked. "Don't be so damned impatient. I'm getting there. OK, OK, I'll cut it short. After the Revolution things were still unsettled. In 1920, the President of Mexico, Venustiano Carranza, was under siege. The army was in revolt against him because he refused to name his successor from the military. He fled Mexico City with the idea of establishing a provisional government in Vera Cruz. He left the capital by train. Sixty cars. In one of them was the national treasury. In gold."

"What?? He ran off with the country's gold?" Kyle said.

"There was historical precedent," Raven answered calmly. "Cleopatra had Egypt's treasury on her ship when she accompanied Marc Anthony to Rome in his fight against Octavius and they got caught at sea in the battle of Antioch. Marc Anthony was so anxious to see she got away safely, it contributed to his defeat. Carranza was an avid student of history, maybe that's where he got the idea. Anyway, he had the country's treasury with him. His train was attacked only a couple hundred kilometers out of Mexico City. He was wounded and committed suicide before they captured him."

"And the gold?" Kylie asked.

"The official word was that a single low-ranking adjutant returned it to the capital." Raven's sneer and curled upper lip evidenced his skepticism.

"You don't believe that," Kylie said.

Raven's toss of the head and raised eyebrows was his answer. "The Revolution was still fresh. The legitimate government had been overthrown. The country was full of warlords, *caudillos*, any one of whom would have fought to the death for such a treasure, and a single low ranking officer with a small contingent of men is said to have returned the gold to the capital. I think that's a bunch of crap. The guys who succeeded Carranza couldn't afford to let the people know the country's gold had been stolen. Biggest damn cover-up in history. And the low-ranking adjutant who escorted the nation's treasury back to the capital? He later became President himself. His payoff for keeping the secret."

"The secret?"

"Pancho Villa robbed that train. Pancho Villa got the gold. Mexico's gold."

Kylie smiled, humoring the old soldier. "I seem to remember Pancho Villa being from the north of Mexico, near the border. How would he have heard about the gold? How could he have gotten there so fast? Most importantly, what did he do with it?"

"He probably had spies," Raven said. "They had telephones and telegraphs back then. He could have jumped on a train. Hell he could have flown."

"Flown?"

"Why not? They had planes back then too. Remember I told you the first time in history our military aircraft ever came under hostile fire was when Pershing was hunting Villa. Hell, it wouldn't surprise me if he stole one of ours. Anyway, he could have gotten there. He had men all over the country loyal to him. And what did he do with the gold? He hid it. He planned to come back and get it later. He was going to use it for the country's good—as he saw it. But he got killed before he had the chance. Look, after he surrendered in 1920, Pancho Villa lived a quiet life. He was shot in 1923 on his way back from a christening, and believe me they did a thorough job. I'll tell you why. Villa was getting ready to make a comeback. He was going to get back into politics and he had the mightiest campaign chest in history. That's why he was assassinated." Raven studied Kylie's face. There were several minutes of silence before he spoke again.

"Don Chuy knew where Villa hid the gold," Raven said. "He was one of a trusted few, and the last one alive of Villa's closest confidantes. He was afraid when he told me. He felt the old enemy was closing in on him."

"So where is it? Where's the gold?"

"He didn't tell me that, exactly."

Kylie stood up and stretched, reaching up and yawning. He put his arms down. "Raven, you've been through a lot lately. It's perfectly normal for you to—"

"Sit down," Raven snarled. "I'm not done yet."

Kylie saw the white knuckles of the fingers grasping the arms of the chair and imagined them around his neck. He sat down.

"Thank you," Raven said. "Rudeness is the behavior of ignorant fools and you're no fool, John Kylie. Now listen. Two things convinced me, in addition to the fact that the old guy had no reason to lie to me about this. First, historians have always wondered how Villa, a small time criminal and a poor farmer, was able to conscript and outfit an army in the early days of the Revolution. Only in the past few years have we learned how he did it. He robbed a train. On April 19, 1913, Villa robbed Northwestern train Number Seven out of Juarez of 121 bars of silver bullion worth $150,000, a lot of money back then. The American mining company who owned the silver negotiated with him and got some of it back, then kept the whole thing secret because they didn't want to appear to be favoring any particular faction in the Revolution. Villa funded his army with a train robbery. Seven years later, he robbed Carranza's train with the same goal in mind."

"You said two things convinced you," Kylie said.

"Yeah." Raven looked around, stood and stepped off the veranda. "Come here." He stood over a bare patch and with his walking stick began drawing in the dirt. Kylie stared down at a rudimentary map of Mexico. Raven differentiated areas with varieties of hash-marks. "This is a map of the country during the revolutionary period, divided into areas by their loyalties to the different revolutionary factions; Villa, Zapata, Carranza and General Obregón. At the height of his power, almost two-thirds of the country was loyal to Villa. Here's Banderas Bay, where we are. It was the southern-most boundary of Villa loyalists; the first part of his territory he would reach coming from Mexico City. Furthermore, he'd done it before; a similar route. Villa escaped from prison in Mexico City in 1913. He went to the west coast, caught a boat north to Sonora and safety. Stands to reason he'd head to the coast again with such a precious cargo. Geographically, Banderas Bay was his first safe haven."

Now Kylie smirked. "So the country managed to keep secret the fact that it's treasury in gold had been stolen, that it was bankrupt? That's ridiculous."

"Is it? Who sees a country's treasury? I mean physically? They say it's there, who's to say it's not? It's kind of like, what did you call it, 'falsifying annual reports'? Damn John Kylie, you of all people should know such a thing can be done."

Kylie slowly nodded his head.

"Besides," Raven continued, "the country had oil by then. Black gold replaced the metal."

"It's feasible," Kylie admitted, "but so what? Even if I believed this crazy story, and I'm not saying I do, you said the old guy didn't tell you where it was, and the old guy, remember, is dead and buried."

"Ah, John Kylie, so little faith, so little imagination." Raven grinned. He leaned forward, resting his elbows on his knees and motioned for Kylie to bend over, too. Their faces were inches apart, yet Raven whispered. "Think for a minute. Say you were entrusted with such a monumental confidence. You see your *compadres* die over the years as you get older and older. You don't trust banks or safe deposit boxes; this isn't something you can hide under a mattress; you wonder about your mind slipping some day or maybe going all together. You trust no one. What do you do? What do you do?"

Kylie stared, puzzled.

"You keep it where nobody will see it. Nobody." Raven leered.

Kylie snapped. "He's got a tattoo. He's got a map tattooed on him," he whispered in response.

"Son, I believe there's hope for you yet."

"Oh Christ, Raven you're not thinking about—"

"Yup. Gonna dig 'im up, check out the old tattoo. Somethin' else I've been curious about, this'll give me a chance to see." He stroked his beard and sat back up. "Always wondered what a hundred year-old pecker looked like."

"Raven, you're one sick bastard."

Kylie stood and walked inside. "Well you can count me out," he said.

"Thought you'd say that," Raven stood and followed him in.

"Glad I didn't disappoint you." Kylie began fixing a fresh cup of coffee. "I can't believe you're serious. OK, you become a grave robber, then what?" But Kylie saw it in Raven's face. "You're not thinking about getting the gold."

"I sure as hell am," Raven said, "and you're going to help me."

"You can forget that idea," Kylie said. "You can forget that right now. Why should I? And for that matter, why on earth should *you*?"

"Tommy." Raven said.

"What do you mean?"

"It's what got him killed, I'm sure of it. Maybe he stumbled across them, maybe they thought he saw something or knew something, who knows; but whoever's looking for this damned gold murdered him. I find the gold, I find out who killed Tommy. It's that simple."

"Raven, there are police for that kind of thing."

Raven guffawed. "Think about what you just said, boy, and remember where you are. Police? Besides," the look in his eyes was that of a man deranged, "police don't know anything about revenge."

Kylie drew a deep breath, shaking his head. "I don't suppose I can stop you?"

"No." Raven walked to him and grabbed his arm firmly. "Look at me," he ordered. "John Kylie, I'm going to tell you something about yourself, and appraising men was my job for almost 40 years. You're not proud of yourself. Maybe you had a goal, maybe you trusted fate to take you where you wanted to go, but once you got there, once you had achieved all you ever wanted, you found it empty, empty and shallow. Didn't you?"

Kylie just stared dumbly into Raven's glaring eyes, eyes with pupils like pin points.

"You're running away from the consequences of what you did, but you're searching, too. You're looking for something to give your life more meaning. Well son, it's not just a matter of giving up limos and first class hotel suites. Living in a jungle shack ain't gonna get it. You have to *do* something. Something meaningful. You gotta take a *risk,* man. You gotta do something to get back your pride or you're going to be a ruin the rest of your life. Your shame will eat at you like a cancer." Raven sighed. "You'll have no dignity."

"And going with you on a Mexican revolutionary Easter egg hunt will restore my dignity?"

Raven let go of Kylie's arm. He waved both arms wildly in the air. "You'll be writing the final chapter of the Mexican Revolution, man. Doesn't that mean anything to you??"

John Kylie had no answer. Raven had succeeded, maybe not in convincing him, but in wearing him down.

---

Colonel Márquez listened to his junior officer's report, his back to him.

"I got as close as I could," Lieutenant Avila was saying. "I heard them talking about the Revolution and Pancho Villa. Then the white haired gringo began to whisper. They went inside. I didn't get the rest of—"

"They know." Colonel Márquez interrupted. "They know." He rocked back and forth on his heels. "But do they know where?"

"I do not think so. I heard the old one talk about the young doctor's notebook. It mentioned our work. He believes we killed the young man for spying on us."

"Well? We did, didn't we?"

"No, Colonel, though I would have if it had been necessary. It happened, just like you said. Accidents happen to gringos, though the woman was about to kill him."

Márquez turned around. "The woman?"

"The Mexican woman. She had a knife. They had been sitting together under a tree, trying to get out of the rain. They began fighting. I swear she was trying to cut his throat, but he got away. He ran, I followed and saw him fall into the river and drown. Perhaps I could have saved him, but I thought—"

Márquez waved his hand as if swatting a mosquito. "One less meddlesome gringo," he said. "But why would the woman—?" He turned his back on the lieutenant, his hands clasped behind him, again the rocking. "You're dismissed lieutenant." As the young officer saluted the backside of his commander, Márquez smiled muttering, "one less meddlesome gringo."

Raven and Kylie had little to say as they topped off breakfast with a beer. The one topic on both their minds could not be discussed in the presence of others. After a long silence, Kylie asked, "When are you going to collect Tommy's ashes?"

"Tomorrow."

"I'm going with you. Is there a public library in Puerto Vallarta?"

"A good one, as a matter of fact," Raven said.

A pall hung over the small beach community as the two men sat at the restaurant under the *palapa's* shade, toes in the sand, somberly sipping brew till the early afternoon as locals passed by their table and paid Raven their respects. He notified them that Tommy's memorial service would be held on the beach when he returned tomorrow, at sunset. By two in the afternoon the word had gone out to enough people to ensure a crowd. Raven's earlier anger had turned to sadness and when tears began to well in his eyes, Kylie urged him to finish his beer.

"Come on," he said, "I'll walk you home."

Raven began to falter as they strolled and his limp returned. "Funny isn't it," Raven said as he hobbled along, "how rage empowers, how sorrow makes one feeble. When I charged up to your house this morning, I had the strength of a lion. Now I'm an old cripple again. What a weapon a warrior chieftain has if he can maintain hatred in his men, keep them from the sadness that death's shadow brings. I can't sustain my anger any more. I can't even rage against my own impotence; just mourn its loss. I guess that's one thing that improves with age, one's mourning."

"Damn," Kylie said, "You forgot Tommy's notebook. Want me to go back and get it?"

"No," Raven said. "Bring it by when you get the chance. It's not important now. "

# CHAPTER SEVENTEEN

The first water taxis of the day left not long after dawn, the "commuter shuttle," Kylie noted as he stood waiting to board the panga. This was far different from the modes of transport he'd used to get from home to work in his days in the real world. The younger of his fellow passengers were easily identifiable by their tidy uniforms, children off to school. But the dark-skinned men sitting hunched over in silence could have been anything; waiters, hotel staff, or even members of road crews like those which had disappeared from the mountain village, kicking off the events which now embroiled him. Raven approached the boat, recognizable by his limp but not his appearance. He wore crisp pleated slacks, rolled up above the knee for boarding and disembarking from the craft, a long-sleeved shirt buttoned at the neck, and a string tie with silver and turquoise bolo. Rarely seen in anything other than faded shorts and T-shirts, his attire had an air of black-tie formality. He carried shoes in his hands, real shoes not sandals, and Kylie would be in for another surprise when they landed and an honest-to-God pair of socks—knee-length no less—would be pulled over those skinny shins. Kylie too sported long slacks, a Polo shirt, and he also carried his expensive loafers in hand. But no socks.

"Bus is about to leave," he hollered, but Raven ambled down to the water line at his own pace, knowing they would not shove off without him.

On the open water the air was cool and crisp. The children pulled their sweaters around them, and one passenger wore a windbreaker, but the remainder of the men had dressed only for the warmth of the day to come, including the bare-footed mate who stood forward hanging onto a rope tied to the prow like he was water-skiing; dressed stoically in only a pair of shorts and a baseball cap worn backwards, he stared ahead as the captain's first set of eyes to gage the water and scout for floating debris, legs planted wide, sunken arches making his broad flat feet look duck-like as he braved the brisk breeze without a shiver. Kylie shivered. Raven did not, but his few words spoken through clenched teeth were proof that he too felt the early morning chill.

They parted when they reached the town, arranging a time and place to rendezvous. Before the solemn occasion promised for the evening, Raven suggested that they have lunch at a good restaurant, price be damned, and give Tommy their own private send-off. Kylie hailed a taxi to take him to the public library.

It was a modern building, attractive in design, the grounds well landscaped, obviously an object of community pride. Kylie felt that with the aid of a dictionary felt he could understand the gist of any historical narrative. He fumbled his initial request, but was received with courtesy and, to his surprise, offered a recently published treatise in English. He took the volume to a far corner behind the stacks directly beneath a ceiling fan and set up two chairs, the second to prop his feet upon. Initially distracted from his primary objective, he couldn't help but peruse the chapters dealing with Mexico's conquest by the Spanish *conquistadors*, the improbable juxtaposition of timing and events that doomed a proud people to subjugation. The woman known as La Malinche, Cortez's translator and mistress, was definitely a part of those events.

Then he skimmed over centuries, seeking the era of Revolution. Reading of the administration of Carranza, he was amazed at the leader's strength of purpose—and fatalism. How he seemed to invite the things which doomed him.

Kylie yawned as he turned the pages, the fan above wafting air which became warmer as the morning lengthened. Eyelids heavy, he blinked as he read; vivid images in his mind of a time when men found glory or death. He closed his eyes for a moment and could almost hear voices, warning, pleading, while others whispered, conspired...

◑◈◐

*May, 1920. It had come to this. President Carranza's train had been assailed, fired upon from the moment it left the Federal District. Now they* could go no further, the way ahead, suicidal. The train had been forced to halt in the rural pueblo. Occasional bullets slammed into the Presidential car even as Carranza sat reading his history, a lifelong passion. On this morning he was consumed by tales of past martyrs. Reluctant to leave, to flee, he had to be pulled from his chair, but once up, the big man moved quickly. His horse had been brought to the train and he mounted, surrounded by the few who remained loyal to the leader and his dream. He took a long last look at the train which he had hoped would carry him to safety and allow him just a bit more time to preserve his legacy. But time had run out. It was time to worry about saving his life.

He had made his way from the capital to the small Aljibes station, barely two hundred kilometers north of the city, cursing all the way the generals he had once commanded, reserving his most vehement approbation for Obregón, the disloyal dog. The general who had once served him well now commanded his demise, not in frontal assault as his wily opponent Villa had done, but from the shadows where he could deny fault and responsibility if the adventure failed. The President thought of the outlaw. Where was Villa now that the fortress of legitimate authority was once again besieged? He smiled. "Villa is everywhere and Villa is nowhere," the American General Pershing had once said. Perhaps it was just as true at this very moment, he mused. In moments of chaos bubbling over, Villa had never missed his chance to stir the pot.

The deposed leader was never more right.

While forces loyal to Obregón lay in wait beyond the village, another had eyes and ears closer to the scene. By the now abandoned train a man in a stolen soldier's uniform gave the pre-arranged signal as Carranza and his small coterie headed away on horseback to meet their own destinies. No sooner had the dust settled from the departing band of horsemen, than another cloud was kicked up alongside the railroad tracks. The arriving group was led by a man whose horse seemed to be running away with him, so fast was his approach, but this rider was well in control of his mount as he reined him to a stop so sudden it seemed the animal's hind quarters had collapsed and his foreleg joints had fused. He jumped off his horse, wincing as his bad leg struck the hard concrete of the station's platform, but not stopping. Even before the men following him reached their leader, he had pulled his pistol from his holster and blasted off the padlock securing a single car in the long train clearly marked, 'explosivo.' He didn't seem to care that he might be blown from the face of the earth with his shot. As he slid open the great door, across the platform another locomotive with a single car backed its way along the parallel tracks.

*Pancho Villa ordered his men to get to work as they dismounted. A line was formed across the platform, snaking from one car to the other. It was not a bucket brigade but a bullion brigade that emptied one coffer, filling the other. When the car in the presidential train was empty, an ice wagon parked in front of the station house was quickly relieved of its light load, four large wooden panels. The first two were painted to resemble bars of gold. These were nailed in position inside the now empty car; the doors were closed. Another set of panels had been even more realistically decorated with end sections of actual wooden cartons that once contained rifles; rifles now in the possession of Villa. These panels were placed in front of the stacked bullion. Villa stepped toward the car falsely labeled "explosivo," took a padlock from his pocket and secured it to the closed doors.*

*"This is a good lock," he joked. "I stole it from Carranza." His men laughed, then several stripped off their riding clothes and donned the uniforms of federal soldiers they had carried in their saddlebags. One bore an officer's insignia.*

*"Report!" Villa commanded, testing the man he had chosen for the most important of deceptions. "Who are you and what is your mission?"*

*"Captain Torres," was answered with a snappy salute, "carrying arms to General Obregón from General Treveño. You will let me pass. The situation is one of grave emergency."*

*"Good," Villa said. "Now go. We'll be with you."*

*Villa was back in the saddle with one hop as the engine with its single car pulled from the station.*

*Through a country in chaos the locomotive chugged. Over flat plains they moved at speeds of up to 80 kilometers per hour, but around mountain passes their velocity slowed considerably. They made their way towards Guadalajara, coming as close to the city as they dared.*

*Less than 50 kilometers from the provincial capital, they stopped. The presumptive Captain Torres sent an eager young man to the nearest village to notify Villa of their arrival. Villa and his men had ridden through the night, over hills and valleys, sometimes alongside, sometimes in front, never far from the train. In fact, two diversionary actions had kept Obregón's forces from detaining and questioning the curious transport. The messenger approached the address given. Two of Villa's men appeared and bid him to halt. Wait a few minutes, they ordered. He heard a woman's rapturous squeal from inside the house and the two men smiled. It wouldn't be long now, they said.*

Villa emerged, tugging his suspenders over his shoulder with one hand, fastening his holster to his waist with the other.

"You are?" he asked.

"I am called Chuy. The train is waiting," the lad said softly.

"Bueno." Villa said, walking to him and clapping him soundly on the shoulder. The young man felt anointed by his touch.

From the single car, the gold bars were loaded onto horse-drawn wagons of the type used for all manner of rural commerce, the bullion carefully concealed. The wagons were linked together and fastened to the most curious vehicle the boy had ever seen. Not a car, not a truck, it was a huge tractor with wheels encased in its own revolving tracks. Metal plated, it resembled a gigantic armadillo. Villa noticed the young man's wide-eyed stare. "Courtesy of General Pershing and the American forces," he laughed. "This thing has the power of a locomotive and can go anywhere."

It was an odd caravan that headed west into the Sierra Madre Del Sur, but the cumbersome and slow means of transport did nothing to diminish the enthusiasm of those who traveled, ready to fight and die at any given moment. Many had thought this chance would never come again, the chance to ride with Villa. Their cargo would travel only half the distance it had already come, but it would take four times as long.

En route, the load was lightened as Villa would draw from his entourage, never more than two trusted confidantes, and carry a portion of the treasure to carefully chosen places of concealment. The majority of the troupe knew the reason for secrecy and did not challenge. When they were within a days travel to the sea, still high in the sierras, Villa called for a celebration, their journey nearly done.

On this occasion he feigned imbibing the rough liquor obtained from the primitive stills of the mountain pueblitos they had passed, while ensuring that the majority of those with him drank their fill. There was not a man among his group who would not hesitate to give his life for him, but Villa knew the temptations of gold. From even this fight-to-the-death band, he selected those to whom he could entrust his own fate; the chosen ones like their leader remaining sober during the evening of revelry. When alcohol-induced sleep silenced the camp, the few headed down mountain passes in the dark, led by the lad named Chuy, from this territory born and bred. They young man knew mining and logging trails over the mountains that would not be found on any map.

It took less effort to conceal the major portion of the gold than Villa had anticipated. The hiding place was ideal, and unloading was a simple matter of dumping the treasure down a deep shaft.

When the gold was safely stored, the group was reunited and Villa—more somberly than might have been expected—received the news by courier. Carranza was dead.

⊰◈⊱

Kylie opened his eyes when the book slid from his lap and slapped to the floor, not sure what he had read and what he had imagined after dozing. He returned the book with thanks. It was time for lunch.

# CHAPTER EIGHTEEN

At the appointed hour, Kylie and Raven rendezvoused. Kylie held open the restaurant's door for Raven, the urn containing Tommy's ashes cradled in his arms.

"Table for three," Raven said to the waiter greeting them, "your best table." They were shown to a corner. Raven pulled out a chair and gently placed the urn upon it. "I'd like to see your wine list, please," Raven said, and took little time perusing it. When the wine was brought, uncorked, and served for tasting, Raven acted the true connoisseur, swirling the wine in the goblet, holding it to the light, studying but not sniffing the cork—he'd ordered a white wine—and finally tasting. He approved. Two glasses were poured and the waiter prepared to leave.

"Wait." Raven stopped him. "We are three at this table. Bring another glass, please." The waiter did so and the third was filled.

Raven lifted his glass and paused. Then he spoke, "I know I didn't always show it, Tommy, but I don't think you ever doubted that I treasured your friendship. You enriched my life. If a man does no more than that for one other mortal, he has merited his existence. Bless you." He clinked his glass to Kylie's; then, as if it were the most natural of acts, clinked the third glass, picked it up, opened the urn and emptied it. "Pouilly Fumé was his favorite," he said, replacing the cap on the urn. He turned to Kylie. "Now, how was your morning?"

Kylie could only smile at the eccentric expression of compassion and loss. He sipped his wine before answering. "I went to the library and read about Carranza, the train, the gold, his death. Now that I think about it, the only absurdity in the whole picture is that the president would leave the capital with the country's treasury on a train in the first place. That's the only thing I find hard to believe, and yet it is an inarguable historical fact. If something that incredible really happened, anything's possible."

Raven's face expressed distraction. At a table in the far corner sat two men, a Mexican army officer and an Asian, the latter in a naval uniform. As Kylie turned to look, Raven's brow furrowed.

"The Asian," Raven said, "he's a sea captain; maybe merchant marine."

Had the Mexican officer's back not been turned to Kylie, he would have offered his own observation.

But for that brief digression, there was no aspect of Raven's conversation throughout the entire lunch which did not include Tommy. He paused when he mentioned his name, as if expecting a response from the urn. His manner was light, almost jocular. There was a bizarre sense of closure to it all. After ordering a second bottle of wine and pouring another glass onto the ashes, Raven said, "And that's your limit, Tommy my boy. You never could hold your liquor."

Kylie called for the check when Raven set the urn in the center of the table and carried on a conversation with the deceased's remains, as if hearing words from the spirit realm. By this time the restaurant was more than half full and the other patrons were staring. Raven let him pay the check without objection, otherwise engaged in discourse with the porcelain.

"Tommy, I do believe you've put on a bit of weight," he said lifting the urn as they departed.

Kylie insisted on chartering a boat for the return trip, and again Raven did not protest. The wine had raised his spirits and he was laughing as the craft pulled away from the pier, "Did you see those two old hags," he laughed, "staring at me conversing with the ashes?" The urn was safely on deck between his feet. He bent over and lifted the lid. "Tommy, that was a hoot. You should've seen them."

He calmed down as they made their way into the bay, looking at the cruise ships in the harbor. One was a vessel not seen before, and not built for passenger trade. "Goddamn, they got one," Raven said. "Good for them."

"Got what?" Kylie asked.

"That's one of those pirate tuna boats like we saw when we went fishing. The fucker's been arrested, I'll bet you anything." Raven stood, cupped his hands to his mouth and yelled, "Good going lads," but of course was not heard, the distance being several miles away. The captain of their own small vessel just turned and smiled at the crazy old gringo.

By now Kylie was a veteran of this journey and even with a belly full of wine suffered neither qualm nor queasiness as they rode the gentle swells on their return. The last of the tour boats was leaving the cove as they entered and their bow gently nudged the beach, deserted in late afternoon.

"Tommy, we're home," Raven said. He rolled his pants up, took off shoes and socks, and jumped into the water. He raised his arms for the urn and Kylie handed it to him. It seemed to slip from his hands. Kylie gasped but it was only Raven's morbid attempt at humor.

"I don't feel like going home," Raven said. They stood on the beach watching as their boat backed away from the shore, turned, and headed into the bay.

"Me neither," Kylie said.

"Beer?" Raven asked. "I'm buying."

Thus began in earnest Doctor Foster Quentin Briery's memorial service. After two beers, Raven and Kylie called the waiter and asked him to join them.

"You know Paco, don't you," Raven said, as if introductions were necessary.

"Sure," Kylie said. "He's served me almost every meal since I've been here."

"And Paco, you knew Tommy of course."

"Sí, señor."

"Well there he is," Raven tapped the urn with his beer bottle. Paco sipped his beer hesitantly. His half-closed eyes opened wide when Raven yet again lifted the lid and poured his beer into the black void. Kylie frowned at him.

"I know, I know," Raven said, "he's had enough already. But hell, he ain't drivin' tonight and this will be his last taste. 'Quoth the Raven, nevermore,'" he cackled.

One by one residents of the coastal village joined them, and were offered food and drink, emphasis on the latter. This was not to be a solemn memorial. With Raven and Kylie already more than convivial, thanks to their by now considerable consumption, and Kylie paying for an open bar for all, the proceeding quickly became a wake with a uniquely tropical flavor. The mood was festive as ranks grew and sunset approached. Only older Mexican women remained in the background, muttering prayers. The others shared toasts and jokes, patting the urn as the back of an old friend. Priscilla tipped the lid and blew a kiss into the murky contents. Raven encouraged them all.

It was finally time. Raven picked up the urn once more and faced his audience.

"Now we say goodbye to our friend," he said.

From the crowd, to Kylie's surprise, a priest stepped forward and said a few words, albeit reluctantly, a cleric at a pagan ritual. As he watched the priest step back into the crowd, he saw her. Malin. She stood behind the Mexican women. He started to go to her, but Raven had begun his march to the sea, the urn in his arms. Others followed him with total disregard for what they wore, and the only gesture of formality had been a manner of dress appropriate to the occasion. Long pants and flowing skirts were soon soaked to waist level. Raven stopped, lifted the lid and handed it off. He upended the urn saying, "Goodbye friend." But nothing happened. All were expecting a cloud of ash to be whisked off onto the waters but nothing exited the upside-down container. Raven turned it right-side up and peered into it, sticking his nose and mouth into the opening. "Hello in there, anybody home?" No one laughed. Then, as several onlookers gasped, he held the urn with one arm, reached down with his hand and withdrew a blackened fist. "Goodbye friend," he said again as he hurled a gray-black mass towards oncoming waves. Feted with wine and beer throughout the afternoon, Tommy's ashes had congealed and now mingled with the forevermore not as feathery wisps but oozy globs; as if even to the last, he clung to this mortal coil. Raven just laughed, and those not aware of his earlier toasts to the dead had every reason to question his sanity. Having finally scraped out as much of the contents as could be removed with his fingers, Raven simply dunked the urn beneath the swirling salt water, rinsing it clean. Tommy's remains were now well dispersed, though those in attendance silently swore off swimming in this immediate area for the next several days.

Kylie made his way through well-wishers, seeking Malin. But she had vanished, like a panther in the night. He turned and joined Raven.

"I'm still going to get the bastards." Raven whispered.

# CHAPTER NINETEEN

These were beach people. Sleeping under the stars came naturally, as naturally as the collective state of inebriation that caused nearly all to collapse on the sand when liquor and energy were exhausted. Kylie lay on his back snoring. The sky was beginning to lighten, but it would be some time yet before the sun's rays rose over the mountain range which fringed the coast. He felt a fly tickle his nose and swatted it semi-consciously. Usually the noise of these winged pests alerted him before they lit, but this one was soundless. Again he felt it tickle. He slapped himself hard enough to stir. Opening one eye he saw her sitting over him, a smile on her face. She held a white feather in her hand, a breath from his nose. Malin put a finger to her lips, urging silence before he could speak. She whispered, "Let's get away from here."

He raised himself to his elbows and surveyed the wreckage around him: a battle scene; home team annihilated. Raven lay dormant a few feet away, his head on the sleeping Priscilla's lap. Both snored like banshees. The rumble and the roar from recumbent revelers kept even the beach mutts at bay, a group of them huddled 20 yards from the scene, not daring to come closer.

"Come on," she whispered. He looked down at his bare feet. His shoes had been kicked off hours ago and were now who knew where. She raised a hand, dangling a pair of sandals from two fingers. Possession conferred privilege in such simple societies—if they fit. Property rights could be restored later. He stood and slipped them on, then put his hand in hers.

Malin wore a full cotton skirt and matching white blouse. The color flattered her dark skin and hair colors. Around her shoulders she wore a ragged shawl. Though rustic looking, it clashed with her outfit and detracted from any sense of style, Kylie thought. Around her waist in lieu of a belt were several strands of yellow nylon rope, also not attractive. But he said nothing as he walked with her at water's edge. They reached the end of the beach, forded the now gentle river, and climbed the steps up to the town.

"Where are we going?" Kylie asked. Malin answered only with a smile. "You know we were beginning to worry about you," he said, "with everything that's happened around here lately."

"I appreciate your concern but I do leave the village from time to time. It's not unusual."

"Where do you go?"

"To places like I'm going to show you now."

Past the town, they headed towards Raven's house but took a left turn onto an overgrown path leading into jungle, but parallel to the coast. For an hour they clung to the path as it wound in and out of thick brush, bringing them to rocky precipices looking down over jagged shorelines. Kylie began to tire—he'd not exactly had the most restful of nights—when they began to descend to the ocean. Sweat stung his eyes and clouded his vision as he took timid steps down a treacherous trail. A steep incline with loose rock made firm footing impossible. They landed on huge boulders jutting into the sea.

"Here?" Kylie asked. He was drenched with sweat, and the boulder on which they stood received direct sunlight. It was a frying pan.

"No," Malin said and walked to the edge of the rock, shimmied down its side, disappearing from view. "Come on," she said. "It's alright."

He walked to the edge. A rope ladder led down to a picture of paradise. Below, protected by rock walls on both sides, lay a pristine beach less than 100 yards long. The water lapping at sugar-white sand darkened as it deepened from clear to turquoise to emerald. The sea bottom was easily visible from where he stood, to depths of ten feet or more. Palm trees lined the beach and gave shade to a sandy area, with impenetrable brush behind. A small hut, like a doll's house, had been built next to the palms. Kylie descended the ladder. He followed Malin's footsteps across the beach. She smiled as he approached.

"You can help me with this." She removed the shawl from her shoulders. Spread out, it was a good eight feet in length and tapered at both ends. A hammock. She took off the yellow belt cinched at her waist and—two separate lengths of rope. The accessories he had criticized were two of the most functional he'd ever seen in women's wear. He watched her thread one rope through the hammock's knotted end, then wrap it around the trunk of a palm and he did the same with the other.

"You're tired," she said. "Me too. Let's sleep."

He gasped at her beauty as she stepped out of her skirt and pulled her blouse over her head. She spread the hammock, then reclined.

"Is there, uh, room for two?" he asked.

"Come and find out," she said. He stepped to where she lay swinging ever so slightly. "Take those things off silly. No one's going to see us here." And he too shed his clothes and all pretension.

"If you can wait," she whispered when gravity brought their bodies firmly together, "I will teach you the art of making love in a hammock. For now, let's rest. It will be better later when you're not tired. I promise."

With a kiss she closed her eyes. Kylie stared wide-eyed at the green canopy above him and the patches of blue beyond until sleep came to him, too.

Malin first demonstrated her hammock prowess in a playful manner when she woke, turning it over with a twist of her body and dumping them both on the ground. She kissed him but jumped up before anything else could ensue and ran into the hut, then out again, a plastic jug in her hand.

"I've got to get some water from the stream," she said. She tossed him a lighter. "Gather some wood and start a fire. There's also a line and hook in the hut. Catch us a fish."

"What do I use for bait?" Kylie asked, getting to his feet in slow motion.

"Find a bug, there are lots of them."

Malin darted into the jungle and was gone. Kylie set to his given chores. Between brush and driftwood the fire was no problem. Nor was the recommended bait. He had doubts about the fishing challenge, with no more than a line and a rusty hook, but waded into the water to his waist and tossed the hook and line like a lariat. The still alive bug kicked when it hit the calm surface of the water and he had a strike before he could count to ten. With a primitive pride in his catch he walked from the water as Malin returned with her plastic container full. Ignoring his own nakedness, he was much more conscious of hers and this became apparent. She came to him. They kissed and the fish fell flopping to the sand as she took him by the hands and led him to the hammock.

"Sit down with it between your legs," she ordered. "Keep both feet on the ground. Now look into my eyes. Only into my eyes."

⊰≫⊱

When the raging fire in him had been reduced to a warm but still flickering flame, they prepared their meal, and after eating sat under the shade of a palm.

"Why do I get this feeling of distance between you and the villagers?" Kylie asked. "I mean, the name they gave you, Malinche. It's not flattering."

"You've been studying our history."

"I opened a book or two. But really Malin, you seem to be so alone. I would think your people would be proud of your accomplishments. They seem to shun you."

She sighed. "Malinche was the mistress of Cortez; his translator, and after earning his trust, his negotiator. She led her own people to defeat, to slavery, almost to extinction." Malin drew in the sand with her finger. "Did she feel remorse in her own lifetime? Perhaps her love for him erased all else. Anyway, she had a son by Cortez, and he abandoned her for his Spanish wife. The first-born son was sent to Spain. The son, the first *mestizo,* was later executed by the Spaniards. She was then given as a wife to one of Cortez's men, who also abandoned her. Them she disappeared from history. There is legend that she murdered her children after the firstborn."

"Fascinating, but I don't see the connection."

"The murder of her children may be nothing but folklore," she continued, ignoring his interruption. "Nevertheless, for 500 years, the spirit of Malinche has appeared to the people of Mexico. That is something your history books do not tell you. To this day, she appears simultaneously to people who have had no contact with each other. Sometimes in the same village, sometimes in different areas, but always at the same time, saying the same thing. She is seeking her children. Some say it is merely allegory; that the legend of Malinche's spirit is collective sadness for the loss of her people, overwhelmed by the Spanish. Maybe she didn't kill her babies, but her apparition is nevertheless terrifying."

"I still don't..."

"When I returned to my village, after completing my education in the United States, several people in the village had visions of La Malinche. They heard her cry one night, and were frightened. They blamed me."

"That's ridiculous."

"Is it?" Her eyes burned through him, irises of soft brown now black as coal. Then with a flutter of eyelids, her gaze softened.

"Then why do you stay?" Kylie asked.

"This is the land of my parents and their parents. I've never felt at home anywhere else."

"I don't know, I guess I just think it's kind of sad you being by yourself all the time; alone in that house of yours so far in the jungle; so remote. Priscilla took me there. We were looking for you. We were worried."

"Any city is more dangerous than the jungle in a hundred different ways, and as for being alone, there's no sadness when it's a matter of choice. I choose to be alone, except when I choose not to be. Like now." She kissed him. "Ready for another lesson?" she asked with a sly grin. "When you get the sense of balance and rhythm," she whispered in his ear, "you'll never go back to an ordinary bed again."

They pleasured the day away. By late afternoon, he had matriculated from novice to intermediate in the art of Kama Sutra, hammock style, but Malin reminded him that their legs would have to carry them home.

"I'd like to come back here," he said as they cleaned up their campsite and prepared to leave. "Share the stillness of night and just watch the stars with you."

"Perhaps soon."

So enamored was he that Kylie took no notice of the three marks, almost healed, in the small of Malin's back. A strange place to scratch one's self, they could have been clawed by fingernails. But Kylie took no notice.

❖

They were approaching the village.

"Do you mind if we stop to check on Raven?" Kylie asked.

"I'm sure he'd prefer to see you alone. I'll go on ahead."

"You sure?" She bussed his cheek and continued on her way.

Kylie knocked on the door. No answer.

"Raven?" he called. Nothing. He tried the handle, it was unlocked. He opened the door and stuck his head in. "Raven? Are you home?" Oh, God. Raven? Where are you?"

The place was a shambles. Everything that could be broken had been smashed. Plates and glasses had been thrown against walls and shards littered the floor. A wooden dining chair had been broken over the sink counter, decorative tiles cracked and ruined. Rage. The wreckage screamed rage. Kylie stood mute amidst the destruction and pondered the question of one's duty to one's fellow man. Could he turn around, walk away, and simply wish the best for this tormented soul? Yes, he decided. Raven needed help that was beyond his capacity to give. Walk away, walk away now, he told himself. And he did. Kylie left the house and ran to the village trying to catch up to Malin, but she was nowhere in sight. He headed home.

The beach had been swept clean of the rubbish left from Tommy's tropical wake. There were no customers at the restaurant. Paco sat sleeping in a chair and Kylie didn't want to disturb him. On one of the empty tables stood the urn, its lid missing, an object now pitiable in its insignificance, but which no one had the temerity to discard. His Italian loafers were on another table, both alien items awaiting their claimants. He slipped off the borrowed sandals and replaced them with his own shoes, which in another world where their value was known a man might have been robbed of, but here no one wanted. Kylie continued on his way. Exhausted, the climb up the hill to his house now seemed daunting, and he realized he'd better get it done before darkness.

The sun was still in the sky when he arrived home and climbed onto his veranda, and when he stepped from his makeshift shower, scrubbed clean. He recalled his amorous acrobatics suspended above the ground, and watched the sun's final gasp as it sunk beneath the waters. He went inside to retrieve the bottle of rum he'd bought. Two fingers neat in a small glass and he returned to his balcony. He thought of Raven's last visit, hollering as he came up the hill waving in hand—Tommy's notebook. Kylie looked around. Where had he put it? On the table out here? No, it wasn't here. He went inside, looked on tables, chairs, under his bed. Nothing. Gone. Taken. He knew by whom, and he knew why. He returned to the veranda, looked to the darkening sky and cursed, "Raven, damn you!"

Kylie paced the small confines of his residence, downed his rum, and refilled his glass. What should he do? What could he do? "I'm still going to get the bastards," had been Raven's surly growl the night before, and he'd come back for the notebook and whatever clues and directions it held of Tommy's last nocturnal sojourn. Having glanced at it only briefly, Kylie tried to remember what it had said. "Aw, hell," he muttered as he weighed the pros and cons of attempting to aid his disturbed—disturbed what? Was Raven a friend—or merely an acquaintance? He sought a descriptive term for the relationship; to define it and thus define any duty or responsibility he owed—or didn't owe. Disclaim. Disclaimer. The words jumped into his mind. Words thrown across boardroom tables by him and his company's lawyers when responsibilities that had once granted privilege were used to confer guilt, and therefore had to be disclaimed. "I disclaim any knowledge of..., I disclaim any responsibility for..." These words had rolled off his tongue. Oh, he'd been good at disclaimers. He had denied responsibility for the suffering heaped on thousands by his executive' actions, he could certainly disclaim any responsibility owed an obviously deranged man that he'd met, what, a week ago? He feared the jungle, especially in darkness, but recalled Malin's words, 'any city is more dangerous than the jungle in a hundred different ways.' He finished his rum and went to his closet. He had proper footwear there for a trek into the wilds.

# CHAPTER TWENTY

Kylie was jittery at first, but as he accepted his plodding pace—essential if he was not to stray from the path—he became accustomed to the ambient cadence of the jungle. The major audio output was that of insects and he was reminded of traffic, not the stop and go of the inner city, but the steady drone of a freeway at night. In the comparison he felt solace. And the more comparisons he made, the more comfortable he became with his surroundings. He was not unmindful of the big cats. He'd looked them up when in the library too, and knew that at any moment jaguars or panthers; mountain lions, pumas or cougars; even ocelots might be watching him from rocks or overhanging branches. The advice had been to show no fear, make noise, let them know you're coming—but he doubted the wisdom of that tactic under present circumstances. There was something out here more dangerous than any wild cat and he had to trust dumb luck that he would see them before they saw him. Wandering through the thickets yelling for Raven was out of the question.

He had decided to start at the point of the trail where he had encountered Tommy that first morning. This was the trail that followed the river, the river that was returning the body when they found it. The logic seemed sound, and Raven would employ logic, even in the mad operation he had set himself upon. Once deeper inland, Kylie had to trust mainly his hearing, and was alert to a cry of help, of pain—alert to the sounds of violence. He did not expect to be aided by his eyes, as his vision was constricted to the length and breadth of his flashlight's beam, but well into his journey he thought he saw a brief flash of light not his own. Minutes later, there was another and this presented a dilemma; should he leave the path to investigate? To do so was perilous. He stopped and sighed. It was exactly what Raven would do. Yes, lights in the middle of the jungle in the middle of the night would be reconnoitered. He left the trail.

Now it did become frightening. He kept eyes frozen down at his feet and the flashlight's beam pointed at his toes, as the razor edges of palm fronds whipped his cheek and thorns scratched his wrists and forearms—he'd sensibly donned a pair of jeans instead of shorts to protect his legs. At one point he walked full-face into a huge spider's web, and momentarily panicked, running blindly, ripping the sticky threads from his face. But he didn't scream. He couldn't, petrified with terror. And then the hand grasped his shoulder.

"You're making more noise than a gang of Girl Scouts. What the fuck are you doing out here?" Raven whispered.

"Jesus, you scared the shit out of me! I'm looking for you! Asshole."

"OK. You found me. Now go on back home."

Kylie aimed his flashlight first at the boots, up the fatigues to the black T-shirt and then the face, painted in camouflage green, black, and tan. Here was Raven the commando; Raven who cut hearts out.

"I'm not going home without you. Raven, you've got to come with me. You're not well."

"Not well?? What the hell are you talking about? Oh. You saw the house."

"It's OK, it's alright. Grief, anger, they're perfectly normal. It's how we express them that—"

"Oh, cut the crap Dr. Phil. I was swatting flies and broke one or two things, that's all."

"You swat flies with chairs?"

"So what? OK, I'm caught. You got me. Set up a tribunal. Find me guilty of man's inhumanity to—household furnishings."

They were interrupted when another beam of light was for an instant splayed on the indigo backdrop of the starless night.

"Get down," Raven whispered. They crouched to the ground. "There's something going on over there and I'm going to find out what it is. You can come if you shut up, or you can go on home. Just don't get in my way."

"I'm coming," Kylie said.

They walked through the brush, standing tall. Whatever was going on was some distance away, and though caution was in order, stealth was not yet the highest priority.

"What made you come looking for me?" Raven asked.

"I went home and found you'd taken Tommy's notebook. I figured you'd be out here somewhere."

"The notebook? I didn't take it. I wasn't at your place."

"Then who took it?"

"Hell if I know. Watch where you're shining that flashlight. Keep it on the ground. No, turn it off. It's interfering with my night vision."

"Shit Raven, I won't be able to see a thing."

"Stay on my tail. Your eyes will adjust. Trust me."

He turned off the flashlight. Kylie was practically stepping on the man's heels, afraid to let any distance come between them. Though Raven's emotional stability was questionable, there could be little doubt of his skills in this arena. Could a man trained as Raven ever be normal again, Kylie wondered. Programmed, that was the word, programmed to meet violence with violence, tranquility would be an abnormal state for such a man. Living in a sleepy Mexican fishing village, he'd probably been one step away from the edge for some time now.

The lights they were headed towards shone at infrequent intervals and for varying lengths of time. No rhythm to whatever it was. But they were getting closer.

"What is it?" Kylie whispered.

"Some kind of vehicle."

"What's it doing out here?"

It was a stupid question and Raven did not dignify it with a response. Now it was crouching time and they duck-walked through the brush. How could Raven do it with his bad knee, Kylie wondered, but his own sharp intakes of breath and rapid pulse gave him the answer—adrenalin. It was mother's milk to some men, maybe all men. Some got a rush from fast cars, some from prowling tropical jungles in the dead of night, some from insider trading. Kylie chuckled to himself. Raven slapped him. "Shut up."

Now they could hear a voice calling out in the distance. Commanding. Giving orders. They crept closer. The total darkness was pierced by a blinding searchlight. They flattened themselves on the moist ground and lay still as the beam passed over their backs. Kylie lay with his cheek pressed to the soil. The metallic odor of earth, mixed with the mold of parasitic growth and rotting leaves gave off a scent of fecund decay. Plants dying, falling, gave sustenance to the innumerable species which survived in this shadowy realm—one of which was trying to crawl up his nostril. He put his finger on the other and blew. Raven tutted with disgust at his unwanted companion's lack of capacity for silence. He crawled away, but Kylie followed him. Twenty yards later, Raven turned, facing Kylie, their noses practically touching.

"They're straight ahead," he whispered, "crawl over to that tree and stay behind it, and for God's sake try to be quiet."

Kylie crawled to his designated cover, Raven behind his own, yards away. The voice was only a short distance from them, still barking orders. Kylie could make out words: *atrás, derecho, izquierda;* directions. The light flashed again, blinding him. He started involuntarily, then froze. He hadn't been seen. The light was extinguished. He blinked. On his mind's photo plate the image of what he had seen in the glare was engraved: a behemoth with open maw ravaging, ripping trees and plants from their roots; raising its arms, tossing their limp forms aside with abandon, while growling, snarling at the path indicated by the momentary flash of light, like a dog given the scent and ordered to attack, maul, and destroy. Here in the jungle under cover of darkness, an earth-mover was at work. Kylie was unable to count the number of men at this task, but there didn't seem to be many. Half a dozen or less. Those he could see in the brief intervals of light had one thing in common—olive drab. Military fatigues.

For nearly an hour they lay, surveying the ongoing activity in silence. Then Kylie felt Raven tap his leg and motion for their return. Reversing their order, they crawled, then crouched, and only spoke when able to walk at a reasonable pace, and at a reasonable distance from the activity they had witnessed.

"What was that all about?" Kylie asked.

"Army engineers," Raven said. "Building something. A road, maybe an airstrip. I don't know."

"Why in the middle of the night?"

"They don't want to be seen. I saw a scanner. They were listening for aircraft. They hit the lights only when nothing was overhead. They were taking advantage of natural cover too."

They walked on in silence and finally came to the river and a clear path homeward. The water was now retained by secure banks and a sliver of moon was reflected in the current. They stopped beside the peaceful waters as Raven mused.

"Doesn't add up," he muttered. "They kill an innocent man who stumbles across them rather than establish a secure perimeter. Then mutilating his body—"

Kylie felt silence was prudent and let Raven continue.

"They didn't want him to talk, but what could he have said? If Tommy saw what we saw, what could he have said? He saw soldiers with heavy machinery? That's not reason enough to kill a man."

"Maybe he saw them doing something else," Kylie offered.

"Or maybe he saw someone else," Raven said. "Tommy's body was mutilated. It was meant to be found and scare others away. That's not soldiering." Raven grasped the irony of his own words. Kylie's blood froze as he listened to the warrior in the dark. "Heh, heh, heh," Raven chuckled to himself, the sound of one deranged.

They walked on, not another word spoken till they reached the mouth of the river, where its murmuring ripples surrendered to the rhythmic wash of waves on the sand.

"Shit," Raven exclaimed. "That's what I heard. Listen."

Kylie heard nothing but gentle waves on the beach.

"Didn't you hear? In the background when that thing would stop? Shift gears or whatever? Waves," Raven said. "I heard the ocean."

This hardly seemed a discovery of major importance. Even with his nonexistent sense of direction, Kylie could see how they had turned from the river and headed through the jungle back toward the coast, but so what?

Raven turned, paced five or six steps and turned. "Look, you go on home. I've got something to do before it's too late."

"Like what?"

"Dig up a corpse."

Kylie turned away. Of that venture he wanted no part.

## CHAPTER TWENTY-ONE

When he reached his house, Kylie stumbled in the dark to his bed, kicked off boots, yanked down his jeans, pulled his shirt over his head, and fell headlong. Something had been stuck under his sheet. He pulled back the sheet and shined his flashlight. There was the notebook. Dropping it on the floor, Kylie resumed his free-fall to slumber, and was out as his head hit the pillow.

He slept till early afternoon and whiled away the hours in passive pursuits till evening; sitting on his balcony, staring at things that moved, lizards and small birds mostly, nothing that required much focus or cogitating. Vegetating was the order of the day. Had there been anything in the vicinity to eat other than foliage and tree bark he would have preferred staying in, but hunger would necessitate a trip down to the beach at some point. When he thought he could stand it no longer, he heard someone whistling his way up the hill. No doubt who it was.

"Hey, Kylie," Raven yelled. "You hungry? Got some sandwiches."

Kylie was sitting on the veranda and Raven threw the paper bag in his lap. "Made 'em myself," Raven said. "No one's seen you in town today and I knew you didn't have anything here."

"You made them?" Kylie peered into the bag. "Hope you washed your hands first."

"That, my boy," Raven sat heavily in the other chair, "is the number one secret to a healthy life in the tropics. My hands are sanitized several times a day."

Kylie pictured Raven's clean hands at the task he'd set out for when they had parted. He lost his appetite and set the bag down.

"Don't leave that sitting there. Bugs as big as your fist will carry it away, then start lookin' to see if you got anything else."

Kylie just stared down at the bag.

"Well?" Raven said. "Don't you want to know?"

"You desecrated a grave to stare at a 100 year old butt. I don't need to know anything about it. I'm not interested."

Raven ignored him.

"They didn't have his stone engraved yet, almost didn't find the grave."

"Raven—"

"En-graved, is that the origin of the word? Anyway, I found it. Not far from his old shack. Just where I thought it would be."

Kylie sighed and looked away, trying to ignore the narrative.

"Old man really looked peaceful," Raven said. "Content, you know? Anyway, it was there. Just like he said it was. On his hip, not his butt."

Kylie turned his head. "He had a map tattooed on him?"

Raven didn't answer, just rattled out a string of memorized words; directions in paces, kilometers, and compass points.

Kylie repeated the first line. "Two kilometers due north. Due North of what? With no starting point, directions are useless."

Raven Smiled. "Don Chuy told me the starting point months. I didn't realze it then, but I do now. The starting point is the rock. I've already mapped it out. I know where the gold is hidden."

"Not too far from here, either. If those soldiers haven't found it yet, they're pretty close."

"Maybe they dug up the body, too."

"Don't think so, the grave wasn't disturbed. Anyway," Raven looked at the back of his hands, examining his fingernails, "I removed the tattoo."

The sandwiches at his side would definitely go uneaten, Kylie swore.

"Raven, why in the hell would a Mexican tell you where a fortune in his country's gold was buried?"

"He didn't tell me," Raven said. "He only told me he held the key. Why didn't he tell his own people? I guess because he didn't know who he could trust. I'd like to think it was because he thought of me as a friend and respected me as another old soldier, but I don't know. Maybe he thought I'd somehow protect it too."

"From the Mexican army?" Kylie stood and stomped across the veranda pacing in front of his visitor. "If, and I mean this is one hell of an if, we find this place and there's something there, perhaps I have to remind you—it's not ours! If there's a grain of truth in this crazy tale, and there was gold stolen from the Mexican government; who gets it when it's found? Those guys we saw working last night; who do they work for? The Mexican government. They're probably on a sanctioned mission. Do you think the government would want media attention on a search for its missing treasury? Those guys last night were doing their job, Raven. They were following orders."

"Or not," Raven said smugly. "Somebody killed that old man and somebody killed Tommy. Maybe Jeb too. Orders?" Raven stood, looked Kylie square in the eyes. "I'm going to find the site. You want to join me, meet me on the beach in the morning. I'm going into town and rent a Jeep. Come, don't come; I don't give a damn."

Raven stepped from the veranda and walked the path down the hill. He didn't look back.

With less than an hour before sunset, the regulars were in place. Raven was spotted as he walked the beach, and hurrahs issued from the table. He waved an acknowledgment and joined them. With his return, death's unpleasantness could be forgotten and lives of ease and without discernable purpose could be continued as before. Raven was ushered to the head of the table, his glass filled, and he was urged to give the benedictory toast. He raised his glass solemnly, then said, "Hell, we're just drunks on a beach. Down the hatch."

"Now that's my kind of toast," Jerry said to a chorus of acclamation.

Kylie joined the group late. Malin was not present and he sat next to Priscilla. She held up her glass and twisted it in her fingers. With no apparent relevance, she offered an observation in a hollow tone of voice.

"You know why mixed relationships don't work?" she asked. "You can't talk dirty during sex. Nobody's that bilingual."

Those who had traversed this territory agreed with her.

Kylie said nothing.

The following morning Kylie was waiting for Raven on the beach.

"Wasn't sure I'd see you," Raven said.

"Thought you might need help," Kylie said.

Raven spat in the sand. "I don't need nobody's help."

"Then I thought you might like some company. Maybe I can still talk you out of this."

"If you're going to yammer at me you can just stay here."

"You invited me, remember? I'm making you a deal. If we get to this place and there's nothing there, you'll forget about it, and neither of us will say a word to anyone. OK"

Raven glared as the panga approached the shore to pick up its passengers. He picked up his pack and waded into the surf.

"I'll take that as a yes," Kylie said.

In Puerto Vallarta they rented a Jeep, drove to El Tuito, and stopped for breakfast. They were an unusually silent couple of diners, caution overriding conversation even in the near-empty restaurant. Raven put a 200 peso note on the table, stood up, and said, "Let's go. It's about 15 miles from here."

Nothing more was said. Raven drove just below the speed limit on the rural road, focusing on the passing terrain and diverting his eyes with almost every click of the speedometer. Twenty minutes later he turned off the highway onto a dirt road. As with most such paths in this country, the further away from the main artery, the worse the road. Raven wove down, into, up, and over ruts, finally hitting one deeper than the wheelbase, and they were stuck. He put the gearshift in neutral and both got out to push.

"We're not far now," he said as they pushed the vehicle out of the rut, "and thanks for keeping quiet on the way here."

"How do you know where we are and where we're going?" Kylie asked.

Raven pulled a small GPS devise from his shirt pocket. It was no bigger than a pack of cigarettes. He took a reading and handed it to Kylie. "Coolest damn gift I ever gave myself," Raven said.

The land they now crossed showed the effects of the extremes to which it had been subjected for eons. Months of baking sun alternating with months of downpour had stripped the terrain of sustenance. Where it had not been denuded of topsoil and worn to clay, the ground was rock. Plant and animal life which managed to survive such harsh conditions shared one common feature—a singular unattractiveness. From branches bearing stunted leaves, condors perched in small groups, ignoring vermin that scampered below them, biding their time for less taxing, moribund prey.

Occasional Brahmas in small groups would amble across the road, hides loose and sagging, ribs exposed. One or more of these unfortunates soon would end up between the beaks and talons of the stone-still observers on high, no doubt. Single strands of barbed wire hung between rude wooden posts denoting ownership of the barren fields. From all creatures eking out their survival, this hard land demanded much and gave little in return. To man, it seemed to give the least of all, yet proof of his feeble efforts were everywhere. Abandoned shelters periodically dotted the landscape, emblems of futility if not mortality. Raven stopped the Jeep past one roofless wreck of a shack and turned to his right, plowing into a cornfield owing its existence more to tenacity than cultivation.

"Would you get out and walk ahead of the Jeep?" Raven asked. "Slowly please. If it is a *cenote* I don't want to drive into it."

"What's a *cenote*?"

"It's a natural shaft. Like a vertical cave."

Kylie got out and walked gingerly, stepping around the stringy corn stalks as if going through a mine field, now recognizing their intended purpose as camouflage. Behind them, the Jeep broke the brittle stalks to the ground. He walked slowly, then stopped. He raised his hand for the Jeep to stop.

"What is it?" Raven yelled.

"Hang on. What does your GPS say?"

"It says you're right on it."

Kylie stamped his foot, then bent over, pawing at the dirt with his fingers. "Oooh, shit!" he said and slowly, carefully backtracked in his exact footsteps. Then he turned and ran to the Jeep.

"You check it out," he told Raven. "I was standing on rotten wood. Over a hole. I'm not going any further."

Raven got out and walked to the spot, brushed some dirt aside and pulled at several planks, then lifted the crude cover and pushed it aside. "We found it." He stood on the lip of a hole, and stared into the void. Kylie came to his side.

"This is it," Raven said in a husky whisper. "This pitiful farm barely gave a living while it hid this country's treasury."

"How deep is it?" Kylie asked.

Raven picked up a rock and threw it into the pit. They waited breathlessly. And waited. The almost indiscernible sound of the rock's landing was muted.

"It's damn deep," Raven said. "And it's flooded. Maybe from the rains seeping through, might be an underground well. That would make it a bitch to pump out."

"How do you know there's anything down there?"

"Don't. You ever do any rappelling?"

Kylie shook his head and just stared at the hole.

"Guess it's up to me then," Raven said. "I'm going to drive back into the pueblo and get some rope. You stay here."

"Why can't I come with you?"

"They're used to seeing me. They see us together again, someone might get curious. Might try to follow us back here. No, you stay. I'll be back within an hour. Stay out of sight."

"Don't get stuck in another rut," Kylie said as Raven drove off, adding as the cloud of dust marked Raven's exit, "please."

Kylie looked at a bird soaring above him, too high for him to identify even if he possessed the knowledge to do so. He looked down at his feet and stepped back from the black void in the orange earth. Three feet from it was not enough. It seemed ready to suck him in. He bent over and picked up a rock the size of his fist, threw it in and started counting seconds. One, two, three. He barely heard the sound of the rock hit bottom, not sure of the exact count, but it was at least four seconds, maybe six or seven. Kylie knelt and drew with his finger in the dirt. The exact formula forgotten, he did recall that accelerating objects were constantly changing their velocity, covering different distances in each consecutive second. Think, he commanded himself and scratched numbers in the depleted soil. First second, five meters; next second, fifteen meters; third second, twenty-five meters and the fourth, thirty-five meters. He calculated a total of eighty meters free-fall in four seconds. Eighty meters, almost a football field. He whistled. Raven had better bring back one shit-load of rope.

With no shade in the immediate area, Kylie was beginning to broil when he heard the vehicle. He crawled to the corn stalks until he was sure it was Raven and the Jeep approaching. He stood and walked to the edge to mark the *cenote*. The jeep slowed to a halt. Raven got out, hoisted a huge coil of hemp rope on his shoulder and a large flashlight.

"Do you have any idea how deep this thing is?" Kylie asked.

"I'm guessing between hundred, hundred fifty meters," Raven said as he bent over and tied one end of the rope to the Jeep, then coiled it around the bumper. He pulled against it testing it. "Deep enough for histoplasmosis."

"Histo what?" Kylie asked.

"Lung infection from breathing mold and fungus. Like you find in pits like this. At that kind of depth, quite possible. We might need to get a respirator. But I won't be down long on this trip."

Kylie breathed deep of the hot but clear air.

"If I yell," Raven said, "you pull me up. Fast."

He walked to the hole, wrapped the rope around his waist. "Lower me slowly. I'm not going to rappel my first trip down." He sat on the side, turned and gave a smile, then went over the edge. Kylie strained against the weight of the man. Sweat burst in beads from his pores as he labored in the glaring sun and soon his hands were slippery with perspiration. It was difficult to maintain a grip on the rope. He heard a scream.

"Holy shit!" echoed up from the earth. Kylie pulled at the rope.

"No, no!" Raven hollered. "I'm alright. Let me down."

"What is it?"

"Biggest goddamn spiders I've ever seen! Jesus, they must be two feet across. Uh-uh-ugleee," he sang. "Damn this is one deep sucker."

"How's the air?"

"Stinks, but I think it's OK. Hot as blazes down here. Guess that's from all the volcanic activity we've got in the neighborhood."

Down, down he went. Kylie nervously eyed the remains of the coiled rope behind them. Suddenly it went slack.

"I'm here." Raven's voice rose to the surface, fainter now. "Bottom's flooded. Can't see a damn thing."

Kylie let go of the rope, wiped his hands on his shirt, reached down and grabbed a fistful of dirt and rubbed it into his sweaty palms.

After several minutes of silence the rope was yanked and Raven yelled once more, calling to be hauled up. When he clambered back over the edge, Kylie fell to the ground exhausted. Raven glistened with sweat, but he grinned like a kid coming off a roller-coaster.

"Man, that was great," he said. "Those spiders, you should've *seen* them. This big." He spread his hands two feet apart. "They're all over the walls on the way down. None on the bottom though, thank

God. Bottom of the pit's like a big room, maybe thirty by fifty. You can't see a thing because of the water."

"So there's nothing there?" Kylie asked, still trying to catch his breath.

Raven pulled out a brass plaque which he'd stuck in the back of his shorts. HOLT was emblazoned across its face.

"You know what this is?" Raven asked, smiling broadly. "Holt Tractor Company. Out of Tennessee. Now called Caterpillar."

"There's a tractor down there?" Kylie asked.

"Nope. Holt was also a military contractor, turn of the century. They made the first tanks. Called them 'tracklayers.' Pershing ordered over 200 of them for his hunt for Pancho Villa. I think Pancho 'relieved' ol' Blackjack of one of them. Those old buggies could haul through any kind of country. That's how they got the gold over the mountains to here. I'd bet the ranch."

"Did you find anything else down there?"

From his other pocket, Raven pulled a handful of gold coins.

"There's plenty more where these came from."

Raven rattled on non-stop as they drove back to the village. "First we've got to pump it dry. Two-phase, maybe three-phase pump like they use in the infinity pools of the rich and famous. They must have just dumped the tank and wagons down the pit. First, we've got to pull out all the junk. We're going to need to gather the gold and put it in crates. There's room for maybe half a dozen men to work down there at one time. We'll need a good winch. Whoo-eee. You realize we're gonna be hauling up tons of gold matey? Aarrgh, it's the pirate's life for me."

The two men chuckled giddily at the challenge, at the prospect of immense wealth passing through their hands even for a moment.

"How the hell are we going to haul the stuff?" Kylie asked. "What can handle that kind of a load on these dirt trails?"

"Remember it was packed into a single train car. One good truck can carry the load, another to carry the crane. Wouldn't worry about the road, one big boy will flatten it into shape in no time."

"Where the hell do we find the trucks?"

"With money all is possible." Raven turned to his companion, a coy smile on his face, "and I know a pirate with a stash of cash."

"You mean me?" Kylie asked. Raven nodded.

"We'll disguise the trucks," Raven chuckled. "Paint *'explosivo'* or something."

"Now wait just a minute," Kylie said. "I don't want to go jumping down some damn hole." He paused then said, "I hate spiders."

"You pansy," Raven taunted. "Afraid of the dark and a few little bugs, well actually, pretty damn big bugs. Anyway, you're in too deep now. Back out at this point and I'd have to kill you."

"Ha, ha," Kylie said dryly. "Your joking—aren't you?"

"I never joke about my work, son." Raven grabbed a small notebook from the glove compartment. Using the hood of the vehicle as his desk, on a dusty country road under the summer sun, he plotted and planned. Hauling capacities, load lifts, sizes, weights and measures were roughly calculated.

"Too bad we can't pay for all this in gold," Raven said when he totaled the estimate. He took Kylie's hand in his, crushing it in a vise-like grip. "We're going to do this," he said, "and you're going to learn what it's like to really live."

"What in God's name am I doing with this madman?" Kylie asked himself, but an abandoned corn field was not the place to argue.

Kylie let Raven rattle on during the drive back to Puerto Vallarta. He ignored him on the boat ride across the bay. They parted on reaching the beach, Raven anxious to return home to mastermind the expedition. Kylie walked up to a restaurant, took a plastic chair and dragged it to where he could sit undisturbed. There under the sweltering sun, his concentration was so intense, even the beach vendors did not approach him. He stared at the sand, one thought turning over and over in his brain. "I should just get the hell out of here."

He felt the lightest of taps on his shoulder. A young girl stood at his side. Her face bore a smile that seemed to match the sun's warmth as she extended her hand, offering fresh-cut roses for sale. He looked into her deep brown eyes. She reminded him of Malin as he recalled that she too had once made her living in this manner. His eyes were drawn to the bandage on the girl's leg and he recognized her as the young patient he had seen with Tommy that morning at breakfast. He bought a flower.

The girl left him and he sat turning the stem over and over in his fingers. He raised his eyes and looked at the point across the bay, then jumped from his chair. Kylie paced. One direction, then another. Then he stopped, planted his feet and said, "Alright Raven, if that's what you want…"

Kylie ran the length of the beach, up the stone steps, through the town. He ran to the furthermost point on the southern arm of the bay, not stopping till he reached the huge wooden door. He pounded on it.

"Raven, goddammit, I've got something to say and you're going to listen to me."

From within a voice answered, "Well, by all means come in, John Kylie."

The man ordered to follow Kylie had quite a challenge. He couldn't run after him; that would have been too obvious. Even his quick stride from the beach and through the town had drawn a few curious glances. But he managed to keep up and did not lose sight of his prey. He watched as Kylie entered Raven's house and found a spot from which he could observe. He could hear raised voices coming from inside, angry yelling he thought, but then whoops and hollers, like spectators at a football game. He was about to sneak closer when the door opened. Both men came out. The older one hugged the younger. They both had tears in their eyes. Damn, he thought, these gringos are crazy.

# CHAPTER TWENTY-TWO

"I hope that will be satisfactory sir. On such short notice it's really the best we can do. I could of course give you a certified check."

Kylie sat across the desk from the bank officer in Puerto Vallarta, amused at the infinite incongruities of life. He'd picked up dinner tabs for more money than he was now requesting, but unless prior arrangements were made, the bank kept limited sums in cash on a daily basis. How unreal, he thought. That's what wealth was, in all its forms. How much labor had gone into the discovery, the mining and excavation of the fortune which had been at his feet? How many had ruined their health? Lost their lives? He fingered the coin Raven had given him. Had the gold in the coin been mined a century ago? Four centuries ago? At least the effort had produced something one could hold in one's hand. In all his years, John Kylie had seen little more than paper trails giving evidence of his own labors, paper trails and numbers. Lots of numbers. That's why his consumption had become so perversely conspicuous. With nothing to show for one's labors but numbers, acquisition of luxuries had become the only proof of accomplishment; a means of justifying one's existence. Boys measured by their toys.

"Will that be satisfactory, sir?"

He snapped from his trance. "Sorry? Uh, no; no check. I'll just take what cash you can give me now. Will two days be enough for you to get the rest?"

The bank officer nodded.

Kylie left the bank with a rather substantial bulge in his pocket; walked around the corner where Raven was waiting.

"That's all the cash I could draw. It'll take two days for the rest."

"This is enough for now. I'd better get started. I don't think we have much time. See you tomorrow back at the beach. Why don't you spend the night in town?"

Kylie decided that wasn't such a bad idea.

A light rain was falling as Kylie's panga nudged its bow onto the beach the following afternoon. Spying Raven sitting under the beach restaurant's palapa, two glasses and a bottle of rum on the table before him. He jumped ashore, chuckling as he approached his companion. Even in shorts and a T-shirt, Raven was nothing if not colorful.

"An eye-patch, maybe a parrot on your shoulder. That's all you'd need and I'd be shivering me timbers," Kylie said.

"Aargh," Raven growled.

Raven slid the empty glass toward him as he took a seat and raised his own. "Here's to," he looked furtively around him, "the *treasure*."

"I assume you found the equipment. That was fast."

Raven smiled and sipped.

"It is incredible isn't it?" Kylie said. "I mean I came here to live a simple life, to forget about—"

"To forget about all the money you stole, and here you are, involved in the biggest heist of the century. Forget about going straight, John Kylie. Some men were just born to be brigands, Harvard degree or not."

"It was Stanford," Kylie said, sipping his rum. "Anyway, when do we do the—?"

"The jump. Into the bowels of hell." Raven took a swallow of rum. "It's not a two-man job. We're going to need help. Another three or four at least."

"And where are we going to find such a band of merry men?"

"Merry men and one damsel. Our local crew."

"You've got to be kidding."

"Why not? I've been sitting here all day thinking about it. They're fit enough, climbing up and down these hills every day. They might be undisciplined, but I've trained worse. We don't need everybody, I'll only recruit the sober ones."

"That'll whittle it down," Kylie said.

"Leave it to me," Raven said.

Kylie looked at the cloud-covered horizon. "Well I don't expect to see any of them out tonight, with no sunset to celebrate, so if you don't mind, I think I'll just go on home."

"Oh, I almost forgot. You've got company. She said she'd wait for you at your place."

"Why didn't you tell me?" Kylie was up in an instant and away from the table.

"Don't worry, this one's on me," Raven said raising his glass to his drinking companion already sprinting down the beach.

Kylie slowed when he came to his hill, not wanting to arrive completely out of breath. Rain was falling harder and thunder could be heard in the distance, rolling across the heavens like coal down a long chute. Lightning flashes were far away and feeble, as if a spirit had struck a match and God had snuffed it out before the flame could ignite. Overcast skies had brought an early darkness this evening, but he could make out her form sitting in a chair on the balcony. Walking slowly toward his home, he allowed the rain to fall and soak him, a preliminary rinsing away of the day's sweat. He reached the balcony.

"Good evening," she said, sitting in the semi-darkness.

"Priscilla. I wasn't expecting you."

"No? I asked Raven to tell you."

"I guess he forgot. How are you?"

"Dry," she said. "Which is more than I can say for you. Come in out of the rain. Don't be shy. This is your house, remember?"

He stepped onto the balcony. She stood and kissed his cheek. Looking down, he spied it on the floor next to her chair. Tommy's notebook. She followed his eyes down.

"It was light when I got here," she said. "I thought I'd read something to pass the time. This was Tommy's?"

"Yes," Kylie said, picking it up.

"I remember him talking to me when I was sick." Her voice softened. "He was confiding in me and I was flattered. He told me he went into the jungle to study the plant life; how certain he was that there were herbal medical remedies for countless diseases, many on the verge of discovery, even more waiting to be *re*-discovered from simpler societies. He saw the jungle as one huge pharmacy just waiting to be cultivated. There'd be no more need for surgical knives or even needles, he said. I can almost hear his voice. Now I understand." She raised her eyes. "I just came to talk, John."

"Of course. Mind if I shower?"

"I'll wait right out here and enjoy the rain."

The hot shower was restorative, but though he rasped the towel across his back as if trying to sand his skin to a smoother finish, he did not feel dry. Even a clean shirt and shorts felt damp and clinging when he put them on. Breaths were shallow and stilted with the moist, heavy air pulled only halfway into his lungs. He lit a candle and joined Priscilla on the porch. Seated and contemplative, her right leg was draped over the arm of the chair, the bare foot dangling and swinging in a small circle. Unladylike though her posture was, there was a girlish innocence in the pose.

"Can I get you anything?" he offered.

"No, I won't be staying long. I just wanted to see you. To talk." Perhaps the oppressive heat and humidity affected her respiration. She barely spoke above a whisper.

"Is something wrong?"

"I—I think I should apologize."

"For what?"

"My bad manners. I've been vulgar and cheap. I'm sorry."

"I didn't think you were—"

"You probably didn't think much about me at all. Not that I blame you. Coming here in the middle of the night. Jumping into bed with you like I did. You've made me stop and think. Take a look at myself."

"And how did I do that?"

"By not asking me back."

Rivulets of rain cascaded from the roof, sustained notes against the percussive background of water pounding the dense foliage and the saturated earth. The now awkward silence between the two of them seemed to be urging him to say something. Kylie cleared his throat.

"Things got kind of busy around here," he said. What the hell was he supposed to say? He didn't want to hurt the woman's feelings. "But really, there's no need to apologize." He reached out and placed a hand on her arm.

She turned in her chair, her moist skin squeaking against the damp leather. "Malin is not good for you, John." The words issued from her lips like rifle bullets. "Don't let it go too far."

"What do you mean?"

"She's not like us, she's different."

"What makes you think that I—"

"A woman knows."

Kylie chuckled in an effort to make light of her observation, but Priscilla's voice hardened and sliced through the soupy night air.

"I think she killed Jeb. I'm almost sure of it." Kylie pulled his hand away from her arm, opening his mouth, sucking a long, slow draft of air till he felt light-headed with the effort. "They were an item for a while. She cooled off; he didn't. God, there's nothing more pitiful than a spurned lover. He couldn't let go. Then he was gone."

"I seem to recall the cause of death being something other than unrequited love," Kylie said.

"Don't make fun of me. I know what it takes to kill someone and I can see it in others. Women especially. Malin had that look. It was like looking in a mirror."

"What?"

Priscilla brought her feet together then stretched her long legs in front of her. "Oh I'm cured now," she said, offering no further explanation, her light laugh like a hiccup, "but I can see—"

"I'll be careful," Kylie said, intending caution to be exercised with present company more than with the woman under discussion. Priscilla stood up.

"I guess I'll be going now."

It was raining and dark. An invitation to stay would have been reasonable under the circumstances, but Kylie did not extend one.

"I think I like you John Kylie. I haven't said that in a long time."

She stepped off the balcony and ran into the darkness, the *slosh, slosh* of her footsteps fading till they were heard no more. And with Priscilla's departure, the rain stopped. A welcome breeze brought a gentle cool to damp skin as Kylie looked up to the dispersing clouds drifting, uncovering the star plane. He stepped off his porch and headed into the jungle. If the fates allowed, he intended to share this night with Malin, the petty jealousies of an insecure woman notwithstanding.

◈

At first glance it appeared Malin's hut was on fire, there was such a glow from her open windows. He ran, then slowed when it was apparent there was nothing out of order. It was candle glow. He called out.

"Malin, it's John."

She stood silhouetted in her doorway, saying nothing till he approached. "I wanted to see you," she said. "I went to your house. You had a visitor."

"Priscilla. She wanted to talk."

"I'm glad she did not stay."

"I didn't ask her to. I wanted to see you tonight."

She stepped forward, pressed herself against him. They kissed their welcome. Muted passion in their greeting, the couple sought only to tune in to one another and so tune out all else that clashed with their gentle, secluded environ.

"I thought we might watch the stars for awhile," Kylie said.

"Or not," Malin whispered into his neck.

She lay at his side. The hammock gently swung. Light from a single candle threw bizarre shadows against the matte adobe wall at their side. Kylie watched the creature crawl from the roof, down the wall. A spider or a scorpion, he did not wish to share quarters with the thing approaching him.

"What is it?" Malin felt him stir.

"I don't know. On the wall there. Look."

She lifted her head. "Just a spider. Not poisonous. Don't worry."

"I don't like spiders."

"No? I do. I admire their industry, their artistry; the perfect geometric forms of their webs." She drew squares on his chest. "They also keep the peskier bug population under control. They are very good house-mates."

"Raven saw some that were two feet across."

"Impossible."

"No, he swore. Two feet from the tip of one spidery leg to the tip of the other spidery leg." He teased her with his fingers, walking them across her bare skin.

"That tickles," she brushed his hand away. "Where did he claim to see such things?"

"They live in a deep pit. He said they had mandibles three inches long with sharp spikes, fangs between their pincers. No eyes. They just feel, feel..."

"Stop that!" She slapped his hand. "He'd been drinking. You'd better watch him. It sounds like his brain is going."

"I swear he was sober, and he swore he saw them."

"If I saw monsters like that, I'd be frightened of spiders too. But they don't exist. Go back to sleep."

He didn't need to be told twice. He closed his eyes as the candle sputtered and died.

## CHAPTER TWENTY-THREE

Next morning, Priscilla paid a call on her friend Alice, at the hilltop hotel.

"My goodness, that was so unlike you," Alice said when her early morning visitor had recounted her tale. "Really Priscilla, I think it was very bad strategy. He's going to think you're a bit—you know—and will be even more intrigued by her. Do you want my advice?"

"That's why I came." Priscilla cupped her coffee mug between her hands and sipped, drawing its fragrance into her nostrils like cognac.

"Let it run its course with Malin," Alice said. "You are right. These things don't usually last. Different cultures don't make for lasting relationships. When the sex is done, what is there to talk about? I mean, does she know who Micky Mantle was? Or Johnny Unitas? Gilligan? Scooby Doo?"

"Scooby who? The two women laughed. "She was educated in the States, don't forget," Priscilla said. "I think she might be up on more current icons than those you mentioned, maybe even cartoons."

"Ah, but he most certainly knows nothing about her culture, does he? All the years I've lived here there is so much I don't know about Mexicans. I'm not talking about their Spanish heritage, but the indigenous peoples. An enigma in their own country."

"I guess I don't see Malin that way. Indigenous."

"I can guarantee you, that's the way she sees herself," Alice said.

❖

Kylie awoke with a singular recognition. If there was a sensation to be remembered, retained forever, it was this feeling. The song of jungle birds, the perfume of morning blossoms, sun glinting on rain-soaked palm fronds, and the soft vanilla scent of the woman in his arms. Escaping a world where senses were dulled by stress and strife, he finally had a taste of paradise and it was waking to a morning such as this. He lay still so as not to disturb her, but Malin sensed his altered pattern of breathing. He felt her eyelids flutter against his shoulder, and kissed her forehead.

She raised her head and looked at him. For an instant he saw the face of a stranger. He saw eyes shrouded with revulsion. Someone he didn't know stared back at him; but the mist cleared and she smiled.

"It's you," she said. "I'm glad it's you." She gave him no time to puzzle over her paradoxical greeting, but jumped to her feet. "You must be hungry." In two steps she was lighting the gas for her single hotplate and putting on water for coffee, then darting outside, returning with a handful of fruit. "Mangoes and coffee," she said, pronouncing the morning menu.

Kylie found the basin and water pitcher placed on the porch for him and washed up, the aroma of coffee wafting through the open door and adding to the potpourri of morning scents. Stepping inside, the simple table setting dazzled with trumpet blooms of fresh-picked *Copa de Oro* mixed with bougainvillea as a centerpiece. Mangoes which had looked like ugly green potatoes had been transformed. Cut in half, sliced in a geometrical pattern, the skins pushed into domes, fruit extended upward, cubed amber arches adorned each plate surrounded by sliced limes and bananas. The coffee was served in clay bowls instead of cups or mugs, almost forcing one to savor, not just sip. He was enchanted.

"Do you have plans for the day?" Malin asked as they lingered at the table.

"I had hoped to spend it with you. Raven and I have something to do tomorrow, but I'm free all day."

"You two spend a lot of time together."

"He's concerned about Tommy's death. He's hoping to find clues somehow."

"Not much chance of that. The jungle washes clean with each rain. Is there anything I can do to help?"

"No. Raven's a do-it-yourself kind of guy. Thanks for asking."

"Well then, if you're free, why don't you let me show you the waterfall?"

"I'd like that."

"Finish your coffee and we'll go."

"I thought I might go home and shower first. You're welcome to join me."

Malin laughed. "You want to shower? Where do you think we're going?"

From her hut it was a trek through thick brush, not the beaten paths used by day tourists for whom the waterfall was high on their short to-do list. The morning cool had evaporated and the sun's rays felt concentrated as if through a magnifier as they crossed the lowland gorge to the cove's southern flank. Iguanas skittered out of their way, as well as smaller creatures too quick for the eye to catch. Malin found a shallow spot to cross the river running rapid with last night's rains, then through a growth of trees, they began climbing. Boulders fifteen feet high did not faze the woman and Kylie had no choice but to follow.

"You did well for the first time. I was watching you," she said when they reached the path and Kylie paused for breath. If she was watching, it was with the all-seeing eye, he thought as he huffed and puffed. She had never looked back.

The path brought them to the side of the cascade. Water plummeted 30 feet into a crystal pool, and then continued its course, winding over and around smooth boulders, inviting the hardy to run the rapids.

"We are lucky. We beat the tourists," Malin said as she stripped and dove into the pool. "Come on," she urged when her head broke the surface. "You said you wanted a shower."

She swam to where the plume of water crashed and foamed, where rocks beneath the surface made it possible to stand directly beneath the cascade. The plummeting waterfall enveloping her naked form was an artist's dream and Kylie stared, then shut his eyes tight to make sure the picture had taken. It was there. Engraved on his mental template forever. He cast off his clothes, then holding his nose, cannon-balled into the center of the cool crystal water.

They splashed and played, then climbed onto rocks and spread out to let the sun dry their bodies. Malin turned onto her stomach to let the sun dry her back. Lying on his side, Kylie stroked the nape of her neck then ran his fingers down her backbone. His fingers stopped.

"What happened here?" he asked. Stroking the three parallel lines scratched into her skin. She rolled over and raised herself onto her elbows. That look he'd seen this morning flashed in her eyes, then passed.

"Nothing," she said. A question had begun to form in his mind, but with her smile, it was erased.

The sound of advancing tourists could be heard. Quickly they gathered their things, dressed and departed. They chose the well-traveled path for their return and, holding hands, bid good morning to those about to discover this natural wonder.

"I hope they appreciate it," Kylie said.

"I hope they respect it," whispered Malin.

She refused his offer of lunch at one of the beach restaurants, instead buying a fish in the village and taking it back to her place and cooking it over an open fire. Even his compliment was spurned as they picked at the bones.

"That was delicious," he said.

"Umm, but it tastes better when you catch it yourself, don't you think?"

It was wildly improbable, this Adam and Eve existence, he thought when again their bodies cleaved in afternoon siesta. Was it merely a temporary fashion with her or was this truly a sustainable lifestyle, he wondered as she lay against him sleeping, her soft breath tickling his chest. Was the pleasure he felt in her company transferable to that world which would someday call for his return? If not, how long could he forestall that sadly inevitable day.

Malin twitched in her sleep, murmuring like a frightened kitten. On waking, she punched him.

"Damn you, it's all your fault," she said.

"What? What did I do?"

"I had a bad dream. Giant spiders."

He laughed, not to mock but to comfort. "You were probably right. There's no such thing. Raven has been pretty stressed lately."

Nightmares did not keep them from venturing out when the sun had set, though they didn't venture far. Malin simply moved chairs to the open space in front of the hut for star gazing. Side by side they sat, legs stretched out, toes touching on the shared ottoman, arms dangling, fingers entwined. Touching was essential for the evening communion.

"My first night here," Kylie said, "I was knocked out by so many stars. I remember thinking I was looking up at the one site unchanged since man's first conscious thought. There's no place left on the planet where you can say that. Our footprints are everywhere."

"And our garbage, and our poisons," Malin added. "It is man's nature to destroy."

"Well, what goes around comes around."

"Exactly."

Hours passed with only occasional hushed whispers, a squeeze of the fingers, a brief gasp as shooting stars animated the awesome expanse. But Kylie had not spent two consecutive nights with a woman in many, many moons, and something told him not to press it this time. It was a sensation too fleeting to be labeled a disappointment, when Malin did not object as he said it was time to take his leave. But of course, he told himself, she was no more used to sharing her nights than he, and after 24 hours together…

He carried her furniture inside and bid adios with a reluctance that surprised him. Walking away, he turned for one last look at her, but Malin had retired for the night, her candle extinguished.

The expat's beach ritual went on much later than usual, outlasting the waiter who served them. Raven had asked select members of the group to stay for an important discussion, and when the sleepy waiter finally left, he reached into the bag at his feet and pulled out an unopened bottle of rum and invited all to share, a tried-and-true military recruitment tactic.

By candlelight he transported them back to the days of the Revolution, telling them of the besieged President Carranza and the train of gold; of Pancho Villa, his interception of his nation's treasury and his trek over the mountains to the sea; of the treasure trove undisturbed all this time—until two days ago. Gently lapping surf provided an ambient background to his tale as he watched the bottle of rum being emptied of its contents.

"Fantastic," Tod whispered and the word was repeated by all at the table, their minds too dulled by alcohol for more creative responses.

"I was able to get all the equipment we need," Raven said. "But there's a catch. I've got the stuff for only 24 hours. I got us a crane too. We'll lower ourselves down the shaft, gather the gold, raise it up and pack up the truck. Nothing to it."

"Are we going to keep it all?" Priscilla asked.

"I'm thinking we keep some, return the rest. Nobody's gonna know how much we found. We'll be national heroes and we'll have enough to live comfortably the rest of our lives. How much does it take to live here anyway?"

"I might want to go somewhere else," Jerry said, then added, "maybe not."

"Hey, it's up to you," Raven said. "You want to go somewhere, you go. You want to do something, you do it. Have any of you ever known that kind of freedom?"

"Actually," Fred said, "ever since I moved here. Don't know if I want to change my lifestyle, but it sure sounds like a cool thing to do. I'm in," he looked at his glass, "and I'm not even drunk yet."

"OK," Raven said, "let's toast. To the mission." Glasses were raised.

"Raven, as a toastmaster, you're getting better all the time."

Raven smiled. "OK," he said. "We'll meet back here tomorrow night, 2 a.m. I want you all to get a good night's sleep and rest up all day tomorrow. Stay home. Relax. Spend the day thinking what it'll be like to be rich. Very, very rich."

Her friends had accompanied her home and Priscilla bid them goodnight at her door. Depending on her mood, to her band of lost boys she was queen bee, den mother, or at times, something altogether different. When she felt like it, an invitation followed the walk home from the beach at night, and she never lacked for a willing escort. But not tonight. Raven's admonition to rest up was taken seriously by all. She traipsed to her bedroom holding a lit candle, stared into her closet and laughed, catching herself from force of habit gazing at her wardrobe, wondering what to wear tomorrow. As if it mattered. She brushed her teeth and extinguished the candle. Nimble fingers undid the few buttons and her garments fell to the floor. She lay down on her bed but did not close her eyes. Think about being rich, Raven had said. For Priscilla, this took no imagining, but remembering. She'd known fine homes, furs, jewels, and fancy cars. She'd also known a loveless marriage and in-laws whose battles over her husband's estate had made her life a living hell—until she walked away from it. She'd join in this little treasure hunt, but as for the gold, they could keep it.

Lying in his bed, Tod thought once again of the high school senior who had come on to him that afternoon then complained to her parents, bringing an end to a profession he had loved. A good attorney might have saved his career, but on a teacher's salary he couldn't afford one. Now he would be rich, but no high-priced lawyer could return him to the classroom where he had spent the most fulfilling moments of his life. "Maybe there's something else I can do with it," he thought as he fell asleep, dreaming of gold.

Fred dreamt of California mansions he had sold and coveted, but into his dreams also came those former clients who bought their palaces only to sell them one or two years later, searching, never finding, a real home. Wealth seemed to bring them little joy. But he would join the hunt for gold.

Sitting in his dark room, unable to sleep, Jerry remembered his bankruptcy. He thought of the construction company he had founded. How it had grown. He made plenty of money, but worked so hard he didn't have time to enjoy it. Then the economy went south. Lawyers. He gripped the arms of his chair. Damned vultures. He thought he could save his company by declaring bankruptcy but everything he had left went to the fucking lawyers. He'd had a taste of wealth. The aftertaste was still bitter. But he was going on a hunt for gold.

Alone in his home before the coming of dawn, Raven could barely raise his arms. His hands shook. He extended his quivering fingers, and by the light of a flickering candle studied them with bemused interest, not concern. Everything was a trade-off. The empty bottle lay beside the chair in which he'd fallen asleep. Alcohol cauterized his psyche's open wounds, expunged painful remembrances. The twitching of a few fingers was a small price to pay for so efficacious a cure. Besides, the unwanted side effects waned by mid-day - with aid from the hair of the dog. He went to his cupboard and found another bottle and returned his chair facing the ocean.

The sea also had a calming effect and was a tranquilizer he employed when alone. He stared at the horizon, opening himself to whatever devils or angels presented themselves. Tommy's companionship had been a sedative, too; a gentle voice in the dark of night when even the booze was powerless to stop the rush of nightmares. Carnage, carrion, bloody scenes of battles in which he'd been forced to participate and which had taken but a few moments of his conscious existence, but now repeated themselves hour after hour, night after night, in tormented slumber. How he hated the dark and the mortal requirement of sleep. Sleep interrupted by screams of terror; to be soothed by the young doctor's calming assurances. Life went on, Tommy would say—as much for his own benefit—and with life the chance to atone. Atonement was Tommy's credo and he tried to pass it on, sometimes with a missionary's zeal. Raven had almost been convinced, but not now. Now he would fall back on a credo of his own; one tried and true and constant as his shadow. Revenge. He took a final drink. Already his fingers were steadier. The sky showed the first hints of the new day. In less than 24 hours these hands would hold a treasure beyond most men's dreams. Enough to buy his revenge.

Colonel Márquez had finally allowed his men to sleep, but not himself. On the field desk in his tent were a kerosene lamp, a near empty bottle of tequila and a picture, unframed. The picture was a printed page, torn from a book. In it an older man wore a fedora at a jaunty angle, seemed to sneer as he lit a cigarette. He wore a silk bow-tie with polka-dots. His sunken eyes were so dark they looked bruised. He had thick eyebrows denoting Andalusian ancestry. It was all Márquez had of his father, a picture ripped from a history book; a picture of a man dressed a little too nattily, a man who looked more like an actor than President of the Republic. In recent years he had kept it nearby, taking it out when alone, talking to it when he was drunk. Tonight he had concluded his last conversation with the picture. He threw it on the dirt floor of his tent, poured tequila on it, struck and dropped a match. The flame burned quickly, then died. He kicked at the dirt, scattering the ashes.

"Soon the world will know what you really were," he said, then stumbled to his cot and fell asleep without undressing.

John Kylie's sleep was undisturbed. He was at peace with the choice he had made.

# CHAPTER TWENTY-FOUR

The sleepy fisherman waited by his panga at two a.m. the following night. He was surprised when Raven appeared as promised, even more when the other gringos arrived, a scraggly band, yawning, scratching and half asleep. Late nights were not unusual for him so, even though he doubted anyone would really show up, he hadn't risked much, and the reward was great. Raven had promised him more than he made in a month for this single crossing. Seeing the crazy American pull a wad of cash from his pocket was an eye-opener, better than a steaming cup of Oaxacan coffee. These crazy gringos, he thought, what were they doing up at this time of night?

It wasn't unusual for there to be no talking as the panga crossed the bay—the outboards made conversation difficult. Raven directed the panga to the north side of the bay, past the town to an empty stretch of the coast. As the panga cruised slowly, about 50 yards from the shore, a light flashed on and off.

"There," Raven said, "head over there." The boat turned towards the beach. Leaning over the gunwale, unable to see, listening as if the sound of water slapping against the hull was his guide to water depth, the fisherman suddenly stopped the engine and the boat drifted. He said something in Spanish.

"OK," Raven said, standing and grabbing his backpack, "everybody over the side. Water's not deep and this is a sandy shore." He swung his legs over and dropped into the water. "Come on, it's only about three feet." Kylie went next but the others were slow to follow, and for a moment Raven thought his crew had mutinied. But Priscilla took her turn and said after landing,

"Come on you wussies, it's not even cold." The other men followed.

As they approached the shore, the skeletal frame of buildings under construction could be seen in relief against the moonlit sky. Raven drew a deep breath. In this light they resembled bombed-out structures he knew all too well.

"How were you able to get the equipment so fast?" Kylie asked.

"Construction," Raven said. "With all the damn development in this bay, there's plenty of equipment around. Getting what we need was just the art of the deal."

"You mean bribery."

"Exactly. We got the, uh, loan of the stuff for the day 'cause the boss is in Guadalajara. Job foreman's an old drinking buddy."

"Can these guys handle this stuff?" Kylie asked, referring to the group sloshing through the water behind them.

"We've got a contractor in the group, remember?" For once, Kylie thought, those stupid games on the beach were useful. "Jerry knows how to handle a crane. The trucks anybody can drive. I got a pump for the water. Nothing to it. Another good thing, the trucks are covered with the name of one of the biggest construction companies around here plastered all over them. Won't be suspicious at all. Great for hiding—"

"—the national treasury." Kylie said.

"Yup. There's my buddy now," Raven said. A flashlight shone from the shore to guide them, the pre-dawn amphibious landing complete.

Kylie drove the lead vehicle with Raven beside him as a lookout and navigator. As the sun began to rise the coastal road heading south turned inland and took them into the mountains. The two-lane blacktop offered spectacular views of the ocean behind them, of distant peaks ahead as they crossed chasms cut by rain-swollen rivers thundering their way to the sea. This was a bold land, defying subjugation. Coexistence rather than conquest, Kylie mused, had maintained the natural integrity of this Eden.

"What are you thinking?" Raven interrupted his meditation.

"I was just thinking that when man worshiped nature as a god he took better care of the planet."

"Yee-ha! Let's bring back those pagan days." He slapped the dashboard. "Actually, the planet was doomed when man started worshiping himself, believing God created us in his image. Slow down. There's El Tuito."

They passed through the quiet village. Raven recognized the turn-off from the main road and guided them through the outback. Their vehicles ably maneuvered the ruts of the dirt trail. They saw no signs of life as they drove over the rugged landscape and reached their second turning point. The entrance to the corn field was still marked by their previous visit and Kylie simply retraced the path over flattened stalks, stopping where they had before.

Waiting for the caravan to reach them Raven slumped into his seat and propped his feet on the dash. "John," he said, "you know my reason for going along on this little treasure hunt, but why are you doing this? Truth time."

Kylie gripped the steering wheel so hard his knuckles turned white. Looking straight ahead he said, "You ask me why I'm doing this." He turned to face Raven. "YOU ASK ME WHY I'M DOING THIS!" he screamed. "I came here to sleep under a thatched roof, to walk a quiet beach and pee out in the open under the stars. Instead I've been dragged all over the country, shot at, spied on. I told you once, I told you twice, I wanted no part of this but, oh no, I've got to *live*, I've got to find some new damn *purpose* for my life. And now I'm about to take a jump half a mile into the ground for some God-forsaken gold—which is the *last* damn thing I want to be doing—and you ask me why I'm doing this."

Raven just looked at him.

"I don't know," Kylie almost whispered. "I think it might be because I'm concerned for you. I haven't had one in a long time so I'm not really sure, but I think you might be a friend. That's all I can come up with. I'm doing this because you're my friend." Kylie sighed. "And I just got sick and tired of arguing with you."

Raven bared his perfect teeth in a wide grin. "Pretty damn good reason," he said. "I am one convincing fucker, ain't I?" He stole a glance in the rear view mirror. "I'd kiss you *compadre*, but the troops have arrived. Let's go get the gold."

Kylie left the truck as the others pulled to a stop and still yawning passengers got out. He circled the entrance to the pit trying to imagine that day, eight decades ago, when the treasure had been secreted. What had been Villa's intent? Extortion, like he'd done with the silver years earlier? Had he planned to use it to finance a new movement? Not only power but the trappings of power seduced the rebel commander, Kylie recalled reading. At one stage, he had even printed his own currency, perhaps due to the exigencies of the time, but perhaps out of pure vaingloriousness. To such a larger than life ego, pilfering his nation's treasury and converting it to his own ends would be all in a day's work—perhaps a step to the Presidential chair he coveted. Had he not been so careless that one summer afternoon, Kylie thought, he might have reclaimed the gold and risen to rule the country.

Raven got out. He pointed to one of the trucks and barked commands. "Unload the gear, then back it out. That one," he pointed to a second vehicle, "has the pump. Offload it where I'm standing then back it out and bring the crane here." A large flatbed had this essential piece of equipment. "We'll pump out the water first."

The pump and generator were set up, and flexible pipe lowered. With their engines sounding like small aircraft, water soon spumed, arching backwards into the corn field. After half an hour, the geyser diminished to a trickle.

"I'm going to rappel down," Raven said, in character choosing the more difficult and adventurous way of descending. "Get the crane over here and use it to pull me up when I order."

Raven selected his rope and threaded it through a figure-eight metal grommet, then attached it to a leather harness. He tied one end to the truck's bumper and yanked it, testing his knot. "I'm just going to inspect the bottom. If it's dry enough, I'm going to yell for you to lower the hook to winch me back up with the crane."

Raven stepped to the pit, pulled the rope taut, then leapt backwards. The rope snapped, slackened, snapped as he rappelled to the bottom. In a short time his voice echoed up. "Turn the pump back on. Got some puddles down here. Looks pretty good though."

For several minutes, water spurted erratically then merely dribbled. The pump and generator were turned off. Kylie stepped to the edge and yelled down.

"You OK down there?"

"Fine," Raven answered. "Bring me up."

The hook was lowered. Raven rose to the surface. Jerry the crane operator swung him back over solid ground and lowered him to earth. Raven stood, legs spread shoulder width, hands on hips.

"Hook up the spotlight. I'll ride down with it. When I've got it set up, send down three men." Priscilla looked miffed.

"I'm going down with you," Kylie said.

"John, this isn't corporate retreat recreation."

Kylie stepped over to him and whispered. "And I'm not the one who's been hobbling around with a bum knee for the past week. I'm going down with you."

"Suit yourself," Raven said. "OK," he yelled, "hook up the spotlight. Glad I brought a long extension chord."

He donned one of two headlamps and was lowered with the spotlight.

It was Kylie's turn. Priscilla waved *adios* and gave him a smile as he descended, his foot in the winch's hook, hugging the chain to his chest. In the narrow beam of his headlamp, the craggy black face of the rock could be seen, its surface not uniform but glistening with mineral deposits, with damp, clinging dew, with—what was that? Kylie thought he could see the rock moving before his eyes, but it passed briefly, then there was stillness. He scoured the rock looking for any sign of human visitation. Kylie wondered if any human eyes had gazed upon the walls of this vertical cave before this day, feeling as one of a privileged few in all recorded time.

"Raven?" he called out. His words bounced back into his ears, startling him.

"Don't worry," the voice came from beneath him, "I'm watching you. You've got about thirty feet more. Doing fine."

He stared down. He could see the surface below in the beam from his headlamp. Its focus became sharper as it seemed to rise up to meet him. He felt Raven's hand touch him to steady his landing and shivered with the human touch in this alien environment.

"You made it. See? That wasn't so bad." Even standing two feet in front of him, Raven's voice seemed to be coming from behind, from both sides, encircling him. Raven yelled up, "He's down. Throw down the chord for the light." The raised voice reverberated off the walls, deafening. "Stand back," Raven said, pushing him against the wall. The chord landed with a slap. Raven picked it up and plugged in the spotlight. "Wait'll you see this. OK, I'm turning it on," he yelled again and his voice boomed in the cavern. Their eyes were blinded, first by searing white light, then the gleaming splendor of the precious metal for which man had sweated and fought, schemed and lied, dreamed of and died for. There it was, a glittering mountain of it before him; wealth beyond measure.

"We've got some coins but it's mostly bullion," Raven said. "Anyway, partner, there it is; the Mexican national treasury, circa 1920. We need Fort Knox and the Fifth Cavalry; they manage with a hole in the ground." He chuckled, the echo of his wry laughter eerie in the subterranean chamber.

One by one, the rest of the crew were lowered to join them. Each gasped at the sight of the gold.

"OK," Raven grunted, "Let's get to work."

Raven gave one of his pre-game pep talks and their labors began. First, the wood and steel refuse was piled in a corner, then material was lowered for the crates that required assembly. Serious injury was barely averted when a cask of large nails came loose and splattered to the ground, sending nine-inch lengths of shrapnel exploding in all directions. It was a small miracle that no one was hit.

Priscilla and Fred were lowered leaving only Jerry above ground, manning the crane. As crates were assembled and stacked against the walls, movement became even more constricted. The temperature was well over 100 degrees and rising with the dramatically increased population. Plus, air was being used faster than it was being replenished. Fred fainted. Kylie also felt light-headed and nauseous. Raven cursed himself for his late response.

"Jerry," he yelled, "I'm sending Fred up in the harness. He's passed out. Then send it back down."

Raven asked if anyone else felt weak or faint. All shook their heads.

'There's too many of us down here at one time," he said. "We're going to load the crates in shifts of two. You need to go up?" he asked Kylie.

"Maybe just for a breath of fresh air."

"Go on up then. Who wants to stay?"

Priscilla stepped forward. "Need a date, sailor?"

Raven chuckled. "I'm regular Army, ma'am."

"Just so's your regular," she said.

"We're gonna work up a sweat," Raven said.

"My men usually do."

Catcalls in the cavern sounded like air raid sirens.

# CHAPTER TWENTY-FIVE

"How's Raven doing?" Jerry asked when Kylie returned to the surface.

"Fine. He'll be up in a while." He drew several deep breaths then said, "I'm going back down."

As he gazed at the wall, again he swore it was moving. He thought he heard a raspy, scratching sound beneath the increasingly faint whirr of the motors above him. He reached the bottom and with a courtly bow offered a hand as Priscilla stepped on the hook.

"Damn," she said, "just when I was getting comfortable down here."

As she was hoisted up, Kylie said, "I thought I saw the wall moving, and this time I heard something scratching. Did you notice it on the way down?"

"It's those spiders," Raven said.

"I thought you were joking."

"I never joke about my work."

The tedium began. Coins and bullion were loaded into the wooden crates using the most primitive construction implements of all - muscle, sinew, and backbone. Hour after hour they labored, two by two, no one ever down for more than 15 minutes at a time. Limiting the number in the shaft prolonged the effort, but there was no more fainting. The day turned to dusk, then to night, which was fine with Raven.

"It was a hell of a risk in the daylight," he confided to Kylie. "I'm glad we've got the cover of night."

"And I'm glad we don't have the sun beating down on us up there," Kylie said. "It was as bad as down here. Since it's cool enough to sit without sweltering, why don't we take a break, all of us. I think the troops would like to hear from their commander."

Raven shrugged, "Why not?"

Bottles of cold water kept on ice had refreshed all day, but that same *agua*, now sipped as a group in the dark, was more than reminiscent of their customary margaritas at sunset. Raven even offered a toast.

"You all worked well today. We're almost done. Here's to us."

Plastic bottles were raised.

"How much of this stuff are we going to keep?" Jerry asked. It was a question on all their minds.

"Been thinking about that," Raven said. "I'm thinking 'finders fee.' You're the business mogul, John Kylie. What's a normal finder's fee in a situation like this?"

"I doubt anyone's ever had a situation like this. In venture capital you've got what is called the 'Lehman formula.' When money is raised for a project the fee is five percent of the first million dollars, four percent for the second, et cetera and one percent of everything over five million. Then there's—"

"How many millions are down there?"

Raven spoke. "History books say Carranza took off with one hundred fifty million pesos in gold." He fingered the coin dangling from the gold chain around his neck. My good-luck piece here is twenty pesos in gold, dated 1917. Its value today is anywhere from 200 to 350 dollars. How many times does 20 go into one hundred fifty million?"

"Two many zeroes for me," Jerry said.

"Seven and a half million," Toad said. "That's over a billion and a half in gold."

"Conservatively," Kylie said. "One per cent of that is 15 million dollars. Then there's what I call the Mel Fisher formula."

"What's that?"

"Mel Fisher found the Spanish galleon Atocha off the Florida keys. He recovered over 400 million dollars in gold and jewels from that one ship. One ship of treasure coming from Mexico and we've got the whole country's treasury. I read the same amount Raven did. I'm not sure I believe it. We could have a whole lot more down there. Anyway, back to Mel Fisher, Florida sued him disputing ownership, the federal government too. The Supreme Court finally ruled in his favor. It was all his." Someone whistled. "But he gave 20 percent of his findings to the state of Florida to keep on public display. I don't think Mel Fisher applies here," Kylie continued. "I only brought it up as a matter of interest. This gold wasn't lost or abandoned, it was stolen and the Mexican government is going to want it back. Guys, this wouldn't be a fight in the courts, and we wouldn't just lose a cause of action if we put up a fight. We'd lose our lives."

"Kylie's right," Raven said. "I say we stick to one percent. They'd probably give that to us as a reward anyway. Well, maybe."

"That's still at least 15 million dollars," Priscilla whispered in the dark, "more than two million each. Look at us. We live in shacks on a beach with no electricity and we love it. What would we do with that kind of money? Do we really want it?"

"Are you crazy?" Fred said. "Why are you here?"

"For the same reason each and everyone of you is. To break the monotonous routine of living in paradise. I don't know if I want to spoil the life I love by becoming filthy rich. I've been there."

"Kylie has an idea," Raven said softly. "He's already mentioned it to me. Go on, John. Tell them."

"I hate the thought of all this getting stuck in a vault where it won't do anyone any good," Kylie said. "Why don't we take our finders fee and do something worthwhile with it."

"Like what?"

"I was thinking of Tommy, his search for cures in the jungle. We could support that kind of research. Any way you look at it, this gold came from this country. I say we use it to help Mexicans. These people have been pretty good to us."

"I think that's a fine idea," Raven said. "I say that's what we do. Is everybody in?"

"I don't know," Toad interrupted. "It's an awful lot of money. I'd like to keep some. I mean, if you want to start a clinic, I could give you some of mine. But I might want to be a millionaire for a while."

"You're a millionaire from now till dawn," Raven said. "We've got to finish up here by then. Anybody starts looking for this gear before we get it back, we might not have any loot to keep or to give away. Let's get back to work."

Raven stood. There was a loud crack and a sharp intake of breath. With a curse the pain in his knee was once again denied. "Let's go. Get that stuff loaded," he said.

# CHAPTER TWENTY-SIX

Through the night they worked. The only casualty was Raven's broken huarache sandal, and, not one to complain, he didn't even mention it. One by one the assembled crates were lifted from the earth and placed on the trucks. There was little conversation among the treasure hunters as they labored, one thought absorbing each of them through the night—wealth, its blessings and its curse. On dilemma's horns they danced till dawn, till the final ounce of gold was loaded.

Raven and Kylie were together at the bottom of the *cenote* when the last crate was lifted. They took one last look around.

"We did it," Raven said. "A bunch of beach bums and we rescued the Mexican treasury from oblivion."

"You know something?" Kylie said. "I hate to admit it but you were right. I feel more alive at this minute than I ever have in my whole life."

"Told ya. OK, let's get topside and prepare to become heroes. Hey up there," he yelled, "send down the hook. We're ready to come up."

But the distant whirr of the winch which had been constant throughout their effort was for the first time silent.

"HEY!" Raven yelled. "Bring us up!"

Instead, all went dark. Raven was about to yell again when something struck him in the face; stinging, drawing blood. It landed at his feet and he bent down. It was the electric cord which had powered their spotlight. "Hey what the fuck are you doing up there?" he hollered, his echo booming. Both men craned their necks looking up. The pitiful morsel of sky that could be seen above was a dull gray with the coming dawn; a dull, distant gray. They heard, coming from the surface, someone laughing. An accented voice yelled down to them.

"One thing I regret is that I never had the chance to introduce myself," the voice yelled. "And that's a pity. You gentlemen have afforded me much amusement lately, but none so much as this past evening. Watching you all sweat and toil has been sheer delight. You gringos, you provide such expert entertainment. And you sure made my job easier. I could quote one of your most famous entertainers as we bid you adios and say 'hasta la vista, baby.'" Again the unholy chuckling. "I'm afraid though, that as a farewell, it's not so relevant in your case, gentlemen, as we do not expect to have the pleasure of seeing you again. I guess I'll just say thank you. *Muchas gracias.* I do regret it must end like this, you have both made such a heroic contribution to my country, but take comfort in remembering that unsung heroes are no less meritorious than those whom history favors." Then he was gone.

They heard the trucks start up, heard them roll away. In the muffled distance they heard Priscilla cry "*Raven—*". Then there was nothing.

The two raved and raged in the darkness which now entombed them no less than if mounds of dirt had been thrown over their bodies. Kylie gasped. He could not draw a complete breath, and the harder he tried the less he achieved. His heart was pounding as if it would explode and shoot through his constricted throat like a missile. The sound was horrible as his larynx contracted, closing off air movement into or out of his body. Two hands gripped his upper arms in a vise.

"Stop it." Raven commanded. "Count to ten. Take a short breath then count to ten again. You're panicking and hyperventilating. Stay calm. There's plenty of air for both of us. That's it, breathe, exhale. Good." When respiration returned, Raven let loose of him. "Now sit down slowly. Breathe normally. Let's talk about this." After minutes of silence, he said, "We can cuss ourselves for being such idiots, but I don't see much gain in that."

"Who the hell was that?" Kylie asked.

Raven drew a deep breath. "I think I believe you when you said you were being followed. Those army troops in the jungle. That officer staying at Alice's place. Damn, I've been an idiot."

"What about the others—maybe they killed them."

"Maybe," Raven said. "That was Priscilla screaming. They took her with them. Not good."

"And left us here to die."

"That we've been left here is beyond dispute. The dying part is conjecture at this point. You hurt anywhere?"

"No."

"I'm OK too. That's something. What have we got down here?"

"What do you mean?"

"Equipment."

"We have one spotlight with extension cord—unplugged."

"Right. Wait - don't we have a couple headlamps down here?"

"I think so; somewhere."

"Sit still. Let me see if I can find them." Raven stood and shuffled off in the darkness. Minutes later a narrow beam restored the sense of sight. With the first piece of head gear the second was soon recovered.

"Let's continue the inventory," Raven said. "See if there's anything down here we can use."

"For what?"

"To get the fuck out of here."

They peered in every nook, covered every inch of the bare rock bottom. Kylie found hammers used for assembling the crates. Raven found a length of broken chain and his huarache sandal with a busted strap. Loose nails and splinters of wood were scattered everywhere. Squatting positions were resumed in the center of the floor.

"We don't appear to be particularly well equipped for escape," Kylie said.

"That's my assessment too."

"Do you think he'll come back for us?"

Raven didn't bother to answer that one. "What I think is that we'd better turn off these lamps. Batteries are running down."

"Yes sir, colonel sir," Kylie turned off his headlamp. "We don't want to die in the dark, do we?"

"We're not dead yet, and I'm not through thinking. If you're going to give up, then do me a favor and shut up."

The silence, like the darkness, was total. It was the silence of death, Kylie thought, but how could one know death's silence unless one were... "Raven?" He needed the sound of a voice, even his own.

"Yes, John."

"What are you doing?"

"Meditating."

"Meditating?? Why?"

"Because," came the calm, even reply, "I once paid $2000 for therapy in a sensory deprivation chamber. This is costing me nothing. I'll let you know when I'm through. Till then, please don't disturb me."

Deprived of speech, Kylie thought of countless things he wanted to say but remained mute and immobile. He thought he heard Raven moving in the dark but said nothing. Didn't meditative pursuits demand one's immobility, he wondered? The rustling noise continued.

"I thought I asked you not to disturb me," Raven whispered.

"Me?? I haven't moved a muscle," Kylie whispered back. "I thought it was you."

Both flicked on their headlamps. Kylie screamed and jumped to his feet. Raven struggled to rise from his cross-legged meditative position, but joints had set and muscles had stiffened in the frozen silent minutes. A dry *'craak'* as he struggled to stand too quickly, and he screamed also, but with pain not fear as his trick knee gave out once more. Kylie jumped to his side, grabbed an arm, nearly pulling it out of its socket. Again Raven yelled as he was dragged, but he'd had a second to look behind him and saw the reason for Kylie's terror. It was as if the floor was moving, their number was so great. In fact, spiked backs and spiny legs covered every inch of surface like a wave rushing toward them. In the front line, pincers as wide as a man's hand snapped open, shut, ready to cut into anything that chanced to come between them.

"My God, look at them," Kylie gasped. Spiders two feet wide were approaching en masse, a hideous infantry.

"Shine your light on them," Raven rasped, and both deployed their headlamps but the creatures, unfazed, continued their charge, bayonets loaded. "They can't see," he said. "No eyes." At his side was the hammer. He took it and struck the ground hard. With the vibration there was an instant retreat and a sound reminiscent of pebbles tossed by waves on a beach as the invading force scattered.

"Timid fuckers," Raven said. "I don't think they're spiders."

"What are they?"

"No idea. Do I look like a botanist? They're probably more afraid of us than we are of them."

"It's entomologist. Entomology is the study of bugs. I disagree with you on the who's scared of whom question. How's your leg?"

Raven gave a deep sigh. "Out again. Bad timing, John. I'm beginning to think we might have a bit of a situation here."

"Well, it's not like we were about to climb out of here. I don't see how we're any worse off than we were. We just have to wait till someone comes, that's all."

"With no food or water? It was over 80 years between visits to this sinkhole, don't forget. No, I think we—" Raven stopped in mid-sentence.

"Are you OK?" Kylie asked.

"Climb out of here. You said 'climb out of here.'"

"What I said was, it's not like we were going to climb out of here before you hurt your knee again and I don't see how—"

"I heard what you said damn it, the operative phrase was 'climb out of here.'"

Kylie began pacing, the beam from his head swinging wildly. "Climb?? Why don't we just jump? It's only ten stories, damn it. Oh, I forgot. Your knee."

Raven said firmly, "I would like you to close your mouth and stand in one place. That's good. Now, listen and focus on the sound of my voice as if it were your only salvation, because if you can't listen to me and concentrate on each and every word I say, then in all likelihood we will die here. Thank you. Now look around you. Gather up as many nails as you can find. Do it."

Kylie scavenged as he was told, returning with a fist full of nine inch nails. Of this commodity there was no shortage.

"Now, take the hammer and pound a nail into the wall about knee high. Cant it upwards and leave about three inches protruding."

This was done.

"Is it solid?" Raven asked.

"It seems to be."

"Test it. Step on it."

Kylie put his foot on the nail and tried to step up but lacking a hold quickly tumbled.

"That's alright. Did it hold?"

"Yes, but I couldn't get my full weight on it."

"I know, I know. Hammer another nail in, three feet higher than the first, about a foot or so to the right."

The second nail was pounded into the rock face.

"OK. Step onto the first nail and grab hold of the second. See if it will support you."

Kylie did and was able to stand off the floor. Now he saw Raven's object and jumped down.

"Oh no. You can't be thinking what I think you're thinking."

"You can do it, John. It is one of the most basic elements of rock climbing. It'll be easier than...than climbing a rope. You've seen it in the movies. Remember Gregory Peck in "Guns of Navarone?" Stallone in, what the fuck was that movie? One nail at a time, one step at a time."

Kylie looked up. The beam from his helmet didn't even reach the height to the entrance of the pit. "I can't," he whined, "I can't."

"No, *I* can't," Raven said, "You can and you must. John, it's the only way out of here."

Kylie walked to his comrade and sat down beside him. "Raven, I've spent my adult life behind a desk. Sex has been my only form of regular physical activity since college and the only climbing I've ever done was up the steps of corporate jets. It's ten stories straight up to the surface hanging on to what, three inches of a damn nail while I'm hammering at another? I won't make it 20 feet before I lose my balance and fall. It's suicide."

"It's not suicide." Raven grabbed his arm again, squeezing it tight. "It will be a noble effort. If you don't make it, you'll fall and die in an instant if only you get high enough. Suicide will be my option if I'm left down here alone. Believe me, if it weren't for this damn leg, I wouldn't be giving you the choice. I'd be going up."

Kylie stepped to the wall and ran his fingers over the rock. "I remember the movie," he said. "Gregory Peck had rope. We don't even have any damned rope."

Raven laughed. "Yes we do. Our humorous friend up there was kind enough to provide it. The extension cord. It's exactly the right length. And we've got the harness I used to rappel down. The nails will serve as pitons, those are the spikes that you use to climb and secure the rope. You've got everything you need. You're equipped to climb Everest."

"It's going to take a hell of a lot of nails."

"Then gather yourself a hell of a lot of nails. Think of it. The higher you get, the lighter the load."

"Raven," Kylie's voice was now a whisper, "the spiders. They're coming back."

"Fuck the spiders. Get your gear together. Let me worry about the spiders."

# CHAPTER TWENTY-SEVEN

Kylie scavenged for nails until he had as many as he could carry. Raven improvised. He ripped apart the sole of his broken huarache sandal and fashioned the pieces into two leather gloves. Covering the palms while permitting him to grip, they were more than sufficient.

Raven lectured from a sitting position and gave a primer on rock climbing; explaining the purpose of each item of improvised gear, the proper use of ropes, climbing holds, knots, how to fashion a sling, and most important of all, state of mind. Courage, he said, was nothing more than mathematics. Element of risk the denominator, skill plus intellect the numerator, achievement the result. Kylie practiced the two knots he would use; the electric cord demanded the simplest. He attached his harness, was given an oral examination, and passed. His instructor congratulated him.

"John, you have what you need and you know what you need to do. I've taught men less physically fit than you and I've never asked a single one to do anything I felt he was not capable of doing. You can do it."

They were being observed. The monstrous insects had ventured within two feet of where Raven sat and stopped, still as death. They looked like gutted, dried carcasses of crabs piled up after a holiday feast.

Raven ignored them. "Go now, John. Good luck." Raven offered his hand and Kylie grasped it with both of his. He was ready to climb.

"Here," Raven said, "take this too." He handed him his headlamp.

"No," Kylie said, "you'll need it."

"You'll need it more if yours goes out before you reach the top. Take it."

From where did Raven draw such strength, Kylie wondered. He felt himself a coward, leaving the injured man, his friend, alone in the darkness, and was ready to abandon his effort before it began. Raven must have read his mind.

"If it weren't for my leg, I'd leave you here in a heartbeat," he said. "Now go."

He shouldered the cloth pouch with his nails - Raven had given him the shirt off his back for fashioning this article - and pounded the first pattern with his feet on solid ground. He heard the spiders skittering away as he hammered, but also the muffled sound of their return when he stopped. He stepped up. The next solid surface on which he'd stand was now the height of a tall building above him. His sling fashioned in the manner Raven had taught, he raised himself, worrying the electric cable would fray and snap but it held and slowly, slowly, he raised himself, then hammered, reaching as high as he could to place nails at the next level.

"Raven, I'm moving up," he yelled.

"Good," Raven said. "Don't talk, just climb. Focus, focus, focus." The man's voice sounded raspy.

Nails were dropped. Nails were driven in too crooked to be serviceable. Kylie became concerned with his waste. What would he do if he neared the top and there weren't enough? He tried to concentrate only on the repetitive routine. Minutes passed. How far had he come? How far yet to go? At least the dropped nails gave him a barometer of his progress with the sound of their hitting the ground below. His progress seemed agonizingly slow. Hoisting himself up he scraped his body across the rock face and soon his shirt was torn away. More than once his bare skin, cut and bleeding, adhered to the rock face as he stretched to hammer above him. It was like ripping bandage from an open wound when he pulled away to step up to the next level.

"Don't think of falling or you will fall," Raven had said, and he focused on only the nail in his fingers, the nail he was driving, the nail he reached for as he pulled himself higher with his hands encased in clumsy leather binding. Attaining some proficiency, no more nails were dropped as up, up he went. How high, he had no idea. The light from his helmet faded and died and he almost fell as he replaced it with the other. The discarded headlamp fell and crashed beneath him. It sounded like a long way down. He listened to hear a word from Raven; encouragement, support, but there was nothing.

Now, from his waist to his neck, it felt like a knife blade was being sharpened against his chest, like a razor against an old barber's strop, with every move he made. The second lamp grew dim as well. His arms ached; the one constantly pulling his weight upwards, the other contorting to reach and strike blows in postures not meant for human musculature. He had only one solace now. If he were to fall from the height he had reached, death would be instantaneous.

Kylie stopped for rest. He hugged the rock face with every pore, could not have made more complete contact had the surface been parallel instead of vertical and he was lying on it like a bed. He banished the thought of beds and of comfort. The nail pouch was lighter now, and the odds against this impossible enterprise had lessened to one of only the highest improbability. With his left arm he reached up once again, and felt the insect's pincer snap against his wrist, cutting open his skin. He screamed with surprise and shock as much as with the stinging pain—and lost his grip. Arms flailed seeking a handhold but there was none. He scraped against the wall as he fell to a certain death. But his left hand clasped the electric cord as it dangled from a single nail. With his right hand he grabbed onto a second nail, trying to hold on. The leather protected his palm but made a secure grip impossible. Scraping the wall, a foot found a nail and he steadied himself, cord in hand, one foot finding hold. He twisted his head and looked down then reached slowly, slowly with the other leg. Finding another nail and a second foothold, his feet were steadied.

How could he have forgotten? He'd seen the wall seemingly moving on his way down. The filthy creatures inhabited the rock face. He looked at his arm. The skin had been cut but it was barely a scratch. He'd panicked. Over a bug. Looking up he could see the loathsome form hiding in a crevice. How he hated them. But there was no other option.

He continued his ascent, reaching more slowly; tapping with the hammer to send vibrations and alert whatever made its home in the wall, hopefully giving the thing time to move out of his way. There were no more encounters. Then his headlamp went out. In total darkness he could only feel and grope but it seemed the loss of one sense heightened another. This was a mixed blessing. Limited now to his tactile senses, the agony of raw skin and throbbing muscles was heightened to an unbearable degree. He couldn't continue. This was his limit. He released a handhold and brought his arm to his forehead, wiping sweat from his brow, and brushing the useless helmet from his head. It fell down, down, and its crash seemed much further than before. Kylie looked above him. In the heavens was a single morning star. He could not see how far it was to the end of his climb but that lone object so far out in the universe gave him hope and the fantastic delusion that he was moving closer to it with each arm-length.

Reaching into his pouch there were only a few nails left. His quest was nearing its end. Alright, if this was the whimper with which his existence would come to a close, so be it, but he still had a few more inches he could climb. A final rung in the ladder, then not a swan song but a swan dive and it would all be over. He reached up and felt not solid rock but dirt. Dirt and blades of grass. He'd reached the surface.

The final two feet were the most perilous. For a terrifying moment reaching over the ledge he had nothing to hold on to, nothing to steady himself. He flung himself forward, kicked and rolled in the dirt, away from the hole. On his back he gulped the fresh air, looking wide-eyed at the heavens above him. He was alive. Then he turned over on his stomach and crawled back to the lip of the *cenote*.

"Raven!" he yelled. "I made it! Hang on, I'll be down for you as soon as I can."

There was not a sound from the depths below.

The scene around the entrance to the pit was that of a work site abandoned in haste. The crane and generator had been left, and loose items were scattered everywhere, their intended use fulfilled. Kylie jumped into the cab of the crane, an alien environment. With trial and error, buttons and levers, he taught himself to control the crane's arm and winch. There were only two functions needed, to swing the arm over the hole; to raise and lower the chain and hook. The chain began its descent. Having observed it raise and lower men and material, he had a pretty good feel for the timing, and was alert to the slackening of the chain. When it hit bottom he jumped down, ran to the hole. The electric cord he had used as a climbing rope was restored to its former function and plugged into the generator. There was light at the bottom of the pit. He stood over it.

"Raven," he yelled, "If I drop the harness, can you grab the hook?"

No answer.

"Raven, are you alright?"

Silence.

He had no choice. Kylie threw the harness into the pit then leapt over the gaping hole in the earth. He grabbed onto the chain but slid before he could slow himself. The metal cut. His hands bled. But he tightened his grip and slowed the speed of his descent, arms and legs wrapped around the chain, sliding like a fireman down a pole. He thumped to the ground at the bottom of the pit and looked around. Raven was nowhere to be seen.

"Raven, where are you? This is no time for games."

Then he saw it. Where Raven had lain was a mound, but not of dirt. Almost imperceptibly, it moved. Kylie stepped closer.

"God no," he screamed and with bare, bleeding hands he beat into the mass of spiny backs and spindly legs of the giant spiders swarming over the body of his companion. There were high-pitched screeches from the insects as they were grabbed and swept from the motionless body. There were loud cracks as he flung them with all his strength at the walls of the cave, breaking their shells, splattering their internal organs against the rock. He kicked against those who came at him with pincers snapping open and closed. He beat them off, uncertain whether they'd accepted defeat or were regrouping for another charge.

"Raven, oh my God, Raven."

The body lay still. There was not a patch of bare skin not covered in blood, and fluids seeped through the cloth on the parts of his body that were still covered. There was movement in one pants leg and Kylie shivered with horror as a creature crawled out at the ankle. Kylie grabbed a rock and beat it to pulp, screaming insensible curses.

Raven's pristine white beard and hair were matted and discolored. It looked like the arachnids had secreted a glue-like substance all over his face. Except the eyes. The sockets where the eyes had been glistened, glimmered as if made of gold. Kylie ran his fingers gently over the face, the eyes. They were...they were coins! Raven had placed two gold coins over his eyes to protect them. Kylie lifted them off. Eyelids fluttered then opened. He was alive. Raven slowly lifted an arm, lowered a hand to his face and wiped the mucus-like substance from his mouth.

"They—they slimed me," Raven rasped. The sound the man made sounded like a cross between a death rattle, a cough—and a chuckle.

"Can you stand? I need you to stand," Kylie said, but Raven only coughed. Kylie grabbed him by the shoulders and pulled him to the center of the pit where the chain hung. "I'm going to put you in the harness," he said, "and get you hooked up."

It was awkward. Raven was immobilized and moaned with pain whenever the injured leg was stressed, but Kylie managed to get him in the harness, then was able to get him to stand long enough to fasten the harness to the chain.

"OK, now you can sit," Kylie said. Raven simply collapsed, but the harness now suspended him almost two feet off the ground. "I have to go back up and start the winch," Kylie said. He jumped up and grabbed the chain, climbing over him, then it was hand over bloody hand straight up. He managed to clamp his feet together between chain links and use his legs as well as his arms for the climb, but the second ascent took more strength than he had. Then John Kylie discovered his own reservoirs of strength. He had to even climb higher than the hole, then for a moment just hung there gasping for air. It was too far to try and jump. There was no choice but to climb up to the crane's arm, then shimmy down to the cab. Drenched with sweat, muscles began to stiffen in agony. Climbing the metal was beyond difficult. Half way down the arm he slipped, hanging suspended for a moment with hands too numb to grip. He fell and landed hard on the roof of the cab. He crawled inside, started the winch, then passed out.

"You son-of-a-bitch get me down from here!"

Kylie opened his eyes. He was seated at the controls of the crane. At the top of the arm, Raven dangled in the harness. Covered in ooze, he looked like the victim of some primitive torture—or a very large gumdrop. "Hey!" he hollered.

Kylie swung the arm over solid ground and lowered the winch. He jumped from the cab, ran to the chain and received Raven into his arms, lowering him gently to earth. He unhooked the harness and both men sprawled in the dirt.

"That was a nice piece of climbing, son," Raven husked between gasping for breath.

"I had a good teacher." Kylie panted. "You have a new career."

"As a fake maybe. That was a first for me. What I know about climbing I learned from Hollywood. But you did it. You saved our lives. Now, can you get me someplace where I can wash this spider shit off me?"

# CHAPTER TWENTY-EIGHT

"See any bodies around here?" Raven's voice was husky, barely audible.

"None," Kylie answered. He looked around, found a bottle of water and gave it to his comrade. The morning sun was full in the sky.

"They took everybody with them," Raven said. "Maybe there's a chance."

There was one vehicle left, the flatbed on which the crane rested. Kylie started the engine.

"Where to, Colonel Allen?"

"Get me to a doctor," Raven said. "Quick."

Kylie drove to El Tuito, calling on Dr. Garcia, the rural physician who had received Tommy's body. The corpse had looked far better then they did stumbling into his office and Dr. Garcia did not hide his shock at their appearance.

"He's worse off than me," Kylie said. "Please take care of him first."

Kylie offered to help but the doctor told him to lie down and be still; he would see to him as quickly as possible. He washed Raven's body as he enquired just what had brought them to this state. Raven mumbled that they were exploring a *cenote*.

"My knee went out on me," he said huskily, "then these underground things attacked us. They looked like spiders. They were all over me. This goo is from them."

The doctor went to his phone, made a call, brought Raven the receiver and as he was lying there, put him on the line. "Describe them to this man," he said, then took back the receiver when Raven was finished and continued to talk to the party on the other end. He returned to his patient.

"My friend is a professor of entomology at the university," the doctor said, "I had to know what these things were and if their bites were toxic. Their bites are not poisonous, but this mucus? I will have to watch for infection. They are not spiders. They are sometimes called scorpions, but they are not those either. Locally they are called *tindarapos*. Most live on the surface but a few species live underground. Usually they don't come near humans. Strange what they did to you. These cuts and abrasions." He was cleansing Raven's flesh wounds with antiseptic as he spoke, the patient's body stiffening with the sting of the alcohol.

"I guess I pissed them off," Raven said through clenched teeth.

"It would appear so," the doctor said.

He then cleaned Kylie's flesh wounds and depleted his supply of gauze and bandages before finishing.

"I am going to have to go out to buy some more bandages," he said. "I'll be back in a few minutes. You will be fine if you just stay still. Can I trust you both not to put your lives in further peril while I'm gone?"

Both lay on parallel beds in the doctor's office and stared at the ceiling. "You feel OK?" Kylie asked.

"If I could move, I'd get up and put some of that alcohol to better use," Raven said.

"There'll be time for that," Kylie whispered. "I'll buy you a case of whatever you want."

When the doctor returned, Kylie had gone pale. The doctor frowned, took Kylie's wrist and looked at his watch.

"Seems I can't leave you two alone for five minutes," he said and went to his medicine cabinet. "Take this," he ordered Kylie, handing him two tablets and a cup of water.

"What is it?"

"A mild sedative. It will relax you." He then took Raven's blood pressure and repeated the prescription. As both became groggy, he said to them, "Now you must rest, both of you. It would not be unlikely for either of you to go into shock. I want to watch these skin wounds for a couple of hours to make sure there is no inflammation. Then," he said to Raven, "I'm going to have a look at your knee. How many times has it gone out on you lately?"

"One, two, three," Raven counted slowly, then lost consciousness.

When Kylie opened his eyes he was disoriented, with no sense of time or place. He was in the doctor's office, he recalled when his head cleared. He heard Raven sleeping on the table next to him, his breathing deep and steady, and wondered whether the absence of snoring was a good or bad sign. He called for the doctor.

"I'm right here," the doctor said. He had not left their sides. He stood over Kylie. "How do you feel?"

"My skin burns from head to foot and every muscle in my body aches."

"Good. If you didn't feel that way I would be worried."

"How's Raven?"

"He's sleeping. He has no fever. I think he'll be OK."

Dr. Garcia was at Raven's side as he stirred then awoke. He stood between their two beds, looking at one, then the other.

"OK," he said, "I think you're both going to live, which may pose a continuing threat to the peace and tranquility of this community. I thought about calling the authorities, but decided I'd give you the opportunity to tell me first. I want to know the truth. What have you been up to?"

Raven turned to look at Kylie. "Think we should tell him?" Kylie nodded. "I don't know," Raven continued. "I still have an obligation to Don Chuy."

"Don Chuy?" Dr. Garcia said. "What does that poor old man, may he rest in peace, have to do with this?"

Raven ignored him. "And I've been thinking what you said John, you know, about the research institute in Tommy's name."

"Tommy? The body you brought here? May he rest in peace. What's *he* got to do with—" Dr. Garcia said. "Oh for God's sake, will you tell me what's going on here?"

"You know," Raven said still ignoring him, "that institute is going to need someone to head it."

"Should be someone from the medical profession," Kylie said.

"Would be good if he were a local too, someone who's proven he cares about people."

Dr. Garcia was fuming.

"Better tell him, Raven," Kylie said. "These guys have ways of making you talk."

"OK," Raven said. He was able to raise himself on his elbows. "Doc, you might want to sit down for this."

Doctor Garcia pulled up a chair. And the narrative began.

⊸◈⊷

"So," Raven said when the story had been told. "Are you in?"

"My God," Doctor Garcia said, "Your friends are in great danger. We must try to help them."

"This guy's got his priorities straight," Raven said. He sat up.

"Wait," the doctor said. His movements were fast-frame as he gave Raven a shot in the knee, then wrapped it in a support bandage. He looked at both. "Neither of you are fit for this mission, but we will do our best." He held out his hand. Raven and Kylie grasped it. "As a boy," he said, "my favorite book was 'Los Tres Mosqueteros.' All for one and one for all. I never thought I'd have the chance—"

Raven stood up. "Doctor, excuse me but we don't have time for literary reminiscences. Let's get the hell out of here."

Doctor Garcia's old pickup was their mode of transportation, the doctor driving as they traversed dirt roads, cow paths, and open fields, as Raven navigated using his pocket GPS. Much of their route was along the coast and not infrequently they forged through dense foliage and over rocks, blazing their own trail. Then thick brush forced them to slow and finally stop.

"We walk from here," Raven said.

As they set out on foot there was a loud explosion. They felt the earth vibrate beneath their feet.

"That's them," Raven said. "Just over that rise."

"Rise?" Kylie said. "It's a friggin' mountain Raven, and it's all rock."

"It's a piece of cake for a spelunker like you. Doc, you should see what this boy climbed out of to save my life."

Dr. Garcia looked at Kylie with admiration. "You are a brave man, Mr. Kylie. You can do this. In life, one must learn to—"

"Oh no, not another goddamn motivational speaker." Kylie stomped away from both.

"What did I say?" Dr. Garcia asked.

"It's OK," Raven said, smiling. "You goosed him. Look. There he goes."

Kylie was already half way up the first boulder, climbing with speed and new-found confidence. He was the first to reach the summit.

The downward side was tricky, and several false steps caused loose rocks to fall. Fortunately, the periodic explosions gave cause for rock slides as well, covering the noise of their own.

"What are they doing?" Kylie whispered after one of the blasts.

As they descended they could see jungle below, and had a clear view to the sea. Raven pointed towards the ocean. "They're clearing a path to the shore. That's what all that construction in the jungle was. Look. Out there."

Miles offshore, a huge ship stood motionless in the still waters.

"You recognize it?" Raven asked. "We saw it that day we went fishing. Its helicopter flew over us, remember? Also, it was in the marina when we brought back Tommy's ashes. Damn thing sure likes these waters."

They continued downward. Reaching ground the brush was thick, and a few more cuts were added to their extensive collection. Kylie wiped blood from his arm.

"I don't think I can feel pain anymore. Is that a problem, Doc?"

"Think of it as a blessing. At least for now."

Raven obviously was likewise impervious, using his bare arms as machetes, swinging and chopping a path through the brush. Then he raised both arms, a signal for all to freeze. He knelt, turned and whispered. "Straight ahead." The two men crawled to his side.

They were mere yards from a man-made clearing. Thirty yards away they could see a group of men and machines. The military engineers. Raven counted six, plus one at the controls of a backhoe. On the other side of the clearing there were two large canvas tents, olive drab.

"If they've still got our team, they're in one of those tents," he ventured.

There was yet another explosion, somewhat smaller than the earlier ones, and with this blast they could see a rock face had been breached. The path to the sea was complete. The men ran to the opening and yelled. From one of the two tents a man exited. They were close enough to see the unlit cigar in his lips. Then a second person came out of the tent and ran to his side.

"I'll be goddamned," Raven said. Kylie gasped.

It was Malin.

"Who's that?" the doctor asked.

"The woman's name is Malin," Kylie spat. "Short for *Malinche*. You know, like the traitor who helped the Spanish *conquistadors*."

They watched as the pair walked to the newly made breach and climbed over the rubble to the shore. The man raised his arm and it looked like lightning flashed from his bare hand.

"Mirror," Raven whispered. "He's signaling to that ship out there. The gold leaves by sea. That's their plan."

"How are they going to get the gold to the ship? That's miles of ocean."

Doctor Garcia interrupted. "We're here to get those people out, remember? I suggest we think about that first."

"I am," Raven said. "They're going to be busy. We've got to circle behind them."

The three snaked their way around till they were in back of the tent. There was perhaps 20 feet of clearing between it and the brush. With all the men occupied at the beach the tent blocked their line of sight. There was no sign of a guard. Raven was about to try to cross the clearing when he heard voices. One was familiar; the voice of the man who had left them to die.

"Lieutenant Avila, how are our guests doing?"

The lieutenant walked out of the tent. "They are fine, Colonel."

"The helicopter will be here in half an hour. Make sure they are ready for their ride."

"They are ready now, sir."

"Don't rush things, Lieutenant. Let them enjoy their last minutes. In fact, why don't you offer them some tequila? I know they like tequila. Yes. Give them plenty to drink, in case there are any long distance swimmers in the group." He chuckled. "I'll be in my tent entertaining my own guest. See that we're not disturbed."

"Of course, Colonel."

After several minutes, Raven whispered, "I've got to get inside that tent. We'll draw that guy out and—"

"Slit his throat," Doctor Garcia said. "I will do it." The two gringos stared at him. "No really, I can do it. Those men aren't soldiers, they're criminals, murderers. Don Chuy. Your friend Tommy. They thought they killed you, and they are about to take—how many more lives?"

Doctor Garcia pulled up his pants leg and ripped off a stretch of adhesive bandage. Taped to his leg was a surgical scalpel. "We must get him to come around to the back of the tent."

Raven looked wide-eyed at the weapon. "I should do it," he whispered. "I have experience."

"No," Dr. Garcia said. "This is my country. You have no such experience here."

"Alright," Raven said reluctantly, "just be ready." He slithered out of the brush across the clearing.

Raven reached the tent, crawled along its back, stopped, and put his face to the ground. He lifted the canvas for a peek, turned to his cohorts, and nodded. Then he crawled around to the side. Crouching in the brush they heard him scratching at the side of the tent. The doctor crept from the brush as Raven ran around the side, the Mexican lieutenant right behind him.

"*Now!*" Raven grabbed the man and the doctor lunged. His arm in mid-air, he halted.

"NOW!" Raven urged, but the doctor's hand, and the weapon it held was frozen in mid-air.

The lieutenant spun from Raven's grip, pulling his sidearm from its holster. He pointed it at Raven, who raised his arms, then at the doctor who had already raised both, the ineffectual weapon still clinging to his open palm. The lieutenant laughed.

"I know you," he said. "You're the doctor from El Tuito. So you're a commando now?" Then he spun around and pointed his pistol in a third direction, the brush. "Come out. I know you're there."

Kylie stepped out, hands raised.

# CHAPTER TWENTY-NINE

Colonel Márquez stood over the group of captives and counted out loud, pointing his pistol at each one. Each was seated with hands bound behind and ankles tied.

"You are going to begin your last journey soon, by a Chinook helicopter—you remember them don't you, Mr. Raven—which is coming to transport our precious cargo to a waiting ship, transformed from a processor of fish to a floating smelter, erasing all traces of origin from the bullion you so kindly recovered for us. You won't be going aboard, I'm sorry to inform you, but don't worry, they say that drowning is the easiest of deaths. Isn't that right, doctor?" He leered at the group.

"Now if you will excuse me, I am going to enjoy the company of a rather special lady. Amazing woman, the one you call Malin. Did you know she killed the young doctor? Lieutenant Avila saw her that rainy night in the jungle. She carried this dainty little knife, obsidian I think, and, hah, come to think of it she did to him exactly what Dr. Garcia tried to do to Lieutenant Avila. I have to say, she was much more accomplished than our good doctor here."

"Tommy drowned," Raven growled.

"Ah, but he'd been stabbed before drowning, isn't that right doctor?"

Doctor Garcia nodded. "I told you that night someone had tried to cut out his tongue."

"And I have no doubt you blamed us," the colonel said. "Ah, we soldiers are so misunderstood."

Heavy equipment was heard outside.

"You know," he said, "I tied the knots myself and I've tested the ropes that bind you, and I'm still nervous about leaving you in here. How did you two get out of that pit? Are you Spiderman?" He grinned at Raven.

"You're closer than you think," Raven said.

"Well, just so you don't get any more heroic ideas, I'm posting armed guards right outside. Automatic rifles would make quick work of you, but it would be so messy. We want a clean disposal, please don't upset our plans." He turned and left the tent.

The first to speak was Doctor Garcia. "I'm sorry," he said. "It's my fault. I just couldn't..., I couldn't—"

"It's alright," Raven whispered. "It was wrong of me to let you try. God meant for you to save life, not take it. I give thanks there are men like you. I just wish there were more of your kind and less of mine. His chin sunk to his chest and he mumbled, but his words were clearly heard. "That goddamn bitch murdered Tommy. Goddamn her to hell."

"Obsidian knife," Kylie muttered. "I saw her use it to cut flowers. It wasn't any bigger than a pen. Why would she—"

But Kylie stopped in mid-sentence. The tent flap opened and in she walked. Malin.

Raven spat on the ground. "If I could move I'd strangle you with my bare hands."

"I was told to come and lead you to the shore," she said softly.

Again it was Raven who spoke for the group. "How ironic, history repeating itself. Once more Malinche is responsible for the deaths of those who trusted her."

"Please," she said. "I didn't know you would be here. You did not tell me what you were doing. I asked if I could help. Tell them, John; tell them I offered to help. But you did not confide in me. I was watching the soldiers. I was going to try to stop them. How did you find it? How?"

"Don't tell her." Raven ordered. "Why did you kill Tommy? What did he ever do to you?"

Malin looked confused. "Tommy? Kill him?? I tried to save him."

"By cutting his throat?"

"How did you—" She stopped. Her eyes glared into Raven's then she looked into each face.

"They saw you that night." Raven said. "Saw you and your knife." He was grinding his teeth in anger.

"What?" Malin's jaw dropped. "Someone was there and didn't try to help me? No, No, you must understand. Yes, Tommy and I met in the jungle. That often happened when he took his walks and I took mine. The storm began and we sat under a tree. We were talking then he...he," She stopped, raised her chin and drew a deep breath. She returned her gaze to the group and continued. She looked at Raven with an intensity that matched his own. "Was Tommy an epileptic?" she asked him.

Raven frowned. "He hadn't had a seizure in over a year. It was under control."

"Was he an epileptic?" Malin demanded.

"Yes."

"I knew it. He had a seizure that night as we were sitting there and talking. He was swallowing his tongue. That's not uncommon with epileptics, is it Doctor Garcia?"

"No," the doctor said.

"He was fighting me. I tried to keep him from strangling himself. I couldn't think of anything else to do. I pulled out his tongue and stabbed it with my knife to keep him from swallowing it. He knocked me down, pulled it out and ran. I tried to follow him—" She lowered her head. "… but I couldn't catch him."

There was silence, broken by Kylie. "But why are you helping these bastards?"

Malin stiffened, lifting her chin. "Come," she said. "It is time for us to go."

She called for the guards. Two entered. One cut their bindings from their ankles and wrists, the other stood with an automatic rile pointed at them as Malin led them from the tent. They crossed the clearing to where the last explosion had blasted through the rocks, clearing a path to the sea. In front of them was a beach with sand white as sugar. The remains of a tiny hut stood beside palm trees blown from the ground. Kylie recognized the scene. This was the beach where he had spent a tender afternoon with the woman who was now leading him to his death. He shook his head in wonder. The crates were stacked on the beach, wrapped with chains and hooks for the off-lifting procedure. Loaded with gold. Mexico's gold. Soldiers began prodding them from behind with rifle butts as Lieutenant Avila ordered them to form ranks on the beach.

"Colonel Márquez has a few more words he would like to say."

The commanding officer approached them. In the distance was the sound of a helicopter getting louder, coming closer.

The Colonel walked past them as if it were an inspection. He leered at Priscilla; sneered at Jerry, Fred and Tod.; shook his head as he stood before Dr. Garcia. His arms were behind his back and he kept slapping the back of one hand against the palm of the other as he talked.

"What an amazing group you are," he said. "You found a treasure hidden for 80 years. You retrieved it, and you two," he was standing in front of Raven and Kylie, "getting out of that pit was a remarkable feat. I want you all to know that I truly respect your accomplishments. When you're out there," he waved towards the ocean, "going down with your last breath, remember you died with my deepest admiration." He chuckled.

"Your friend Malin respects your accomplishments too, don't you, my dear?" He held out his hand for her and Malin walked to his side. Colonel Márquez put his arm around her waist.

"I believe you truly surprised her. She kept telling me you didn't know what you were doing or what you were looking for. She said she had discouraged you from trying, didn't you, my dear. But I thought otherwise."

He turned and lifted Malin's chin as if to kiss her. Their lips almost touched. Her movements were too quick for the eye to catch. Grabbing his wrist, she twisted it over her head as she stepped in back of him, pinning his arm to his back. Her other forearm slammed into his larynx, choking him, causing eyes to bulge. She brought to his neck a small blade, obsidian.

"Throw down your arms," she shouted at the soldiers, "or I'll kill him."

No one moved. Rifles remained pointed in the direction of the captives, and at the two on the beach, now locked in a deadly embrace.

The obsidian knife pressed into the flesh of Colonel Márquez. A trickle of blood ran down his neck. "Do something!" he shouted. "Shoot her!"

"No!" Lieutenant Avila yelled. "You might hit the Colonel."

"Kill him," Raven shouted to Malin.

Raven rocked on the balls of his feet, ready, eager to jump at one of the armed men even if it would be a suicide leap, then he felt the earth rumble beneath him, or was it the shaking of his knees? The droning of the helicopter was getting louder, but over its air-slicing rotors they heard another sound, a high pitched wailing. Higher, higher in decibels, splitting the eardrums. Soldiers dropped their rifles, clasped their hands to their ears. Lieutenant Avila flung his pistol to the sand, grabbing the sides of his head. The wailing came from all around them, from within their own skulls. From within their own souls.

As the rumbling grew the earth began to vibrate beneath their feet. The siren scream grew louder, louder. Nothing else could be heard. All eyes were on the beach. Colonel Márquez had fallen to his knees, but not from a stab wound. He too had his hands clasped to his ears, shaking his head and screaming in pain with the wail that cleaved his brain. Words seem to form in the din.

"¡Mis hijos, mis hijos, donde estan mis hijos?"

Did the cry come from heaven or hell? It could not have issued from any mortal throat; certainly not from the woman Malin, now with her arms at her sides, her head raised to the sky, and her feet— two feet off the ground! The woman was suspended, levitating as the lament deafened one and all. Still the earth rumbled and shook. Then the wailing stopped, its echo receded, as Malin returned to earth. But the rumbling did not diminish. It became a roar as chasms opened, splitting, swallowing the earth on which they stood. Malin turned her back to the others and faced the sea. The waters roiled. The beach began to slope and the loaded crates slid toward the water.

"Noooo!" Colonel Márquez ran toward the containers of gold. Malin turned and followed him, walking slowly, purposefully.

Water lapped at the bottom of the wooden crates as the Colonel reached them and, mad with the fear of losing something neither he nor anyone else could ever possess, threw his arms around one and tried to drag it back from the deepening waters. Malin turned. Her eyes were on John Kylie as she raised a hand and waved. Once, twice.

There was a deafening roar. With the earthquake's tremors the beach sank from sight and disappeared. Waves that had fallen on sand now slapped against firmer earth where the new bank formed. In the sound of the coast collapsing and sinking to the ocean's depths, Kylie swore he heard children laughing, tens of thousands of children laughing.

With the ringing in their ears, all blinked in disbelief. What their eyes had beheld moments before was no more. The beach. Gone. The Colonel. Gone. Malin. Gone. And gone was the gold.

"*Aieee,*" screamed the first soldier to recover his wits. He ran towards the jungle and the others followed him. Overhead, the huge Chinook helicopter made a pass, then headed back out to sea.

"My God, what just happened?" Priscilla asked. "Did you see her—"

"Yes, we saw," Raven said. "We saw."

# CHAPTER THIRTY

Dazed, the treasure hunters returned to their homes. For the next few weeks their lives were marked with a sense of loss, though each tried to banish such thoughts. How can you lose what you never had? Indeed, what had they lost? A dream. Only a dream. There were no sunset celebrations on the beach. They kept to themselves and would lower their eyes and say nothing when they passed each other during the day.

When Kylie thought of Malin, as he did with each waking breath—with no respite from her memory in his dream-filled sleep—he wondered whether she, and what he had felt for her, had been real or like her namesake La Malinche, more fancy than fact. And that surreal manner of her death, what was that? Had she induced some sort of mass hypnosis? One night he swore he heard her cry, "*mis hijos!*" Kylie rose from his bed and walked to his porch. In the brush, moving just beyond the clearing surrounding the house a five foot tall blue-green flame glowed. He walked towards it. The evening was still, not a whisper of a breeze, yet scents of vanilla, of coffee, of bougainvillea and mangoes wafted towards him. She was there. He reached out for the light and felt damp warmth on his fingertips.

"Malin?"

The luminescence took form, a woman's shape. "I could not stay," it said.

He wanted to talk to the apparition. He wanted to ask Malin who and what she was, and what, if anything, they had been together, but he couldn't speak. His throat was dry. He couldn't swallow.

"It is my destiny to wander," were the words he heard, "to wander forever. To return to my people that which is theirs, that is the task I've been given."

The light became dim, the sounds drifted away and far off in the jungle he heard a wild cat scream. This time it did not fill him with terror. He knew the spirit that had visited him had taken another form, not human, but flesh, blood and a living part of the jungle that no longer threatened, but welcomed. Now a breeze caressed him and beckoned him to stay. And John Kylie knew that he would.

Next morning he walked across the bay to share his spiritual visitation with Raven.

"I've had a couple visits myself," Raven said, as he sat in his home staring out to sea, "and I was sober."

"What do you think it means?" Kylie asked.

"I don't know. Maybe they want us to be better. You know, better than we are. Hell, I've sure got room for improvement."

"Me too," Kylie said. "You feel like walking down to the beach for a beer? I'm buying."

"In the whole English language, those are my two favorite words," Raven said. "Hand me my walking stick, would you old buddy?"

Thought was given to recovering the gold. Mel Fisher had done it. But Raven asked a diver friend.

"The San Andreas fault runs through there," the diver said. "Jacques Cousteau couldn't find the bottom with a submarine. Nobody knows how deep it is." That was sufficient to doom the idea.

It was John Kylie who called for resumption of their evening homage to the setting sun. All joined once again on the beach and this time a newcomer had been invited, Doctor Garcia. In another break with tradition, Kylie stood and addressed all before Raven's opening toast was offered.

"We had a good idea when we thought we had a fortune in our hands." There were several frowns. By tacit agreement, the incident had been banned from discussion as if it had never happened.

"The research institute," Kylie said. There was a chorus of "oh yeah's." "Well, I think we should do it."

Toad blurted, "If you think I'm going to the bottom of the ocean, you're nuts. That damned pit was deep enough for me."

"No," Kylie said, "that gold is gone. It is—" a vision of Malin flashed before his eyes— "where it belongs. But I know where there's more."

There were groans from the table. One adventure had been more than enough for the group. Doctor Garcia stood. Before speaking he dabbed his lips with a napkin.

"I enjoy quaint English sayings," he said, "though there are many I do not understand. One that took me a long time to figure out is "never look a gift horse in the mouth." I believe this expression means to accept gifts without question and with gratitude. Am I right?" There were nods. "Mr. Kylie has informed me that he is making a large amount of funds available to this research institution which we, every one at this table, will organize and bring into being. In a way, the gold we were going to use for this purpose has been restored to us. We should accept, not question his gift."

"Actually," Kylie said, "it comes from a lot of people who God will reward for their generosity in his own way." He looked at Raven sitting at the end of the table. His toothy grin stretched from ear to ear. "Anyway, what I have comes to almost the same amount that we were going to contribute. I can live without it. So, we are going to do what we said we would do."

After a round of 'hurrahs' someone shouted, "A toast!"

Raven stood and cleared his throat.

"Here comes a long one," Fred whispered.

"Stand up everybody," Raven ordered and all did so. He turned and faced the sunset. Its brilliance was blinding.

"Out there is all the gold I ever want to see," he said, "To Mexico's gold."

And with thanks for the simplest and truest of treasures, glasses were raised to the setting sun.

THE END

# AUTHOR'S NOTE

To those who perceive errors in this effort, I recognize there is a new road between Puerto Vallarta and San Sebastian. The journey today, though scenic, is not nearly as exciting as the one I described. Not too long ago it was an adventure. Yelapa now has electricity and the descriptions of that magic village came as much from fantasy as memory. Much in our beautiful bay has changed since I first moved here. By God's grace much has stayed the same. The process of fiction allows me to choose the images I wish to employ. Some will think I confused the historical character of La Malinche with the folkloric myth of La Llorona. I did merge them into one, but am not the first to do so. The two have been melded in national stage and screen productions as well as Mexican literature many times.

It is of course ludicrous to think the nation's treasury could have been stolen (which history acknowledges), then stolen again and the public deceived (which history refutes). But that's the fun of fiction. One can build on the unbelievable to create the impossible. I had fun. I hope you did, too.